RAISING KANE
FOR THE LOVE OF KANE

JANETTE ANDERSON

Raising Kane: For The Love Of Kane

Published in the USA by:
BearManor Media
P O Box 71426
Albany, Georgia 31708
www.bearmanormedia.com

ISBN 1-59393-350-9

Printed in the United States of America.

Dedicated To
Frank Stallone

CHAPTER 1

"And crossing the line now for the very last lap is car number 3, John Camery. Behind him the red-hot favorite, the Italian Alexander Vincentia, in car number 9. These are Formula One practice laps at their finest here at Silverstone racetrack!"

The English commentator's voice reached fever pitch as he adjusted his collar and tie. The unusually hot July heat was suffocating, mixing with the stench of fuel and the choking odor of oil.

These would be the pole positions. Camery first and then Vincentia second place.

"Wait!" The commentator peered down through the steamy glass windows of his grandstand box. "Something's wrong. Vincentia is swerving across the track. He's losing control of the car as they round the bend. There is nowhere for him to go...nowhere. Four more cars are behind him. Oh, my god, oh, god no, he's going to hit the wall. At that speed he'll never make it! Dear god, sweet Jesus, help him!" and he crossed himself as he poured with sweat.

The other cars swerved to avoid Vincentia and the speed slowed immediately. Car number 9 careered across the track and the explosion rocked the over-crowded stands, as Italy's number-one driver Alexander Vincentia's car hit the balustrade head on and exploded into a ball of orange flame.

The warm Santa Ana wind wrapped itself around their half-naked bodies. Spending the night on Malibu beach was nothing new for Kane Branson, spending it with his wife in his arms was. He watched the swell of the water and glanced out across the Pacific Ocean toward home and Australia, while the smell of salt filled his nostrils. Tonight they would be on a plane for Heathrow, England and to the world of Formula One racing. His thoughts were distracted as he felt her move in his arms. Kane altered his position slightly and sat up just a little, his long hair falling down onto his muscular arms.

"Morning." Kane looked down at her. "Did you sleep well?" Kane pulled strands of hair from his wife's face.

Kelly turned in his arms and looked at him with seductive, sparkling eyes. "Make love to me?"

She reached for her husband, and slid her hands into his long blonde hair pulling him down onto her young, taut body. In the crisp Californian morning she could see his tan and supple body. Kelly ran her fingers through the gray on his chest and let her fingers slip on down across his stomach, inside his jeans and down to the course patch of hair.

"You know just how to get to me, don't you, lady?" His mouth covered the uncovered butterfly tattoo on her breast.

"Oh, I hope so…" and her breathing became labored as her husband seduced her to meet his every wish. Her hand clenched around the sand on the beach, and the water seeped through her fingers.

Neither of them had noticed the incoming tide as it washed at their legs, soaking anything in its path. Nothing could stop the sands of time. It crept up their clothes, and languished there. Warm wet waters of Mother Ocean.

Kane turned over in the spray and pulled his wife with him. Her hair hung over him and she looked down at a man she loved so much. Water swirled around them, warm and sensual, like them.

"I'm wet," she murmured in his ear as she lowered herself down onto his body.

"Yeah, I know that," he replied huskily.

She giggled. "I mean, I'm wet all over."

"It's called salt water. Makes you taste good," and he mockingly licked her neck, and then carried on kissing the side of her face.

Kelly giggled. Kane still liked her to do that, and Kelly knew it.

Finally Kane moved back from the sodden blanket, and leaned his back against the rocks. Reaching in the pocket of his shirt that lay on the rock, he pulled his cigarettes out and lit one up. He watched the smoke float into the air, while Kelly stretched out across his legs. The salt water reached its mark, and for now they were safe, even if their clothes had taken a beating.

"What time is our flight?" She closed her eyes as she spoke, leaning back on him.

"Seven tonight. We have a few hours. What do you want to do, aside from getting dry?" He puffed hard on the weed.

"You!"

"Aside from me. You wanna ride down PCH? Motorbike back there is calling my name," he teased, as the rented silver Harley sat waiting on the side of PCH. "Gonna be a thousand people here soon. We should get going. We'll get in trouble if we're caught here."

Kelly snuggled closer to him.

"Since when has trouble bothered the infamous Kane Branson? And anyway, we have to get caught first."

His finger touched her nose. "You are a bad influence on me, young lady. And this time we're not on any mission and the people over here don't know who I am. We're just the Bransons on vacation. And you can have me anytime you like."

"Yeah, I know. But this is kind of exciting. Like when we first came to the States…" She didn't get to finish her sentence.

Kane's cell phone began ringing in the saddlebag on the motorbike. "Damn. No one at the department in Sydney knows we're here, 'cept Dan. Fact, no one knows where we are except Alexander and Maria. And they're not expecting us till tomorrow, and they don't have this number."

The cell rang until the voice mail picked up. The phone rang its melodic tones again.

"Man, persistent buggers, whoever they are." The monotonous ringing was irritating Kane.

"Thought you told Dan not to call us unless it was really urgent? Damn, can't the Australian Federal Police function without you for two weeks? Commander or not! Maybe it's about the kids. Want me to fetch it for you?"

"Yeah, but put my shirt on first. Geez, man. Has to be important or some fool got the wrong number."

She pulled on the black shirt and it blew in the morning breeze. Kelly returned with the cell and handed it to him. Kane flipped open the cell and answered it.

"What the fuck do you want? I'm on vacation, Dan. What can be so important to call me halfway 'round the damn world? Did I see what? Television? Not unless they've installed them on Malibu beach. Yeah, we spent the night on the beach." He paused. "What's wrong? Is it one of my kids? Sage or Star in trouble? Not the baby, not something wrong with Kene?"

He put his arm round his wife and listened hard. Kane's pallor changed. He handed the cell to Kelly, who took it from him, and he moved away from her.

"Dan? What's wrong? Oh, my God! When? We're due to fly to Heathrow tonight. They're sending a car to meet us. Some big event we're going to. The practice lap? You at the department? I have to go. Kane's gone down in the water. Call you right back."

She dropped the cell on the sand and moved towards her husband. He stood a couple of feet in the waves staring at the horizon.

"Is Alexander…?" Kane couldn't finish the sentence.

"He's still alive. Severe injuries and first degree burns, but alive. Dan saw it on the sports news. Figured you'd want to know. What do we do? We still goin'?" Kelly moved into the water, looking up into her husband's face.

"Hell, yes. Let's get to the airport. Maybe we can switch flights and get in earlier. Get your things together. Stick the bag on the motorcycle. Leave the blankets."

"Told Dan we'd call back. You do it and I'll pack up the gear."

"Yeah, right," Kane replied. He picked up the cell and shook the sand off it.

Kane and Alexander had grown up together as kids in Australia, almost like brothers. The Italian's father was stationed in Sydney. When Nam hit, Alexander went back to Italy. Kane went to Nam and came back and joined the Australian Federal Police. The two men had stayed in touch. Kane Branson was now the head of the AFP. while Alexander was Italy's top racing driver. They were planning a reunion for the first time in twenty years at the British Grand Prix, a celebration and a vacation all in one. Kelly needed one after the birth of their second child, Kene, who was now six months old. Kane's oldest daughter, Sage, was babysitting not only her father's children but her own. But most of all Kane needed to get away. Becoming commander-in-chief and completing a hundred missions had taken a toll. Almost fifty-seven, he needed some time with his young wife. Kelly kept him on his toes. At twenty-six, with two children by Kane, a stepdaughter older than her, and a thirty-seven-year-old stepson, Kelly had grown up fast. She would do anything to keep Kane happy, even to the point of becoming AFP herself.

"So, what did he say? Any more news?" she asked, and handed Kane his shirt back while pulling on her own T.

"Yeah. Maria called the department."

"What? Why? She knows we'll be there tomorrow. You gonna call her?"

"Yeah." Short, sharp answer from Kane.

Kelly continued to pull her clothes on; shorts and high-heeled boots completed the picture. Kane was on the cell to Maria for sometime. Kelly saw his expressions change like the clouds overhead. Looked like a storm. He closed the cell and slid it back into its usual place in his handmade, snakeskin boots, that he had just pulled on.

"I thought Maria said he was asking for me. Couldn't understand everything she says. That damned accent. Did find out the car was totaled, and something about Alexander wouldn't play ball. There seems to be some doubt about the crash. He was driving well and nearly at the end of the race. No reason on earth for him to crash."

"And you think what?" She'd seen that look on his face before. "Sabotage?"

"Alexander is always a careful driver. He's never crashed, not ever. Doesn't smell right. I called the airline, also, and managed to switch the flights to one leaving in two hours. You ready? We'll grab food at the airport and anything else we'll pick up there."

"What about the cases we left at the hotel?" Kelly asked.

"They're sending them on to the Vincentia's address in London. Got your passport and papers?" And Kane climbed up on the motorbike, donned his helmet and gloves, and then steered it out onto the main drag.

"Of course." Kelly thought that was a silly question. Hadn't he taught her better than that?

A helmeted Kelly climbed up behind him on the Harley. They didn't have to go back for anything. Kane was always ready: passport, credit cards, and gun. And Kelly had learned to follow suit, even down to her birth control pills. She could feel his body, tense and alert and tightened her arms around his waist. He revved the throttle and hit the dust.

The Harley flew down PCH. Kane never obeyed the speed limit and stoplights were an inconvenience. When he had to stop, Kane kept the bike revving, his gloved hand tight on the throttle. Weaving through the traffic in Malibu, Kane picked up a tail. The siren echoed in his ears, and the cop flagged him down.

"Fuck!" Kane pulled the motorbike over and removed his helmet.

The Malibu cop strode over to the cycle. "Sir, do you know what the speed limit…"

Kane reached for his credentials from the back of his jeans and the cop pulled his gun. Kelly froze.

"Man, I'm on your side." Kane flipped open his wallet, complete with badge and handed it to the cop.

The cop stared at him. "Commander Branson, I'm sorry. I thought I recognized you." He glanced at Kelly. "Ma'am. You won't remember me, sir. But I was one of the cops that helped you when you went down the side of the ravine at Malibu."

Miles Stratton and his merry band of drug dealers flashed through Branson's brain and he felt Kelly tense behind him. "Then officer, I owe you, but right now I have to get to LAX. Our flight leaves in two hours. Can you escort us?"

"Absolutely, sir. Follow me. I'll take you right to the plane," and handed Kane back his credentials.

"Not necessary, but you can take the motorbike for us when we get there."

Kane replaced the helmet and pulled his handmade snakeskin booted feet up onto the bike. "Hold on, baby," he yelled back to Kelly.

Kelly clasped her hands on his black T-shirt. Around her waist she'd tied her thin blouse and slung her purse across her chest. These clothes and one extra T-shirt each was all they had, and like Kane said they'd just buy what they needed. And where they were going, they needed. Following the cop was easy. He cleared the way and they reached LAX with a little time to spare.

Kelly climbed off the motorbike and Kane followed her, tossing their helmets back on the bike. He pulled the bag from the back of the Harley while Kelly clutched her purse and waited. The siren still sounded on the police car, and the lights flashed red and blue. The cop had parked in a no-parking area and cleared a path for Kane. Nine-thirty was busy at LAX.

"Thanks, officer. I'll make sure you get recognition with your boss. We have to get the tickets and grab some food." He stretched his hand to the officer. The officer reciprocated, and Kane turned to Kelly, saying to her, "Let's go, darling."

He took off the long, black shirt. Kane pushed it into the bag along with T-shirts, a camera and their guns. He saw Kelly's pills in there and smiled. Kane grabbed her hand and they bailed right through the crowds at Branson speed. Kane held her hand and led Kelly right to front of the British Airways desk.

"Hey, pal. Don't you see the line?" yelled someone from the very back of the line.

"Yeah, I see it. I don't wait in lines," Kane shouted, and stopped at the next first class window. "Have two tickets to change for the flight to Heathrow. Leaves in thirty minutes."

The BA attendant stared at him. "There are people in front of you, sir. I hope you don't mind waiting…"

Kane pulled his badge. The girl stared. She was obviously flustered.

"Commander Branson. I'm sorry, we were expecting you. Your luggage, sir?" and the BA looked around for some.

"Don't have any except this bag, and this goes with us on the plane." He opened the bag and she looked inside. "They're not chambered and I have the bullets."

She looked a little shocked at the .38's in the bag and called her supervisor on the phone to come over to help her.

"Problem?" Kane asked looking more than a little exasperated.

"No, sir. We're going to escort you through customs and onto the plane," replied the starchy supervisor.

"Kane," whispered Kelly, tugging on his arm. "I need to pee. I mean, I really have to go." She crossed her legs in mock gesture.

"Can't you wait?" he inquired, glancing at his watch.

"No," and Kelly shuffled in her boots.

"My wife has to use the ladies room," Kane mumbled to the starch, almost embarrassed.

The supervisor stepped forward. "This way, Mrs. Branson."

Kelly smiled at Kane and followed the BA uniform to the bathroom. While Kane waited patiently, Kelly did what she had to do, and then stepped out and washed her hands. She grabbed handfuls of perfumed tissues and sachets of hand-cream. Kelly felt like she was supposed to tip the attendant. She didn't have cash; neither Kane nor she did, only credit cards. She had nothing with her. There was complimentary everything in the bathrooms, even showers. Now that was tempting! She picked up soap, some tampons, and a face cloth. The watching attendant smiled and handed Kelly a goodie bag. Kelly looked at her watch and raced out of the bathroom and back down the airport to Kane.

"Where the hell have you been? And what are you holding?" her husband asked.

"Just a bag of necessities. You get anything to eat?" and Kelly peered into the bag that Kane was holding.

"Yeah... some fruit and bagels. Good job they take credit cards here. Couple of magazines for you. Here, put your things in the bag."

Kelly unzipped it and a little white bear sat inside, its head peeping out of a jet-black sweatshirt with 'L.A' on the front.

"For me?" she asked, looking expectantly up into Kane's face.

He nodded. She still held the charm that had captivated Kane when he first met her.

Kelly still wasn't used to Kane buying her things and poked further into the bag where a couple of pairs of underwear with USA on them stared back.

"Well, the shirt's not my size and I'd look kind of stupid clutching a teddy bear. We don't know what the weather will be like over there, and also the temperature on the plane." He whispered in her ear about the underwear in the bag.

"Thanks." She smiled and reached up to kiss him.

He ruffled her hair.

With their passports and their tickets in hand, the supervisor and an attendant ushered them to the waiting plane. They were the last to board and Kane smiled at the other passengers as they hustled down the aisle. Kane was used to traveling first class... Kelly wasn't. Only once had she had that privilege...to Hong Kong on Kane's hundredth mission. She noted the look the stewardess gave him. In fact, she saw the looks the whole cabin gave them both. They weren't quite the fashion for first class. Kelly smiled. If only they knew whom they were traveling with and what Kane had in the bag, they wouldn't be quite so snotty.

"You want the window seat, baby?" asked Kane ushering her into their numbered seats.

"No, you take it. Hey, these look like the seats on the Qantas flight. You know the ones that turn to beds. Are they?" She sat down and settled in, examining everything around her.

"Not quite as good. But we get blankets and pillows and all the best treatment. Buckle up. Couple of minutes and we'll be under way," and he did up his seat belt.

He had stowed the bag under the seat in front of him. That bag wasn't going anywhere but with him.

As the plane taxed down the runway and lifted effortless into the cloudless blue sky Kelly clutched Kane's hand.

"Something wrong, baby?"

"Strange feeling," she said, and shivered.

Kane stretched his long legs out in front of him and leaned back in the seat. "Here, Kel, lean on me and get some sleep. Gonna be a long day, baby."

Kane unfolded the fluffy blue blanket he had found in the seat-back in front of him and wrapped it around her. Kelly nestled into him. She smelled of salt, but more importantly to Kane, she smelled of him.

"Sir, would you like a drink? All complimentary," asked the perky flight attendant with the British accent.

He wanted a drink, but he needed a clear head. He'd told Maria not to send anyone for them. They'd get there on their own, their way.

"No thanks." He refrained. What he wanted more than anything was a cigarette.

Kane dozed. He dreamed. He made phone calls courtesy of British Airways. He talked to Maria. He talked to Sydney while Kelly slept on. He pulled one of the books out of the bag...Vogue... he pushed it back in the bag. That was Kelly's. He looked at his magazine. Silverstone stared back from the front page where Vincentia's face commandeered half the book. The more he talked to Maria, the more he realized something stank. He turned pages till he found advertisements for hotels listed by the track. One in particular caught his eye. He glanced over at Kelly. Kane figured it was about time she had somewhere nice to stay, some luxury in her life. It was time.

First they needed to check into the one in London, a home base. That one he had booked some time back. Kane looked at a sleeping Kelly. She would like this hotel. The idea had been to take time to get over jet lag, and generally relax. He had a plan, but plans had changed. Now they had to make other arrangements that included buying clothes, renting a car, and forming a new identity. He didn't want them to go in as AFP or the Branson's on vacation, but he did need to contact MI5. Somewhere down the road he had the feeling he would need their help.

London looked big and expensive when he'd made his initial plans. Hyde Park and the Strand looked good in the brochure at the travel agents. Kane had picked the Savoy for a reason. He'd ridden by it on a trip to England and wondered what kind of people stayed there. Now it was his turn to find out. Commander of the AFP and with the money he had inherited from his grandfather, Kane was more than comfortably well off, in fact he was what one would call wealthy. He'd never really told Kelly how much he was worth, but if anything happened to him she and his children would never have to worry about money. Kelly awoke disturbing his thoughts.

"Hey, sleepy, you want to eat?" Kane nudged her.

"Guess so. It's cold on this flight." She shivered. "This what it's gonna be like in England?" and Kelly pulled the fluffy blue blanket tighter around her.

"No. Maria said right now it's hot."

"You spoke to her? How's Alexander?" Kelly sat upright and the blanket slipped down around her.

"Unconscious. He was in a lot of pain and they put him out. Helps him, not us. So… we're gonna stay in London a night or two before we go to some place called Buckinghamshire. I have an idea…"

Kelly dreaded that look on her husband's face. "And that would be?"

"They don't know me from Adam at the racetrack. Think I've just become an Australian racing driver." A smug smile crept across his face.

"You're gonna what? I don't think so, Kane Branson!" She almost jumped in her seat, and grabbed hold of his arm.

"You think you get a say in it, Kelly Branson?"

"Yes, I do. You're the father of my kids and I know you when you get these ideas." She pulled back from his arm. "You don't know how to race cars? Do you? Or is this another little one of your accomplishments I'm not aware of?"

He smiled at her and then winked.

"Oh, god! Did Alexander teach you at some point? You race motorbikes and cars? Oh, my god. Here we go again."

"Darling, Alexander didn't teach me, I taught him. And I am sure the man behind your seat didn't catch everything you just said." Kane smiled. "I learned when I was very young. Didn't say I was great, but I can race enough to 'get by' over the pond. And you still don't get a say in it."

Then she whispered in his ear.

Kane laughed at her. "That, darling, is not an option."

Kelly slumped back in the seat and pouted. She tucked her legs up on the seat. She pulled her hair up on top of her head and held her long, curly hair in a knot. Then she let it cascade down onto her shoulders and turned her eyes and pouting mouth to Kane.

"That won't work on me either." It did, but he couldn't show it. "If I want to race, I race. And if it helps us to find out about Alexander then I'll definitely do it." He talked quietly to her. "Baby, think about it. It would give me the inside edge. Maria was mumbling again about him not playing ball. Someone was telling him what to do. I know Vincentia, always been his own man. It's very likely he was sabotaged. It's strange really. Last time I talked to him he was guarded." Kane was thinking out loud.

He thought for a moment longer. Yeah, he was guarded. Things were beginning to make sense. He pulled out the phone again from the back of the seat. Funny, he had never realized how much the seat-backs held before.

"Operator, please get the number for MI5, then connect me to them." The phone clicked and he was connected.

Kelly sulked. He put his hand on her leg and let his fingers slide up to her shorts.

"You want not to do this anymore?" and his fingers slid just under the bottom of her shorts.

"No," she giggled.

He tried to concentrate. "Yeah, connect me to Inspector Graham. My name…Commander Kane Branson, Australian Federal Police." He spoke quietly.

Kelly swelled with pride. Little Kelly Walker married to the commander of the AFP.

"Peter Graham? Long time, man. Yeah, it's the same old Kane Branson. Just happen to be commander now. I need to see you and talk over old times. Where am I?" He peered out of the window seeing only dark skies. "Over the big pond somewhere. Can't see a damn thing except darkness. We're arriving in London Heathrow in about an hour. My wife and myself." He paused. "No, not Sage Jay. I'm remarried. Yeah, two more kids. We're staying at the Savoy. Nah, don't send a car. Well, if you really want." He winked at Kelly. "Okay, so send the car. Unmarked though, okay? Oh, and we need to stop at some stores on the way to the hotel. We, er, left L.A. in a hurry. No luggage." Kane paused again. " Oh, right, too early for stores. Sure we can meet you tonight. Yeah, man, we'll be rested by then. You still married to Gina? Three children? I have four altogether."

Kane paused. "Hey, Peter, I need a favor." He whispered into the phone. "Over dinner then. Say eight in the lobby. I'll reserve a table. And, Peter, thanks." He hung up the line.

"Well, Commander Branson, just what are you planning? Thought you were going to be a race car driver." She pulled the oversized sweatshirt out of the bag and tugged it over her head, pulling her hair out and over the top of the collar.

"I am. All racing drivers need protection. What's better than MI5?"

"And you just happen to know the highest ranking inspector from where?" she questioned, wrinkling her eyes at Kane.

"Long story. Now, when we disembark there will be a car waiting for us. We'll go shopping later. We can't arrive at the Savoy looking like this, then again might be kind of fun. Yeah, man. Why not?" He laughed the laugh of mischief in full swing.

"Wow…that was a bumpy landing. Kind of reminds me of the way you land planes, choppers anyway. Where they gonna meet us? Not like we have any luggage. That's at the Vincentia's, right?" Kelly babbled on.

"Are you excited or something? You haven't quit talking for a half-hour. Yeah they're going to send someone to find us," he replied.

"How will they know us? You don't exactly look like a commander of anything, 'cept maybe Malibu Hell's Angels," she teased and looked him up and down.

"They'll know. It's their job to. Ready?" He pulled his black shirt back out of the bag and slid it on over his T.

"Yep."

He looked at his wife. Long black boots, huge sweatshirt, and the shortest shorts it was possible to be decent in. That was Kelly. That was part of the reason he married her. She sure was going to be a shock for the prim and proper Peter Graham. For the Vincentia's she would be refreshing, and Alexander would most definitely approve.

Disembarking the plane first, much to the relief of the now very curious passengers, they were escorted through customs, .38's and all. Kane pulled his hair back in a ponytail, and pulled the shirt round him. Kelly bustled alongside him swinging her purse in her hand. Two men dressed in plain black suits moved toward them. Kane felt the now- loaded gun down the back of his jeans and held tightly onto Kelly's hand. He was licensed to carry in any country. So was Kelly. The approaching men removed their sunglasses, and Kane thought the guys looked kind of starchy. One of them was brave enough to step forward.

"Commander Branson? Inspector Graham sent us to escort you."

They both flashed ID badges at him. Steven Asher and David Goodman. One blonde and one dark haired like salt and pepper.

"Good guess," replied Kane.

"Not really that hard, sir. You're the only ones in first class that looked like..." the Englishman paused.

"Like Australians?" interjected Kane.

"Something like that, sir," came the reply.

"This is my wife, Kelly." Kane ushered her forward.

"Ma'am," and the blonde Englishman bent his head slightly.

'Ma'am,' thought Kelly... "Name's Kelly, mate...and pleased to meet you," she replied.

"Likewise, I'm sure." The blonde 'mate' turned his attentions to the Commander. "So, where would you like to go, sir?"

"The Savoy," replied Kane.

"*The Savoy*, sir?" The blonde policeman looked astonished.

"Yeah. That a problem? Steve wasn't it?" boomed Kane, giving one of his withering looks at the young man.

"No, sir." Steve replied. "David and I are assigned to take you wherever you want to go."

"Not dressed like that, mate." Kane looked them up and down. "Where we're going you'll stick out like couple of sore thumbs. You, my friends, are coming to the world of Formula One. But first, let's get to the Savoy. So, escort us, my man. Take us to the Savoy and its splendor." Kane waved his arms in mock gesture towards the exit sign.

Kane Branson was enjoying this. Sudden acknowledgment and the good life. Maybe when he got back he'd retire. Maybe not. He swaggered through the airport like he owned it. One man on Kelly's left, and one of Kane's right.

Parked outside the airport in the no-parking zone was a silver-gray sports Mercedes. Steven Asher opened the backdoor for Kane.

"Pay well over here?" Kane commented as he climbed in the car, while rubbing his hands along the red leather interior.

Dave opened the door for Kelly and she sat in the car next to Kane, crossing her legs as she did.

"No, sir. Inspector Graham sent this for you. He did ask that you not drive too fast. He has to return it in good condition." Steve turned the key in the ignition and the headlamps flipped up.

"Steve, right? My husband always drives fast. The chances of your boss getting this back in good condition are slim to none," stated Kelly.

"Cute, darling. What my wife means is that I'll be careful. David, okay if I call you Dave? You like racing?" Kane leaned over the seat resting his arms on the supple leather.

"Actually, sir, I do. My brother races. Amateur of course." Dave pushed his dark hair from his eyes.

"So, you know about cars then, Dave?" Kane's eyes gleamed.

"Yes, sir," he said in his very proper English accent. "Grew up with them. Both Steve and I spend most of our weekends messing with cars."

"You do, huh? Well, isn't that gonna come in useful. Think you could pass as mechanics, like in a pit stop?" and Kane propped his boots against the expensive leather.

Dave glanced at the blue-eyed, blonde-haired Steve. "Yeah, we could do that. Inspector Graham's orders were very explicit. We go where you go. You're meeting him for dinner tonight, sir. Why don't you confirm that with him just so we don't overstep our bounds? You want to go to the shops later, sir?"

Steve was driving. Dave half turned to look at the passengers in the back seat. He was taken by the difference in his boss and the man in the back. He couldn't imagine the inspector in jeans, boots, black T-shirt and a wife that looked like this one. Immediately, he liked Kelly. He figured they were about the same age.

Kane noted it. Steve was a little older, by maybe five years. Kane liked them both on sight. Kane could smell a crooked cop a mile away and these two were honest. And he needed a couple of guys like these two. He could have done with three, but he had three people. He had Kelly. But back to the question in hand.

"Yeah, later. Let's go straight to the Savoy. I'm tired. Need to take a nap. Right, Kel?" asked Kane sliding his arm around her shoulders.

"Uh huh. Would like to shower. My body is all mixed up. What's the real time?" she asked yawning.

"Six, ma'am." From where Dave sat her body was anything but mixed up.

Kelly rubbed her sleeve on the glass, and then peered out of the window. First trip to England always made the best impression. The sun was coming up over the Thames with shades of morning shining down on the river. The palace sat in all its glory: bold and majestic, casting shadows in the first light of day. The hustle and bustle starting early, heralding a new day in the lives of the Queen's people.

She amused Kane. She'd been to such far off lands that people only dreamed of and sailed ships on the seas of Orion. And still the smallest things to him were the greatest pleasures to her. His arm tightened around her and Kane whispered in her ear.

"Sounds good to me," she murmured and snuggled into his body.

Kane's cell rang. He bent down and pulled the phone from his boot. Dave leaned across the seat and stared. He'd never seen a cell produced from a boot before.

"Kane Branson. Hi, Peter. How's the rest of the world doing? Don't you ever go home? Yeah, we're fine. Your blokes got us. Tired? Yeah. You want these guys sent back to you this morning? We won't need them till later. Kelly wants to sleep some. Don't know why. She slept the whole flight." Kane looked out as the street lamps died and they drew up into the Savoy's driveway. "Seems we're here. Did I get in? Great, man. Thank you. Speed, in your car? Nah, I'll drive slowly. Better still, send the boys with us. Good idea, yeah, I thought so. Later." Kane disconnected the line and pushed the cell back down his boot. "All set. You guys are in."

"In *what*?" asked Kelly looking questionably at Kane.

"Just in," he replied. "By the way, you two up front. Drop the sir. Kane is fine."

Dave glanced at his partner and raised his eyebrows.

"Yeah, you two. I guess you're not used to calling Inspector Graham anything but Sir. Well, I'm not him and you're working for me for now. I guess you're not carrying either?"

"No, s...Kane. You and your wife?" Dave asked tentatively.

"Always. Don't worry. I'm not gonna shoot up London and I am allowed to carry."

The British policing system still fascinated Kane. He waited for Steve to stop the car. Kelly went to open her door.

"No," Kane whispered and he held her back.

Eccentric wealthy racing drivers and their women didn't open doors. Two doormen in top hats appeared; regally opened the doors, and Kane and Kelly stepped out. She stood on the curb and her eyes widened. Kelly knew it was nice, but not this nice.

The doormen had seen worse than Kane. They'd seen better, but he'd never seen a Kelly before, not at the Savoy. They'd never seen sunshine on two legs and happiness shine from deep blue pools that called themselves eyes. They were all watching Kelly excited from arriving here. Everyone except Kane. He saw the black car with tinted windows pull into the side street as the Mercedes pulled into the Savoy. Kane glanced back and saw it turn its engines off. He watched the two men step from the car and the glint of a camera lens with a flash. Kane turned to face them and he caught the taller man talking on a phone. Not a regular police walkie-talkie. And the guys were not English. Too dark skinned. Italian maybe, trouble definitely. And without a shadow of a doubt following them.

CHAPTER 2

Steve tossed the Mercedes keys to the valet. Kane felt for the gun in the back of his jeans. Steve saw him do it and then looked in the same direction that Kane was staring, all the time moving closer to Kane's side.

"Inspector Graham filled us in about your mutual friend." Steve stood and watched the other men on the street. "They're Italian, right?"

"Think so," Kane mussed. "But why are they tailing us? And how come so quickly? I figured they pulled in behind us about three miles back."

"I saw them in the mirror. I thought they'd turn off. You want me to radio for backup?" Steve asked, looking away form the Italians and back to Kane.

"No. You and I will deal with it. Get Dave to take Kelly into the lobby, and have them wait inside the door. You get behind these people, and I'll approach them directly. Er, Steve, you got some ready cash? I can't even tip the doorman." Kane was embarrassed at having to ask a near stranger for such a favor. "Had planned to go to a bank, but you know, plans changed."

Steve fished in his pocket and handed Kane a wad of money. "You can pay me back later."

"Good on ya, mate. You know, Detective Steven Asher, you and I might get along just fine." He thumped the young man on the back. "But you have to get into some jeans and T if you're gonna ride shotgun for me. By the way, Kelly is good with a gun if ever she's needed. Young enough to be my daughter, but old enough to give me two of the finest kids in the world. You married, Steven?"

"Yes, for five years," Steve paused. "Sir, I don't feel right calling you Kane."

"Man, I have a son thirty-seven, a daughter twenty-eight, another little girl of four, and a baby boy of six months. All of them call me Kane, 'cept the baby of course." Kane laughed at his own joke and continued, "I have a very checkered past. If you're going to work with me the name is definitely Kane."

Steven Asher nodded. It was going to be hard keeping up with this bloke. Commander Branson may look like Crocodile Dundee with long hair, but the man had brains to back the brawn. He'd reached this position by seeing action from the ground up.

Steve turned to his partner. "David, why don't you take Mrs. Branson into the entrance and wait there? Commander, I mean Kane, wants to step around the corner a moment. We'll be right with you." Steve nudged his partner, and whispered. "Get her into the hotel."

"Of course." Dave turned to Kelly. "Mrs. Branson? Shall we go inside?" Dave took hold of her arm.

She pulled back instinctively. This she wasn't used to.

Kane leaned down to her. "Kelly," whispered her husband. "Just go with him for a second. Be right with you, baby."

"What's wrong?" Kelly asked immediately.

Kane shot her a glance. She didn't need a second look like that, and let Dave take hold of her arm. Kelly glanced back at Kane, who had already turned away from her gaze and was standing right next to Steve.

"Go." Kane strolled across the road and approached the men standing outside the unmarked car in a friendly manner. "Say, mate. You blokes want something? Maybe an autograph, something like that?" He took in every detail of their faces. "You were following us. Maybe you speak English?" Kane stood in front of the one and Steve came up right behind the other.

The second man turned to climb back in the car.

"Going somewhere?" Steve asked and shut the opened car door.

The dark man in the shades stopped dead.

"I repeat. You speak English?" asked Kane a little more impatiently.

The man looked to his companion and spoke fluent Italian. Kane replied for him.

"So you do speak English and I understood every damn word you said. What did you hope to gain? You knew I'd spot you. Maria didn't pick you very well. And why the pictures? She knows me well enough. I haven't changed much in twenty years."

Kane thought about that. Last time the Vincentias had seen him he had short blonde hair, was clean-shaven, somewhat thinner, and didn't have a young wife on his arm. He rubbed the stubble on his face. Perhaps that should go and also the long hair. Maybe, if he wanted to incur Kelly's wrath and sleep in the spare room for a few weeks. That didn't appeal in the slightest.

"Okay, so I have changed," Kane conceded.

Kane bent down and retrieved the cell from his boot. He stood up immediately as the number one Italian made a move forward. Kane put his hand on the man's shoulder to stop him.

"I don't think so, mate. You stay right here till I talk to Mrs. Vincentia." Kane flipped the cell open and pushed buttons. It took just a few seconds. "Maria, Kane." He was careful not to say his last name. "Two blokes in front of me…and not particularly good at their job. One's tall, real dark, aquiline nose, and thick black hair, while the other is short and stocky." Kane looked him up and down. "Reminds me of Alexander's father when he was younger. Would these blokes be someone you know?"

Kane never took his eyes off the taller one. The man stared back. He didn't like Australians, especially tall good-looking blonde ones. And Maria had sent them to watch Kane's movements. But Maria Vincentia paid well and one call was all it took.

"You do? Good, then they can help." He turned away from his audience and continued the conversation with Maria. "Remember, I taught Alexander to drive? I'm coming to see you as a driver. We'll stay here in London today and tomorrow. Kelly and I need to get some traveling clothes. How is he? Still unconscious? Probably best. Out of danger? Good. These two guys can bring us to you, right? Maria, why were they taking photos of us? You don't know? Interesting. You're sure they're working for you? This gets deeper by the minute. Okay. You have my cell number. If Alexander wakes, call me. If you need me we'll be right there. Just some things I need to do first. We're not that far from you. I'm gonna bail." He turned out of earshot. "We're at the Savoy under Branson, just in case. Talk soon." He closed the cell, replaced it in his boot, and turned back to face his new Italian friend.

Steve caught the look in Kane's eye. "All set?"

"Yeah, they're clean." Kane reached forward and straightened the lapels of the man's jacket. "Looks like you're working for me also."

"For Mrs. Vincentia," the Italian replied in his thick accent.

"Same thing. Run along now and be back here at eight tomorrow morning. You have names?" Kane was irritating to the point of abuse.

Steve watched carefully and figured he could learn from this man.

"Bruno Van Camp and my partner is Sergio Caboni." He pulled out his credentials.

"Very impressive." Kane slid the .38 slowly around his waist till it sat at the front of his jeans. "But I like my credentials better." He patted the handle of the gun.

There was no way that they knew he was the commander of anything. Kane figured they thought that all Australians carried guns for one thing or another.

"Then we understand each other? We work for you as long as Mrs. Vincentia says so. She is paying for that privilege. You will go to Silverstone tomorrow?" Bruno asked.

"Possibly. I need to practice a little. Been a while since I drove. Mrs. Vincentia told you I'm gonna race, right?" Kane asked knowing Maria couldn't have told them because he hadn't told her the plan till just.

"She said you taught Alexander back in Australia. That is all. *Si*, she told us you race." Bruno replaced his ID in his jacket.

'Very clever,' thought Kane. The guys were hedging. Maria had told them a lot. Why? To them he was just some bum that taught people how to race. And these guys weren't only working for the Vincentia's either. Someone else had filled them in. Kane left the gun in the front of his jeans just to remind his new friends where they stood.

"Then, Bruno and Sergio, return tomorrow morning at eight. I imagine you can dress so that you don't look like the Mafia in mourning?"

He saw them both bristle. Now he was getting the picture. Wasn't the first time he'd worked with Italy. But he didn't think they were behind sabotaging the car. They'd want an Italian to win. He was a little confused still as to the motives.

"Come on, Steve. Let's go find my wife." Kane ignored the formality of goodbyes and turned and walked away.

"What do you think that was about?" asked the Englishman keeping a good pace.

"Not sure. They were very much on their guard. You notice that? Do me a favor. Don't mention this to your partner and I won't mention it to mine."

"You mean your wife?" asked Steve.

"Yeah, man. She's my partner in everything. But let's keep this between us till we're sure exactly what is going on here."

Kane smiled at his new friend. He had liked Steve immediately. Kane pulled his shirt around his chest. He didn't want everyone else to see his credentials, but he also noted the chill winds that suddenly blew around them.

Kelly sat cross-legged on the black leather sofa in the hotel lobby. She'd dipped her fingers into the fountain on her way through the Savoy doors. Satisfied the water was for real she joined Dave on the couch. She was trying hard to fit in with this new Branson image, but everything was new to her, especially this kind of luxury. She considered that the bellboys were better dressed than she was, but then again they hadn't spent one night on the beach and one on a plane. She glanced at her silver-banded watch: seven o'clock. She was hungry, a usual scenario for her lately. She missed baby Kene. But Kane had looked tired of late and when he suggested a vacation she jumped at the chance to spend time together. Kane had been a patient man and waited for her to settle in again to being his wife, and not just a mother. Now he was making up for lost time. She laughed. The thoughts amused her, and tried to suppress the laughed and failed miserably.

"You okay?" asked Dave looking at her.

"Fine, thanks." She looked at the young guy next to her. "You got a girlfriend?" She slid her hand in her shorts pocket and pulled a packet of gum out, sliding a stick out into her hand. She unwrapped it, smelled the flavor and pushed the gum into her mouth.

"Kind of." Dave blushed.

"Kind of? Either you do or don't?" She turned around to face him, pursed her mouth, and then blew a bubble, which cracked with rapid force on her face.

"I work so much and help Steve with the cars that my girlfriend kind of comes in second. I would like to see more of her, but you know how it is," he rambled, embarrassed, and he stared at this woman popping gum and tried to figure why the gum was not stuck to her face.

They may have been the same age, but they were light years away from each other. Then Kelly saw Kane come through the revolving door and she was gone from the seat to meet him.

"So?" She popped again.

"So what?" He put his arms around her. "Do you have to do that?" asked Kane.

"Who were those guys?" she asked, as she snuggled into him ignoring his plea.

"Just a case of mistaken identity. You checked us in yet?"

Kane directed his conversation to Dave, who had now joined them.

"No, sir. Didn't know what name you'd be using," replied a cautious Dave.

'Very good,' thought Kane. There was definitely hope. "Branson is fine. A relative of mine is Kene Branson, an amateur racing driver. Named our son after him. Name comes in useful now, so let's go do this."

For once in her life, Kelly was out of her depth. Glancing at the chandelier and plush red carpets, she pulled her sweatshirt as far down as it would go, clutched her purse, and walked in line with Kane. She'd be glad to get into some real clothes, but dinner was something she was really dreading. She popped again. Maybe this wasn't the place to do this and swallowed the gum. Kane signed in. The Branson's had arrived.

"Ready, baby?" Kane picked up the keys. He turned to Steve. "You guys get something to eat and take a break. Be back here this afternoon around three and we'll take the *lady* shopping, and see in a few sights. Meet you in the lobby, then." Kane looked at his wife. " I need a nap. And I know you do." Kane slid his arm around her back. "Let's go, baby."

Steve watched the pair walk away, especially Kelly. "How come my wife doesn't look like that?" he mussed.

Dave turned to his partner. "Because your name is not Commander Branson." He laughed, and slapped his partner on the back.

"What floor we on?" Kelly asked still with girlish glee as they rode in the glass elevator.

"Top one. Penthouse suite."

The bellboy hit the button for the Penthouse floor. He was far better dressed than the Branson's.

"We playing pimps and prostitutes again, baby?" Kelly rolled her eyes at Kane and suppressed a laugh as she saw the bellboy stare at her husband.

"My wife has a weird sense of humor," and Kane stared at the door wishing it would open.

"Can't afford that. Can we?" Her eyes still large and round.

"Pimps can!" Kane smiled and took hold of her hand.

The elevator stopped and the confused bellboy escorted them to the suite door, turned the key, and let them in. Kane looked around and smiled.

"Very nice. Ask the desk if they can send us up some breakfast." He slipped the boy two twenty-pound notes. The bellboy stared. "Anything's fine. Continental, orange juice, coffee, fruit…just so long as it in the next ten minutes," and he escorted the bellboy to the door.

Kelly went in search of the rainbow. "Now, he really thinks I'm some hooker you picked up on the way here," she yelled. "Look at this place. Kane, come look at the bedroom. There's a Jacuzzi in it, right in the bedroom! There's soaps and perfume, robes, a fruit basket, even a bottle of champagne and glasses by the bath. And an envelope…"

Kane heard her crying. It would be a shock finding your birthday card next to the champagne, with a diamond ring attached to it. Kane had managed to arrange for the gift to be there when they arrived, even if they were several hours too early. He pushed the door open a little wider and peeped in the room. Kelly sat on the side of the tub holding the ring in her fingertips. She looked up at him, her eyes wide open and tears streaming down her face. Kane leaned on the door frame silhouetted in the morning light.

"You thought I had forgotten? I had this planned for months. It coincided nicely with the trip and it almost got screwed up with switching the flights. Happy birthday, Kelly."

He moved to her side, took the ring, and put in on her finger along with her wedding band. "We never had time to do things the conventional way. Now, it's time."

Kelly flung her arms around him and cried into his shirt. "You didn't have to do this," she sobbed.

"I didn't have to. I wanted to," and nuzzled into her neck.

Slowly he pulled her shirt over her head, and bending down he unzipped her boots. Kelly could feel the pleasure welling up inside her as he unbuttoned her shorts and slid his hand inside, almost pushing her back against the soft white towels.

"I love you, Kelly," Kane whispered.

There was a knock at the suite door.

"Damn! Don't move. I'll be right back."

She could hear him in the other room as she moved herself to the bed and pure silk sheets. Kane was back quickly with the cart of food. She lay in the silk sheets wearing nothing but the rings, the butterfly dancing eagerly on her breast. Her hair hung seductively down her body as she waited with anticipation for Kane. It was then he saw her and now Kane had an appetite… and it wasn't for food.

"Breakfast can keep." He pulled back the bedcovers and climbed in beside her.

"Never made love on silk before. It feels kind of sensual." She ran her hand over the sheet. It was soft and the silk spilled through her fingers.

He leaned across her. "Kelly Branson, you talk too damn much," exclaimed Kane.

"Sir, yes, sir." Kelly giggled.

Once wasn't enough for either of them. He played with her hair as she crept inside his loving arms. She could feel his muscles against her, his arms tight and caring. She wrapped her legs around him and held him inside her. Her way of keeping him with her.

"Kelly, you ever regret marrying me?" he whispered in her ear.

"I don't believe you asked that. You know I don't. You saved me, Kane. God knows where I'd be now, probably with some pimp or dead from drugs. You gave me your trust and your love and two wonderful kids. But most of all you made me respect myself and made other people respect me. Where's this coming from?" Kelly asked. She was shocked to hear this from him.

"I gave you those things and I gave you wealth. What I didn't give you was a young man."

He gently slid out her body and she lay back on the sheets. Kane sat up naked as the day he was born and moved to the jam-packed food cart. He sat down on the end of the bed. She watched him a second, then crawled across the sprawling bed to him, pulling the sheet with her, wrapping it around her body. Kane popped the champagne bottle and filled two glasses to the brim, and then handed her one. Kelly caressed the stem seductively, still with her eyes on Kane.

"What the heck would I do with a young man? He couldn't possibly make love to me like you do and he certainly wouldn't have a body like you… and," she ran her fingers down his chest, "he wouldn't have the stamina you do. Don't underestimate yourself, Kane. Most women would kill for a man like you. And I love you more than my own life." She paused. "What do you think your friend Peter will say when he sees me? He knew Sage Jay, right?"

Kane stood up and slid into a Savoy robe, tying the belt loosely around his waist, and then sat down on the end of the bed next to her.

"Yeah. Alexander, Peter, and I used to go on vacations together. Sometimes to Europe, back to Alexander's family, and sometimes to other parts of Australia. We were all young and single. You know the kind of things young guys get up to, baby? Peter was the first to marry, and then Alexander, finally me. Peter and I drifted apart whereas Alexander and I stayed closer. We'd spent more time together as kids. More like brothers, I guess. That's why I have to do this, Kel. Whatever it takes. Peter will help me and with the two guys he sent and you we can manage. I need you in on this. I need you to get close to Maria. She'll like you. Get close to her. Find out if Alexander had enemies. Who are their friends? Where do they go, what they do? Anything that will help us." Kane paused. "The two guys outside in the street. I lied to you. They were following us. I also need you as my back up." He swallowed the champagne down in two gulps.

"Well, if Commander Branson needs me then I can't disobey him. But I want something in return." She crunched her face up and let the sheet slide down her body.

"Name it." He munched on a fresh, crusty croissant that he had cut in half and doused with cheese, expecting Kelly wanted to climb back under the sheets.

"To be in the pit stop with you. One of the guys." She sipped her champagne and stole a side-wards glance at her husband.

He almost choked on his croissant. "Don't be ridiculous. You really think you can pass as a guy?" He looked at her body. "Anyway, it's too dangerous?"

"You can play racing drivers and you argue it's too dangerous for me? I'll be careful. And who the heck is going to know? Everyone dresses in all that gear. That's my deal, Commander. Take it or leave it?" She buttered a slice of toast and piled jam on the top.

He watched her a minute. "You're not pregnant again, are you?"

"Why do you ask?" and Kelly bit off a couple of sections of the tasty treat.

"'Cause you're eating for the whole football team. Are you?" He took another bite.

"Not that I know of, but it's an idea. I mean you're so old it may be your last shot!"

Kane dropped the croissant onto the tray.

"Why you! Come here and I'll show you who's too old." He grabbed the sheet and pulled Kelly towards him. Pinning her against the Victorian bedposts, Kane held her there.

"Now, remember, you need me. You know what I want. No pit stop deal, no more..." Kelly didn't get chance to finish.

"Yeah, right, Darling. I know exactly what you want."

It was three-thirty. The phone on the bedside table made a horrible noise. Kane reached for it and pushed it under the bed. A few minutes later, someone knocked on the suite door.

"What time is it?" Kelly murmured, turning towards Kane.

He looked at his watch. "Oh, fucking hell. I told those guys three. Pull your clothes on and let's go. We'll come back and shower after we go shopping. Don't know about yours, but my clothes stink of the ocean."

Kane fell out of bed and pulled on his jeans and shirt. Kelly ran to the adjoining bathroom, fixed herself up to her liking, and reappeared complete with large sweatshirt and short shorts. Hearing voices coming from the other room, Kelly opened the door slowly and saw Dave and Steve chatting with her husband. All the rooms were a mess. She viewed the discarded food trolley that sat by the suite door. The totally dismantled bedding lay strewn between the bedroom and the room the three men now sat in. Kelly felt uncomfortable, and closed the bedroom door behind her. She moved across the room and perched her rear end on the arm of Kane's chair. Dave and Steve stood up in acknowledgement of her entrance into the room, and then sat back down. Kelly liked them standing for her. Australian men didn't do that.

"Sorry, guys. We, uh, overslept," Kelly muttered somewhat embarrassed.

"Darling, they're English, not dead," replied Kane.

"Thought we'd take you to the shops first. Mrs. Branson? You want to go to Harrods?" asked Steve eyeing the young woman again with some humor. The thought passed by his brain as to why his wife didn't look this good after sex, and he sipped the ice water Kane had given to quell the rising thoughts in his mind.

"Do I? I mean, can we, Kane?" Kelly was excited at the prospect, her eyes gleaming with excitement.

"Why not? You need something for tonight. If I know Peter and Gina they'll dress for dinner. And we need some clothes for traveling: sweats, jeans, T's; and that's only for me," Kane laughed. He pulled the cigarettes from the back pocket of his super tight jeans.

Steve wondered how the heck he managed to get the cigarettes in there in the first place. He leaned forward and offered Kane a light from the bookmark packet of Savoy matches. The cigarette lit and Kane inhaled deeply, blowing smoke out in the non- smoking room.

"Can I get some fancy dress?" Kelly's eyes were wide with anticipation.

"Sure," replied Kane. " I'll even pick it out for you. Something strapless and sexy. Black high heels, you know, something that you could wear in a pit stop at Silverstone?"

Steve nearly swallowed the ice in his water and spluttered uncontrollably.

"My sentiments exactly. She wants to go with us into the pit. Imagine that. Kind of silly, don't you think?" Kane took another drag on the cigarette, a habit he had never dropped in all these years when he was either angry or being cautious.

"Not silly," she argued. "You need all the backing you can get. How do you know they won't hit on you next? You're Alexander's friend."

He'd thought of that. "Still a ridiculous idea, so forget it right now." Kane turned toward the two men.

"You two don't carry, do you?" asked Kane.

"No, but we can get permission in an emergency." Steve paused, and then braced himself. "Maybe Kelly should be in there with us." He set the glass of water down on the table.

Kane looked at Steve like he had lost his mind. "I thought you, of all people, would say no. You said you were married?"

"I am. But Linda is a housewife, not an agent in the AFP. Kelly's your wife, sir, but I think she has a point. At least you'd know where she was. And I'm sure Mrs. Branson can hold her own. I would think, Commander Branson, she would have to," he paused, mainly to get more confidence. "She is, after all, married to you." Had Steve said the last sentence out loud? He thought maybe he had gone insane.

Kelly had never heard anyone stand up to Kane like that before. Not someone new. She was astounded. Dave's coffee cup never reached his mouth and even Steve realized he had gone too far. But he had watched Kelly. She may be young, but very competent. Now, Steve sat virtually cringing, and waited for the outburst from the Australian.

Kane squashed the cigarette between his fingers and dropped it into the ashtray. Standing up, he moved to the window. London was bustling this time of day. Across the Thames he could see the Tower of London. That's where they locked up prisoners. Wasn't that what he was doing with Kelly? He was her jailer. Hadn't he taken her to Hong Kong where she'd proved herself over and again, and she was pregnant then. Why was this so different? They weren't on a mission. All he wanted was time with her. Instead, here they were again in some hotel room, albeit the Savoy, making plans to do just what they came not to do. He liked Steven and he was right. Feeling three sets of eyes on him, Kane turned around.

"Steven Asher! Anything, and I mean anything, happens to my wife and I will kill you." Kane's eyes made contact with the other man's.

"I know that, sir." Steve thought he had actually gotten off lightly with just a death threat.

Kelly took a short sharp breath. While his hand shook, Dave managed to replace the cup in the saucer.

Kane headed for the door making only one statement. "I'm driving!" He grabbed the room keys and his gun from on top of the dresser by the suite door, and forcibly shoved the .38 down the back of his jeans.

Kelly had never seen Kane so angry. His face was flushed red and his steely-blue eyes narrowed almost to a squint.

"We still going to the store?" Kelly asked tentatively, clutching her purse tightly to her body.

"Only because we have to," replied the arrogant Australian.

Kane marched in front of everyone else, with no one daring to speak on the way to the lobby. He'd expected support from Steve and he hadn't got it.

When the valet fetched the car and pulled up by the front entrance, Kane snatched the keys from him and jumped into the driver's seat. The valet opened the door for Kelly and she climbed in beside her husband. Steve glanced at Dave and shrugged his shoulders as he opened the door, and the two Englishmen climbed into the back seat. Kane hardly waited for them to close their doors before he started the engine and took the car straight out of the drive. At the Branson speed of high acceleration, Kane headed for the motorway. He had a pretty good idea where he was going, he hoped. Kane accelerated to the point that the car went into overdrive. Kelly pulled her seat belt tighter as Kane wove in and out of the traffic. The car handled like a dream. Built for speed and comfort, this one had both totally in tune. He drove the car like he did the Harley, with no hesitation and no fear. Still he didn't speak. Passing everything on the road, Kelly looked at the speedometer: seventy, eighty, ninety. They left the city and the Mercedes flew through the countryside, turning with precision on every bend. The clock read four-thirty. Kelly turned her head towards him. The speedometer caught her eyes: a hundred mph. This was crazy, even for him.

Kane glanced in the rearview mirror and seeing Steve's face, figured if there was any fear he hid it well. But Dave was nervous, with huge beads of perspiration running down his face. Steve would be good to have around. David Goodman, he wasn't so sure of. Kane shifted his gaze to Kelly's direction. Their eyes met and he winked at her. She smiled. He followed her eyes to the time, and Kane nodded so slightly she almost missed it. He dropped gears. Kelly smelled rubber burning and sat back in the seat now, enjoying the ride. Kane was pretty certain they'd lost the tail the Mercedes had had with them for half the trip. And in the back of their car one man sat convinced Kane Branson was not a man you would cross the line with more than once.

CHAPTER 3

"You like this one?" Kelly asked flaunting her body in a short, strapless black dress.

"It's okay," muttered Kane. Then he saw the dress that draped itself around the mannequin in the department store known as Harrods. "That's the one," he whispered.

Kane jumped up from the soft couch he had been sitting on, and walked across to the mannequin. He felt the silky material between his fingers, and immediately could imagine it wrapped around Kelly's body.

"I can't get in to that!" Kelly protested. "I'm too fat. And it's really glamorous. I'm the regular T-shirt and jeans girl." Kelly looked amazed that Kane would even suggest it.

"Well, maybe it's time to change your appearance! Just humor an old man and go try it on. I'll wait right here."

Kane hovered outside the cubicles as the stern looking sales person took the dress from the mannequin. The assistant ushered Kelly back inside the cubicle and stared at Kane, wishing with all sincerity he would disappear.

"Yes," came a voice from outside the dressing rooms. "I'm here with my wife and she doesn't look like you. Do us all a favor and try it on. Give your man a treat."

Kane walked back to the couch, turning to look at the fat little man who had made the comments. He sat smoking a long Cuban cigar. Kane glanced up at the no smoking sign, which even he obeyed in this store.

The rotund cigar-smoking man just kept on puffing. Gold jewelry dripped from his hands as he fished for his pocket-watch and held it to his ear. He shook the watch, and looked back at Kane's not so friendly face.

"Something wrong? It was just a joke. Most of us guys get to sit here and wait for our wives. Not every day you see one as young as your lady in here. Not unless she isn't your wife? Maybe your mist…"

"She's my wife," Kane cut in. There was something familiar about the fat little man. Kane had seen him before. "We met somewhere? You ever been to Australia?"

"Yeah, long time back. You're right. We have met someplace. You're not a man one would forget easily. Bet you're the same age as me." He stuck his hand out to Kane. "Jimmy Rogers. Part owner of Mercedes Racing. You would be?" Rogers figured he had to be someone if he was shopping in Harrods.

"The luckiest man in England today," Kane murmured and shook Jimmy's hand. The handshake was clammy. "Branson. K…Kene Branson. I race cars down under. My wife and I are here on a trip. Came to see a friend of ours race. You probably know him, Alexander Vincentia. I taught him to drive cars."

Enthusiasm streaked across the fat man's face. He was red and quivering.

"You know Vincentia? Taught him to race? What the hell are you doing driving cars down under?" Then Jimmy's tone changed. "I assume you know he crashed in practice yesterday?"

"Man, I heard that. Not like him. Probably go up and see him." He didn't want to appear over eager. "Some function at Silverstone we were going to be guests at. Guess that's off now." Kane leaned back on the brown leather sofa. Trying to act like he had money wasn't hard. Trying in dirty blue jeans and shirt, a little more difficult.

"Where are you staying, Mr. Branson?" asked Jimmy.

"Savoy." The hand-made snakeskin boots looked good though. "Lost our luggage on the flight over, and it's my wife's birthday. Special treat, along with the diamond ring I gave her. Wanted her to have something other than shorts to wear for dinner tonight with my friends from MI5."

Jimmy Rogers almost swallowed the cigar.

"You okay, mate? Those things will be the death of you. You must know my friend, Chief Inspector Graham? He knows all the top racing guys. He was on the front of Fortune magazine." He paused for effect. "That's where I've seen you before. You were inside the magazine with a brand new racing car or something like that."

"Mercedes teamed up with Vincentia's tire company. He races for me you know. You really race cars down under? Maybe that's where I've seen you? In some racing magazine."

'In a magazine all right, probably the Federal Police Times', thought Kane. 'Or Firearms weekly!' "That must be it," Kane replied.

Kane happened to glance up as he heard a rustling noise. Kelly appeared in the dress, and Kane did a double take.

"My god, Kel? Is that you under that?" Kane stood up and moved across the floor the greet her..

"You like it?" She glowed.

Her hair had managed to stay on top of her head for exactly thirty seconds. The dignified sales assistant had found Kelly shoes to match. Long drapes of red satin wrapped itself around Kelly's perfect body, with her breasts rising just above the button-up top. No straps to the dress, just a suntan. Her hips gave a perfect shape to the red material, and that in itself made the gown hit the floor just right. Her own chain with a K hung down her cleavage.

"Pearls" Jimmy Rogers was shaking as he spoke.

"What?" muttered Kane, his eyes never leaving Kelly's body.

"Pearls would look good on her. White stoned pearls, or maybe diamonds to match the light in her eyes, and the ring on her finger." Jimmy Rogers stopped. "Mr. Branson. I'm sorry." He was flustered. "I once knew someone that just looked like your wife does right now." Jimmy Rogers stared at the girl. "Ma'am, I'm sorry, but look?"

Jimmy stood up and pulled the tie from his collar, then unbuttoned the shirt. A gold locket protruded through. He fumbled with the clasp, and it popped open. Kane looked first. It could have been Kelly in the picture, and then she leaned forward to look.

"My god. Who is she?" asked Kane, his eyes not believing what he saw.

Rogers held the locket in his sweaty little palm and his voice choked out the words.

"I met her in a little town near Sydney about twenty-eight years ago. She was quiet and pretty. I was there on business for Mercedes. On my own, wife at home. Wasn't such a big shot back then. You know how it is, Mr. Branson? On my own in a big new land." He paused. Did Mr. Branson know? He doubted that. He figured Mr. Branson never had to go looking for a woman in his entire life. Rogers looked down at the locket and fingered it lovingly, and with some regret.

Kane saw that all too familiar look in the man's eyes. A look of love from a man for a woman. Kane happened to glance at Kelly. She'd perched herself on the arm of the sofa. There was an expression on her face that frightened him. Taking hold of her hand, he squeezed it. There was no response. He tried again and this time she responded. But the look stayed in her eyes and Kelly held her breath. Like she was afraid of the next statement, Kelly's gaze was fixed on the locket.

"I saw her a few of times before I realized what she was. She was on her own at first, then one night this guy appeared with her. Threatened he'd cut me up really badly if I didn't pay over a great deal of money. He'd been watching the last twice, even when… well…that doesn't matter. He said he would go to my boss. Figured correctly I was married. He also said he'd beat up the girl. So…I paid up. He beat her anyway, and me. When I finally came round they were gone and so was my wallet complete with credit cards, everything. My company took care of my indiscretions. Flew me back home. That was the last time I saw her, until…" Rogers hesitated.

Kane felt Kelly's hand tighten so hard around his that her knuckles turned white.

"What was her name?" she whispered.

"Jenny. Her name was Jenny."

Kelly's release on Kane was immediate. She stood up and smoothed down the dress.

"Excuse me. I should go and get out of this. Don't we have to get back to the hotel?"

Kane heard her words, but they were bland. It wasn't Kelly speaking.

"Yeah, baby. We can grab a few things on our way through the store. You want the dress?" asked Kane.

"Yes, please. I want the dress," and Kelly turned back towards them, slowly and seductively, her hair cascading down her back, and her eyes resting on Kane.

"Mr. Branson, I'm sorry, I hope I didn't upset your wife. She looked very uncomfortable when she left us. I shouldn't have told you all that. Don't know what made me do it. Haven't told anyone in years. My wife thinks this is a picture of my mother. It's just that your wife looks so much like Jenny. Kelly, that's her name?"

Kane nodded.

"Where does she come from in Australia?"

Good question. He doubted if his wife really knew, and Kane looked towards the lavish cubicle.

Kelly stood in the dressing room and looked in the mirror as Jenny looked back.

Outside Jimmy Rogers continued, "Mr. Branson, could we meet up tomorrow? I may have something to offer you. I would like to see how you perform on the track. Here's my card, call me around ten. Again, I am so sorry if I upset your wife. Have a very pleasant time this evening and give my respects to Inspector Graham."

Kane took the card. "Yeah, I will. Kelly's fine. Just a little sensitive right now. We have a six-month-old baby back in Sydney." How stupid did that sound?

He didn't seem surprised at the statement. "Ah, that would explain it. I hope to hear from you." Rogers shook Kane's hand with a surprisingly firm grip this time. "Better go find Mrs. Rogers. We have dinner plans also." He bustled away.

Kane waited for Kelly. It took a few minutes, but she appeared, calm and collected. Kane put his arm on her shoulder finding she was cold to the touch.

"You okay, darling? He apologized if he upset you. Tactless, I agree. But he had no way of knowing your background." Kane tried to reassure her.

"I'm fine," she replied rather too quickly. She glanced at her wristwatch. "You know its after six? We have to go back, shower, and we still didn't get clothes to take with us to, er, Silverstone, right?" She looked flustered and spoke much faster than usual.

"Kelly, slow down. We can pick up more clothes later. We have jeans each and a couple of T's. You got underwear from LAX, that's when you wear any, and I picked out a couple of black shirts for myself and some black pants while I was waiting for you. You got shoes right? The rest we'll get in the morning. Don't panic. I did see a couple of matching sweatshirts that I thought you might like. Got Harleys on the front. Tossed them in as well, along with shorts for you. I kind of like this buying spree thing." He was trying to snap her out of the obvious black mood she as in. Now was not the time to ask her where she was born.

Kane paid for the goods, and ushered Kelly out of the store. Outside Dave and Steve sat patiently waiting with the car parked on a meter. Steve jumped out of the car and took the packages from Kane's overloaded arms. This time Kane let Steve drive, and Kane opened the door so that he and Kelly could take the back seat.

Traffic was heavy on the bridge, but it wasn't too far back to the hotel. Kelly never looked at Kane the whole way back, and stared blankly through the tinted windows, all the time seeing absolutely nothing. Kane busied himself with his cigarettes.

As they arrived in the driveway of the Savoy, Kane noticed foot traffic had increased around the hotel entrance. After they disembarked from the car, the valet took the car-keys and drove the Mercedes away. The bellboy rushed forward to get the packages, hoping another twenty-pound note might slip his way. It did. They crossed the lavish lobby, and the elevator took the party up to the penthouse suite. The bellboy, complete with his load, hurried behind the Branson's. They stopped outside the penthouse and Kane unlocked the door with the keys. Once inside, the packages were placed on the nearby couch. Steve shuffled about unsure of what he should do next. He hadn't failed to notice the atmosphere in the car.

"You want us to hang around till the Inspector arrives?" asked Steve.

"Yeah. You blokes can take a break here in the suite while Kelly and I get ready. Order anything you want. This one's on me. Then when Peter says, you can go." Kane tossed the mini-bar keys to Steve.

Kelly still hadn't said a word since they left the store. Kane tried to draw her into the conversation, but it hadn't worked. Kane was trying to be patient, but he needed to talk to her…alone.

"Turn on the TV. Help yourself to a drink. The bar's fully stocked. There's fruit and crackers. If you don't see it, order it. I'm gonna take this long awaited shower." He pulled his shirt over his head as he walked into the bedroom, and closed the door behind him.

Kelly was heading for the shower when Kane laid his gun on the dresser.

"Kelly! Stop right there. What the fuck is wrong with you? A guy shows you a picture and you go to pieces. Kelly, did you hear me?" He threw his shirt on the overly spacious bed.

"How can I not hear you? The whole floor can hear you." Kelly shook as he spoke.

"Turn around." He banged his fist against the wall. "Damn it, Kelly. Turn around!"

She jumped, but kept on going through to the bathroom. She had never turned her back on her husband before. Kelly pulled her T-shirt over her head and unzipped the shorts, stepping out of them as she went.

"Don't you ever walk away from me again, you hear me?" Kane was angry. He followed her and slammed the bathroom door behind him.

"Don't you order me about, *Sir*! I'm your wife, not on an assignment for you. I do what I want." She was shaking uncontrollably. With tears streaming down her face, Kelly held her ground.

Kane sat down on the white whicker chair, pulled off his boots and unzipped his jeans. She kept her back to him. Kane knew he had to ask, and he knew the answer before he asked. Kane was interrogating his own wife. He watched her intently, noting once more how great her body looked, even after two children.

"Kelly, come here." His tone was less intimidating.

"I have to shower, and we have to get ready for your friends," Kelly replied, almost too civilly, all the time slowly but surely stripping her underwear from her.

It was then Kane lost it.

"Fuck my friends! Who is she, Kelly? Who is Jenny?" he yelled.

Kelly turned around, her nude body in front of him. "You know exactly who she is. You know," she screamed. "You're not stupid, Commander Branson. You married a prostitute! You knew my background. You know goddamn well who she is!"

"Then say it, Kelly. Let's get it out in the open right now." Standing, Kane grabbed hold of her arms. "Say it!"

Her hands grabbed his wrists and she held on tightly. "She's my mother! Happy now? Your newfound friend paid for sex with my mother. Told you she liked older men. She always did, just like m..." She stopped.

"Just like you? That's what you were going to say? You want me to leave you some money for what I'm about to enjoy?"

From the back of his jeans he pulled some of the bills that Steve had loaned him. He slapped the money on the small white table next to the shower.

"Make you feel better, Kelly? More like her? That's why you're so angry, isn't it? You think you're like her. You're nothing like her. Your father made you feel like that," he yelled. Kane realized he wasn't even making a dent on her.

"But I am just like her! I picked you up on a plane. What the hell is the difference? And we both know who the man was that beat her. You killed him, and I watched!"

Kane let go of his wife, and opened the shower door, turning on the water at the same time. He left it on cold, and turned back to Kelly, picking her up with one arm and putting her under the water. She screamed, loudly. Very loudly. Loud enough to be heard right through the bedroom.

Within seconds there was banging on the bedroom door.

"Commander Branson, is everything alright in there?" Steve yelled outside the door.

Kane closed the shower door leaving Kelly slumped down on the floor, and hurried back through the bedroom. He opened the door slightly.

"Fine, everything's fine."

Steve looked at the man in front of him. He could see the water down Kane's chest and the front of the commander's unzipped jeans.

"I'm sorry, Sir," he stammered. Steve was visibly embarrassed.

"Yeah, well. Understandable. Just wait in the room," and Kane closed the door behind him and strode back through the bedroom. At the bathroom door, he stepped out of his jeans.

Kane had to follow this through to the end. He had to let his wife know that it didn't matter that half of the world had slept with her mother. But there was another thought in his mind, and he knew it had to be in Kelly's, too. Jimmy Rogers.

Kelly sat under the cold water which poured down her naked body. She sat on the tiled floor oblivious to how cold she was. The door partially opened and Kane climbed in with her, turning the temperature to warm and pulling her up to him. She was still defiant her eyes fixed and round daring him to take her.

"This is how it's to be now, Kelly? You gonna act like a prostitute? Great. Then I'll treat you like one. Remember how it was, Kel? Those first few times, sex initiated by vengeance? You remember?"

He pushed her back against the shower wall, his hands around her hips, lifting her up till she was waist high then roughly entering her body. She cried out, her hands smacking his face, and she fought against him. He was incredibly strong, and he held her there thrusting into her with all the strength he had. Without warning he pulled out of her still holding her to the wall.

"You had enough, lady, or you want some more? Maybe I didn't get my money's worth from you yet. Is that it?"

He moved forward again into her body just as hard as before, bending his head slightly as he did. He wanted her to hit him, to put up some kind of defense against him.

After all he was raping his own wife. Blows landed on his head and as he rose up in front of her the blows hit his chest one after another. Kelly yelled and screamed at him trying to force him to quit, but by hitting him she only fueled the fire. He wouldn't stop till he had succeeded in getting to her.

Slowly, she stopped hitting, and her legs wrapped around his body. Kelly looked down at his face as he lowered them both to the floor as warm water gushed over their bodies. Kelly arched her back on the tiles and Kane lay on her. He felt the softness of her breasts under him and the now willingness of his wife. He ran his hands down her face and gently kissed her rounded mouth. She responded to him with an urgency that took his breath away. He whispered in her ear, and she closed her eyes tightly.

"You're nothing like her, Kelly, nothing. The only thing you had in common is that you are as beautiful as she was. And it wasn't her choice, Kel. Your father made her do it. Darling, you know that? Deep down you know that."

Kelly opened her eyes and looked at him, and then she cried, deep meaningful sobs that racked her body. He held her to him and rocked her in his arms, all the while leaning back on the shower door. Deep down inside he knew this had never been over, just in remission. Even from the grave her parentage haunted her.

"I'll make an excuse for you downstairs. Tell them you are tired from the flight. Not far from the truth." Kane buttoned up his black silk shirt as he spoke. "It'll be okay. There will be other times to show off my new and young wife." As he combed his hair, he watched her in the mirror.

Kelly sat on the bed bundled in huge white bath towels with her knees tucked under her chin. She fluffed her hair with her hands making sure it was drying.

"Kane, I'm sorry, I let you down, just when you need me the most. One friend's in the hospital, you have another one waiting downstairs, and tomorrow you're gonna race track. Kane, I'm so sorry. I don't know why it got to me so much…"

"Hey, come on." He sat on the bed next to her. "It's okay, baby." He slid his arms around her. "It had to be a shock for you. I won't call Jimmy Rogers. There has to be another way in to the circuit. Mercedes isn't the only group around."

"No. You call him," she urged. "I can deal with it. I'm not a child. I'm the Commander's wife. Just stall them downstairs and I'll be down. Okay?" She nudged his chest.

"Sure, baby. You want Dave to wait for you?" His tone was gentle as he rose from the bed.

"No. All of you go down and I'll join you. Just give me a few minutes alone."

Kane turned to look at her one last time before he left her. Kelly's eyes started at the top of him and went down and back. He smiled at her obvious implying looks. Tight black jeans, black silk shirt and his blonde hair shining in the lights of the bedroom.

"Kelly, you take women's lib to the extreme. Aren't I supposed to look at you like that?" he asked.

"You will, baby. Now go," and she scooted off the bed and pushed him to the door. She let her hand rest on the backside of his jeans far longer than was necessary.

"Think I'd rather stay with you, Kel…" he protested.

"Go!" she ordered.

She heard him talking to the blokes in the other room. Then it was quiet. She didn't cry. Now was not the time. Now was the time to stand beside her man.

Kelly dropped the towels to the floor. Pulling her long hair on top of her head, she pinned it there with a couple of clips. Kelly looked in the full-length mirror and had to admit she did look good. She had already decided no underwear. Stepping into the dress, Kelly did the buttons up the front which were so tight that they pushed her breasts up high. The matching K on the chain hung low. She sat down on the stool in front of the mirror and pulled strands of hair down the side of her tanned face. She wanted to look good for Kane. A subtle shade of beige eye-shadow was all her sparking eyes needed. She added some lipstick and a touch of class, natural class. Kelly stood up and looked again in the long mirror. Slipping on the high heels gave her three more inches height. The woman from the locket smiled back at her with approval. Kelly laughed with a gentle tone in her voice.

"But you don't have a man like Kane, mother," and Kelly slipped the brand new sparkling ring back on her finger.

Kane strode across the lobby flanked by the two men who were in stark contrast to him, English to the core with their short haircuts and pale complexions. Branson smiled to himself. Both men were out to prove themselves just like he had done all those years ago and one had a good chance of doing just that. Kane saw the Inspector first.

"Peter, long time no see, my friend." Kane didn't wait to shake hands. He embraced Graham in a bear hug.

"My god, Kane! You haven't changed a bit. It's amazing. You found the fountain of youth or something? Stand back," and he held Kane at arms length. "It's amazing, Kane. I'm lost for words. We're the same age and look at me!" Graham patted his rounded stomach. "I started losing my hair years ago. Seems it came to Australia and found you. Yours is even longer than when you were a young man."

"My wife likes it like this, and the facial stubble that goes with it. Sorry about no tie and jacket. We didn't have a whole lot of time today. Thought a silk shirt would be fine though." He smoothed down the front of the shirt and flipped his long hair back, considering maybe he should pulled it back in a ponytail.

"Looks great from this side," a woman's voice rang out from behind Kane.

Kane turned around. "Gina. You look terrific!" He planted a huge kiss on the cheek of the woman in front of him.

She did look good but older. Long black dress, with sleeves. Finely brushed, slightly graying hair, but she still held the charm that she always had. She hugged Kane to her. Gina was Gina, very sophisticated, yet bold and overwhelming. Classy and yet warm.

Inspector Graham acknowledged his men.

"You looking after my friend here?" He turned towards Kane. "Are they, Kane?"

"Very well. Went for a nice *spin* in the car this afternoon. Did some *shopping at* Harrods," responded Kane.

"How much do they pay you for being Commander?" Peter whispered. "I can't get over the way you look. And you're a father again? Twice over?"

"Yeah. Little girl almost six, named Star, and a boy, Kene, six months old and a thirty-seven-year old son." Kane waited for the reaction.

"A son how old?" asked Gina very much taken aback.

"Six months," repeated Kane.

"No, not that one, the other one," replied her husband even more shocked than his wife.

"Long story, Peter. My life is very different from when I was married to Sage Jay." Kane paused. "She was murdered a few years back. Wasn't far from our home." He stopped and took a deep breath.

Gina glanced at her husband.

"We're so sorry," she said.

"It's okay, now. My daughter, the one you met, came back home after trying the hard life. She's married to my deputy, correction, the guy who took over as SFA after me, and they have a daughter older than my youngest kid. They live with us in a huge house near Sydney. House goes with the position," stated Kane. 'Lie number what?' thought Kane. He continued out loud. "Made Commander after my hundredth mission, and that's when I discovered I had a thirty-odd-year-old son named Sam."

Peter looked at the ground. "Big discovery. Your first mission was Lantau, right?"

"Good memory, Peter." Kane was impressed, "And it produced a son."

Gina was looking around for the missing link. Kane noticed.

"You looking for someone?" asked Kane.

"You said you were married again?" replied Gina, tossing her hair back over her shoulders.

She was looking at every woman around forty that went by. Kane always had a thing for younger women. She remembered that.

"My wife was feeling tired. Long day you know, but she'll be down in a minute. So, that's my life in brief." He decided that was enough info for now. "What have you guys been up to in the last twenty years?" Kane went straight to the point.

"Is it really that long? Guess it must be. Your Sage had been at school a couple of years. Kane, I'm really sorry about Sage Jay. Did they get the bloke that did it?" His tone was sympathetic.

"I got them all; one by one. Five in total." His tone was very deliberate. "You may as well know. My wife is the daughter of one of the guys I took out. He was one of the main drug dealers in Australia. It's complicated but I am very happy with Kelly. She joined me in the force, and so far has given me two wonderful children." Kane smiled.

"So far? She found the fountain of youth also?" asked Peter.

"No, sir. She *is* the fountain of youth," Dave grinned, and pushed his dark hair from his eyes.

He and Steve stood hovering at the back of the group the whole time.

They were so quiet that Kane almost forgot they were still there. Dave's comment amused Kane.

"Very good. I'm impressed. Speaking of which?" a smiling Kane interjected.

Peter caught Kane staring at the young woman getting out of the elevator and that woman was more than stunning. Red satin clung to her body as if embroidered onto her skin. She walked with an air of confidence and yet she was still a child compared to them. Kane took a step forward letting out a breath of admiration. Peter caught Kane by the arm.

"Better not let your wife see you staring at a beautiful young woman in that manner." 'Nor my own,' he thought.

Kane Branson smiled and pulled away from Peter Graham, striding boldly across the lobby to Kelly. Steve moved to his boss's side.

"Sir, that *is* his wife," remarked Steve, smiling.

"Good grief, Peter. She's young enough to be his daughter. Younger women, yes, but..." Gina hesitated.

Peter reached for Gina's hand and squeezed it tightly.

"Gina, it's his affair whom he marries. If Kane's happy, that's all that counts." 'How could he not be happy married to her?' thought Peter, " No wonder he looks so damn good."

"What?" Gina bristled and turned to look at her husband.

"Nothing. How old is she, Steven?" asked Peter.

"Twenty-seven. Today is her birthday. You look shocked, sir? I have to admit we were a little surprised...by them both. Kane, I mean Commander Branson, isn't quite what we were expecting." Steve slipped and corrected himself very quickly.

"*Commander Branson* always did have a penchant for being different, even as a rookie. And *Mrs. Branson* definitely isn't what we were expecting. But that's okay. We'll get over it. When we go into dinner you two take the rest of the evening off. Be ready bright and early in the morning."

Kane put his hand round Kelly's hand. He held it tightly, and looked her up and down.

"Told you you would!" Kelly giggled.

"What, baby?" replied Kane a little curious.

"Look at me like that," and she laughed out loud, a precocious and endearing laugh that Kane loved for.

"You look wonderful. I have to be the proudest man in the world right now. Look at their faces. They're speechless, like I am when I look at you."

Kelly's hand tightened around in his. "I'm terrified. The heels are too high and I feel like my boobs are gonna fall out the dress… and I didn't put on underwear."

The last statement caught Kane off guard. Kelly giggled again and Kane would not have been surprised if Kelly had popped gum right at that point.

"Now you'll be thinking about that all through dinner," laughed Kelly. "Under that dress, you're the same Kelly that I love. Don't you really have any on?" He slid his hand down her backside. There was no panty line. "My god, Kel, you don't. Good girl. Let's go introduce you to world, and the world to you." 'And I'm not sure that this world is ready for either of us.'

Kane held her hand tightly and led Kelly across the highly-polished marble floor till he reached his friends. Her heels clicked as she walked.

"Peter, Gina… this is my wife, Kelly."

Gina put her hand out to her. Kelly reciprocated the gesture, both tight and fast grips.

"Nice to meet you, Kelly. Kane tells us you have two children, one only six months old," quipped Gina. "And what a wonderful dress and that ring…"

"My pleasure. My husband speaks very highly of you both." She turned to Peter. "Especially of you, sir, and the ring is a birthday gift from Kane."

"Kelly, the names Peter. *Definitely* a pleasure meeting you, and now I know why Kane looks so young. You two planning on any more children?" Peter couldn't resist the question. He looked at Kelly and then his own wife. Kane Branson was indeed very lucky.

"I'd like another one, before I'm too old," Kane replied casually.

"You'll never be too old, Kane," she replied, smiling demurely at her husband. Kelly remembered where they were, and turned back to his friends. "So, has my husband changed much over the last few years?"

"Yes and no. But whatever he's doing, it suits him," put in Peter. Kane was doing something right.

"Sir, I think the Maitre' D is trying to let you know your table is ready," Steve whispered in Kane's ear.

"Steve," muttered Kane. "Stop calling me *sir.* It makes me feel old."

"I have to, Mr. Branson." He nodded towards his boss.

"Peter," Kane turned to Graham. "Tell these guys to call me Kane, better still Kene"

"Kene, why Kene? Don't you have a relative by that name? He drives racing cars back in Aus…"The penny dropped. "Kene Branson, that why you wanted it set up like that…" Peter Graham touched his forehead. The penny had dropped.

"Like what?" questioned Kelly, looking up at Kane.

"Nothing, darling," and Kane very noticeably slid his hand around Kelly's waist and down onto her backside and left it there.

Gina looked disapprovingly at Kane. Peter envied the hand.

"Shall we go into dinner, ladies and gentlemen?" Kane remarked and ushered Kelly through the door in front of them, still with his hand on a tight cute butt.

Kelly's eyes widened. The dining room was simply aglow with chandeliers and candles. Red velvet chairs, drapes to match, and the richest looking people Kelly had ever seen. The place was crowded with the high society of London. Jewelry appeared to drip from the anointed few, and Kelly noted even the waiters looked better dressed than her on a bad day.

"Darling, try not to look so surprised. This is the Savoy. It's time we had some good times in our life. Maybe time to be Mr. and Mrs. Branson. This could be the beginning of a different kind of life," whispered Kane in his wife's ear.

"Kane, what are you saying? You're not gonna quit the force 'cause I won't let you. It's your life." She walked side by side with him. Even with high heels she was still tiny next to him.

His reply was too quick. "No, baby. You are. The job is secondary to you."

The Maitre 'D pulled back the chair for Kelly to sit down. The others followed suit. With napkins fluffed on their laps and their glasses filled with ice cold water, Gina started the conversation first.

"Kelly," gushed Gina, "how did you meet Kane?" She leaned on the hand, elbow just on the edge of the table, her eyes piercing into Kelly's.

Kelly looked at Kane first for his cue. He raised his eyebrows and smiled.

"I propositioned him up on a flight to Brisbane." Kelly sipped her ice-water.

A pin dropped.

Kane chimed in. "I let her. Well, come on, Peter. Wouldn't you let her, too?"

"You're damn right I…" He stopped, probably because his wife's foot had sent gnawing pains up his right leg.

"You often do that, Kelly?" continued Gina trying to contain herself.

"Not since Kane. Before that I made a good living at just that. Girl has to be inventive and do something to put food in her stomach." Kelly kept a straight face and helped herself to a bread roll instead of waiting for the waiter to offer the breadbasket.

"Is she serious, Kane? Or is she pulling our leg here?" commented Peter.

"Dead serious. That's why she makes such a good cop. She knows both sides of the fence. She can fire a gun, pursue a victim and bring them down better than most. I'm very proud to have her as my backup," acknowledged her husband.

"And that's why I want in when Kane goes in as a race car driver. I know how to do all that stuff. He thinks I can't do it, and that someone will spot me, me not being a guy an' all." She turned to him. "You just said yourself how good I am. Steve said I should go. Dave thinks so, too. He's just to afraid to say so." She popped a piece of the crusty bread in her mouth.

"Afraid of who?" retorted Kane looking surprised.

She swallowed. "You. You scare him to death. You half agreed anyway."

"When?" he exclaimed.

"This afternoon in the bedroom when we were making…." She nudged his arm, and her eyes flashed mischievously.

"Oh, yeah, right." Kane interrupted and smiled, ignoring Peter and Gina's stare. "Okay, on the condition that you give me what I want in return," replied Kane.

"And that would be?" Kelly crinkled her face at him.

He leaned round the table and whispered in her ear.

Kelly laughed, and from the far side of the room the laugh echoed back.

CHAPTER 4

Kane heard it and turned in his seat. Jimmy Rogers and his party sat at the far end of the palatial restaurant.

"Oh, great!" muttered Kane.

He glanced back at Kelly. Her back was to Rogers' group, and for once Kane wasn't sure how to handle this. Jimmy Rogers would see them at some point during the evening, especially the woman in the red dress. He could either tell Kelly now and get it over with, or wait until the obvious event happened. He thought about it for a few seconds and then Kane slid his arm around Kelly's chair and whispered in her ear.

Kelly's face turned ashen. Her hand reached for Kane's and she gripped his fingers tightly. Slowly Kelly turned her head and looked in Jimmy Roger's direction. Kane stared at Kelly's face. He could see the hatred in her eyes not for the man himself, but for what he stood for. Jimmy Rogers puffed smoke rings from his Cuban cigar into the air, while Kelly's eyes followed them and Kane's followed Kelly.

Peter Graham observed the whole situation. He leaned back in the chair and watched as his friend exerted an authority over Kelly. He looked in the direction that the Branson's were intently starring. Peter was fascinated.

"Excuse me, I need the bathroom," stated Kelly and started to stand.

Kane held her by the hand and pulled her back down on the seat. "No, you don't, Kel. You're not gonna run anymore. He's there and we're here. Get used to it. Otherwise you'll be running forever," Kane whispered. As he leaned across her, Kane's shirt rippled across his muscular body, but his face depicted that of a stone statue.

In slow motion, Kelly turned to look at her husband. He was right and it wasn't her problem. If she ran now she would always be on the run.

"You're right as usual. I'm fine," but her grip still stayed on her husband's fingers.

"A friend of yours, Kelly?" asked Gina in a sarcastic tone.

"Gina!" Peter said angrily at his wife. "A problem, Kane?" Peter asked turning to his friend.

"No problem. Just someone we met in Harrods. He..." He felt Kelly's fingers tighten on his. "He offered to let me go drive a car tomorrow at the race track. You must know him? Jimmy Rogers? Head of Mercedes racing."

"Yes, I know him. Decent enough guy by all accounts." He leaned forward and spoke softly to Kane. "Your wife okay?"

"Fine. She's fine. She just doesn't want me to go race. You know these women. Get protective." Kane didn't believe this stuff was coming from his mouth. It was crap and he knew it. And he knew Peter Graham knew it.

Gina picked up her menu and viewed the contents of the pages.

"Well, I'm hungry." She gazed up from the menu and made Kelly her objective. "You need to eat. You need to keep up your strength for goodness knows what." Her tone was less than friendly. "After all, you are a growing *girl*."

The pain in her toes from her husband's shoe was not pleasant. Gina stemmed the scream that wanted to leave her mouth. She buried her head deep in the Savoy's menu.

Meanwhile Kelly regained her composure very successfully.

"Kane tells me you all grew up together," she commented, and focused on Peter.

This was the Kelly Kane knew.

"Don't believe anything Kane tells you about those days. We were just kids having a great time, the three of us: Kane, me and Alexander. It was always Kane and Alexander that were the center of attention, always in trouble, or being chased by the ladies. Mostly your husband really. I was the innocent bystander," laughed Peter, and pulled his stomach in to make himself look thinner.

"Sure you were, Peter. That's not how I remember it." Kane replied. He was still concentrating on Kelly.

Peter noted that Kelly still kept her hand tightly on Kane's. Kane was indeed a lucky man. He may look like a very well dressed Hell's Angel, he may talk with an accent, but he had a wife and a lifestyle that Peter Graham could only dream of. Indeed, his friend was fortunate. Why did he have the feeling that Kane had not told him everything in the conversation they had had? He knew Kane was close to Vincentia. Everyone knew that, but there was more.

Kane sat back in the chair and never let go of Kelly's hand, pulling it down on his lap, letting both their hands rest there. His eyes searched Kelly's face and knew what she was thinking without her even saying. Kane also knew that Peter was watching him. He needed MI5 on his side. He needed the AFP. He didn't need the Mob. But he was Kane Branson and he could deal with it.

"So, you want me to order for you, baby?" Kane asked, Kelly knowing full well she couldn't read French.

"Yes, would you?" her seductive blue eyes gazed at him.

She'd glanced at the menu and didn't understand a word it said. Kane had never taught her how to read French. That had been the last thing on his mind to teach her. While she thought about that her pinned up hair began to irritate her. She pulled at the clip that was sticking in her head letting half the hair tumble down. Kane reached over and pulled the other clip, that he could see, out from its resting place. Kelly shook her head sensually and the long curly hair cascaded down her back.

"And you want to go in the pits as a guy!" Kane raised his eyebrows as he spoke.

"Certainly doesn't look like any guy I ever saw," Peter added, without even stopping to think about it, and totally ignoring his wife's piercing stare.

"Me neither." Jimmy Rogers intervened.

So intently were they watching Kelly, none of them noticed Jimmy leave his table and walk across the floor. Now he stood behind Kelly's chair admiring her hair. He stretched his hand out slowly to Kane.

"Mr. Branson, you are a lucky man." Rogers' eyes were moist.

Kane pushed his chair back and stood up, shaking Rogers' hand as he did. Kelly also went to stand.

"No, Jen..." Rogers stopped speaking.

Kane interceded and introduced the rest of the party.

"I believe you know Inspector Graham, and this is his wife Gina. Peter, Jimmy Rogers, the driving force behind Mercedes."

Peter stood and extended his hand to Jimmy. Rogers' confusion over Jenny lasted momentarily. He let go of Kane's hand and shook Peters'.

"We've met before, Inspector Graham. Mrs. Graham." Then he turned his attentions to Kane. "Kene, I wanted..."

"You wanted to confirm tomorrow. I had planned to call you about coming to try the track out before I leave for Silverstone." Kane rested his arm on Rogers' less than broad shoulder. "How about my guys and I arrive around ten. Just need to practice some." In the back of his mind he was thinking *some* was an understatement. "I believe the address was on the card you gave me. You having a pleasant meal…good, mate. Let me walk you to your table."

With his arm round Jimmy's shoulder, Kane all but ushered Rogers away from their table. Kane glanced back at Kelly and winked at her. Kelly smiled back. She knew what Kane was doing, and watched them walking through the dining room, back to Jimmy's party.

"Well, why don't we order some wine?" asked Peter, trying to break the tension that shrouded the table.

"Kane and I don't drink that much. He has the occasional whiskey, but that's about it. I tried to get him to quit smoking, too. We made a pact. I kept my side, but he failed." She picked up her water and took a long drink, staring into the glass like she was expecting something to emerge from it.

"Not like Kane to fail at anything. What did you give up, Kelly?" asked Peter with some apprehension.

"Cocaine." She paused, and watched the reaction on their faces. Satisfied, she had stunned them, she continued. "Kene suits Kane, don't you think?"

"Uh, yes." That was all Peter could think of and his glass of ice water hit the table with a thump.

Kelly suppressed a giggle at Peter's loss of words.

"You look shocked, Inspector Graham. I'm sure Kane told you I'm an AFP agent. My father was a man named Walker, who participated in Kane's first wife's death. I was a prostitute back then and a drug addict. That was before Kane, who changed my life in more ways than one. We have two really great children, and hopefully maybe in the next year we'll have another. Where he goes I go, and that includes to Silverstone and the pits!"

Kelly was back where she belonged on top of the situation. She flopped back in the chair and draped herself seductively over the arm.

"Don't you think that's just a little bit dangerous? Kane going in to see what happened to our friend is one thing. You going in also is another. I can give him the entire backup he needs from MI5."

Peter was on a fishing trip and Kelly knew it. So the Inspector didn't know the whole story, but then again did she know exactly what Kane was planning?

"I'll be fine, Peter. I'm used to Kane and the way he operates. I trained under him at the academy and you know what? He nearly killed me. What everyone else did, I did twice. He's a hard taskmaster, but I kept going and I ended up going on his hundredth mission with him to Hong Kong. I saw things that changed the way I thought. And saw the things that changed his life. We have a bond that nothing can break. You understand that, don't you?"

She looked at Peter with an expression that penetrated through his British suit of armor. Peter Graham did understand. He understood that this slip of a girl was on to him and nodded his head at her.

"So, you missed me?" Kane's question was directed at Kelly. He leaned over her chair and his hair hung down near her face. Pushing it out of the way he continued,

"Think I should get this cut..."

"Don't even think about it. Or I'll cut mine so short you'll think I'm a boy," chirped Kelly.

Peter doubted that last statement. Kelly? A boy? Never.

"Smart lady you have, Kane. Your friend Jimmy get seated again?" asked Peter looking around.

"Yeah, man. Peter, is it okay if I borrow your boys for the next few days? Got two more joining us, some of Marie Vincentia's friends, and, of course, Kel here."

Kane raised his eyebrows at Peter in mock gesture. Kelly didn't miss the look, but she had her own plans.

Dinner was pleasant. The Savoy served some of the best cooked food in town. It smelled good and it tasted great. With each course she watched which cutlery Kane used and followed suit. The roast duck and orange went down well and the salad only complimented it. Kelly was careful to leave room for the sweet stuff. She had seen the tray circulating the room and this kind of food cost a lot of money. Kelly also decided she could get accustomed to this kind of lifestyle really fast.

"You enjoying that, Kelly?" asked Kane with much amusement.

Kane had been watching his wife tuck into the roast duck and orange sauce. He wondered with some amusement, where she was putting all the food, maybe in a hollow foot. She patted her stomach and then he saw the butterfly wings rise on her breast. Kane saw Peter notice also. And she wanted to be one of the guys.

"It's a butterfly. Pretty isn't it, Peter?" asked Kane.

"Very." Peter looked away knowing Kane had seen him watching her breast. "Kane, I was thinking. Mind if I come with you guys to Silverstone? I don't mean tomorrow to Jimmy Rogers place, but when you go up the road. I can work in the pits, keep track of Kelly for you, and I always had this desire to be around cars."

Kane smiled and had been expecting that request half an evening back. Gina's eyes popped and turned to face her husband in total amazement.

"You want to do what? Have you gone insane? From Kane I would expect it. Alexander also. But you? You're the quiet one. The slippers in front of the fire guy. What the heck can you do there?" Gina said with raised voice.

"Actually, he can do quite a bit, Gina." Kane thought his plan was working just fine. "I like the idea. Man, the more I think about it, the better it gets. You, your boys and the Italians, and us. I did mention the Italians, didn't I? Yes, sure I did. Okay. You got a deal."

Kane leaned across the table and shook Peter's hand.

"Just like old times, Peter. Just like old times," and Kane leaned back in the plush chair. "Oh, by the way, mate, put the check on my room." Kane was arrogant in his self confidence.

Now Kelly knew what Kane's plan was in keeping everyone together. She marveled at his maneuverings.

"I'll call you later tomorrow, after I visit Rogers' place. Have to see how I do first. Been a long time since I raced anything," added Kane.

He stood up, his silk shirt pulling tight across his chest. Kane pushed the chair back, and leaned down for Kelly's arm. She took hold of it and stood up, her slim body encased in red. And the Grahams stood also.

"It's been a pleasure meeting you both." And Kelly extended her hand towards Gina.

The two women shook hands. Kelly's shake was firm, where as Gina's was not. Peter couldn't help notice how well Kane and Kelly complimented each other. He wasn't jealous…

"I'll let you know how I do in the morning. Have to be there bright and early so I'll just take the guys." He squeezed Kelly's arm, praying she would not object right there, and then let go of her. "Gina, always nice to see you." Kane hugged her. "Peter, talk to you in the afternoon."

"Absolutely. Kelly," and Peter pulled Kane's wife to him and whispered in her ear. "Whatever you are doing keep doing it. My friend looks happier than he has all his life."

Kelly blushed and she pulled away from Peter very slightly.

The Grahams watched the Bransons walk away.

"Want to trade me in for a Kelly model?" asked Peter's wife.

Peter put his arm around Gina.

"Nope. I haven't got the stamina for a Kelly model. Nor the looks. I'm not Kane Branson." 'Unfortunately,' he thought.

Kelly leaned on the rail in the elevator. She was tired. The lift attendant pushed the buttons. Kane watched Kelly. He had never realized till tonight, when he saw her come out of the elevator, just how much he loved her. Without her his life would be nothing. As though she read his mind, she leaned forward and slipped her hand into his. She squeezed it tightly, and cocked her head on one side. She understood Kane Branson very well.

They walked hand in hand to the penthouse suite. He unlocked the door, then picked Kelly up in his arms and pushed the door firmly shut behind them.

Kane woke first and was tempted to wake Kelly. She turned in her sleep and her arm rested on his chest. She looked peaceful and he thought better of waking her. He slid out from under her and flipped the silk sheets back across her. Showering in the luxurious bathroom, he left the towels lying on the floor. He stepped back into the bedroom and pulled clothes from the closest. Champagne glasses still sat by the Jacuzzi from last night, along with the empty ring box. Kane chuckled to himself as he thought about Kelly and her birthday surprise. Kane slipped into jeans and a black T-shirt he'd picked out yesterday. He pulled on his boots and slid the cell phone inside and looked at the gun still lying on the dresser. Aside from down the back of his jeans, there was nowhere else to put it. It was too warm for a jacket. But the black shirt he pulled on covered Kane's credentials nicely. He scribbled a note and left it on the pillow for her. On top of it he placed a red rose from the teacart, and closed the bedroom door quietly behind him. It was eight A.M. exactly. He had one thing left to do before he left the suite. He needed to call Maria.

In the lobby, Sergio and Bruno sat. Sergio shifted uneasily in his seat, and in his clothes. He wasn't a jeans and sweatshirt kind of guy. Bruno adapted more easily. His dark features were emphasized by the bright blue jeans and white T- shirt he wore. They still stood out in the crowd, but not so predominantly as before. Two men approached them. Bruno recognized the one immediately from yesterday. Short blonde hair and dressed in black, a younger version of the one now alighting from the elevator.

Kane strode across the floor to greet his happy teamsters. Never had he seen such an odd looking collection of people. He smiled to himself. If this worked it would be a miracle.

"G'day, mates'. Man, you should see yourselves. Two salts and two peppers."

The two parties sat together yet apart. That was going to change right then and there as far as Kane was concerned.

"Steve, you met Bruno yesterday. Meet him again today. He's your new partner for the racetrack. Dave, this is Sergio. Now all shake hands, kiss and make up and let's get the hell on the road. Just us guys today and we need to get to Mercedes by ten. Steve, you got the car?"

An astounded looking Steve nodded a yes. "Valet parked," he spluttered.

"Let's go, then," and Kane slapped him on the back.

Kane strode across the lobby with his entourage in tow. Leader of the pack. Outside Steve hailed the valet and they waited in silence for the Mercedes. When it finally drew up, Kane climbed in and sat behind the steering wheel. The others jumped in the remaining seats for fear they would be left standing in the dust.

"Sir, I mean, Kane…don't you think I should drive?" stammered Dave.

"Nope. I'm driving here. So get used to it." Kane shifted the automatic into drive and took off at the usual 'Branson' speed. He adjusted the rear view mirror to suit his eye level and viewed all three occupants of the backseat.

Steve watched him. Sitting alongside Kane was an experience, and he tightened his seat belt an extra notch. An experience maybe, exciting definitely.

"It's only eight-thirty. Let's go for our own *spin* first. Your M1 motorway makes a good track. Lot of traffic, but that's okay. You guys in the back better buckle up there." Kane grinned, and his boot bent the metal.

The silver-gray Mercedes took off. "You blokes alright back there?" He heard the seatbelts click in unison.

"Fine, just fine," boomed Dave above the roar of the accelerating engine.

Steve smiled. He knew Kane was testing the water not the car. In the outside lane Kane powered the car to ninety, then a hundred and they all could smell the burning rubber of red hot tires.

"Sir, Kane, better watch the speed limit. Would be kind of embarrassing if we got a ticket, especially in Inspector Graham's car," Steve reminded Kane.

But Steve had to admit Kane was a good driver, and he himself was enjoying the speed. He doubted that hear no evil, see no evil, and speak no evil in the back were. He turned to look at his partner, the real one. Dave was ashen and he mouthed words to him.

"Think you better get used to this way of doing things, *mate*!"

Dave cocked his head on one side and starred back at Steve. "Funny."

The two Italians showed only an emotion of fear. Kane inclined his head just slightly and caught Steve's comments. It amused him. This little test was to sort the men from the boys. So far he could see one man. He did need Peter Graham and he did need Kelly after all. Admitting it was another thing. His mind returned to the pace he had set. Maybe he was going too fast. He slowed the vehicle down to normal speed, and glanced at the clock. Nine-fifteen. They needed to get going to Rogers' place. Fun time was over.

"Okay, Mister shotgun rider. You worked out the route to his place? Thought I saw you with a map earlier. Can't be that far away from here." Kane glanced at his co-pilot.

Steve pulled the crumpled map from his jeans pocket.

"Did some checking last night. Mercedes headquarters were pretty easy to find on the map. Should only take about twenty minutes to get there, and the way you drive, ten!"

"That's true. You don't scare easy, do you Steve?" questioned Kane.

"Not paid to scare. Just to do my job and sometimes even to enjoy it. Like now," came the reply.

"That's what I thought. We need to toughen those guys up in the back. You game?" laughed Kane mischievously.

Steve grinned. "Just what did you have in mind? No, don't tell me.

Probably something illegal. I'll just go along with whatever it is." He threw his hands in the air.

"Good man. I knew you'd be the right choice for back up. Your boss is coming also."

Kane looked dead ahead as he spoke, his broad hands gripping the wheel tightly.

"My what? Inspector Graham at Silverstone? Our Inspector Graham?" Steve asked nervously.

"The very same. You look surprised. Peter Graham is a good mechanic. We also used to mess with cars back in Oz. Peter, myself and Alexander, when we were kids and still growing up."

"By the way, how is Mr. Vincentia doing?" asked Steve. "They didn't say anything on the news about him today."

"They won't right now. Few things need to be kept quiet. Sabotage isn't something you publicize across the silver screen." Kane paused. "You had figured out that's why we were going, right?" He glanced quickly at the man next to him.

"Obviously. Mr. Vincentia is too good a driver for it to be an accident of that kind. You wouldn't be doing all this, and Inspector Graham would not have sent us with you, let alone going himself. You think your new friend can help us?" Steve kept his voice low on purpose.

"Mr. Rogers?" Kane uttered.

"Yes," replied Steve.

"He can get me a car to drive. Probably last pole position, but a car nonetheless. Depends how I do this morning. Need to be able to pull off some good speed. That's why I didn't want Kelly along, that and…well you don't need to know anything else yet."

Steve gave him a quizzical look. Commander Branson was deep. He was sure he would find out when Kane was ready to tell. Steve peered at the map and commented to Kane.

"Turn left at the next traffic light. Then the next right and we are there."

Steve turned across the seat to look at his partner. Dave was still ashen. Steve chuckled to himself. All the times they had driven the old wreck cars Dave had never looked like that. Sergio and Bruno looked a little healthier. Good job they didn't have to get in the racing car with Kane Branson he mused.

Kane turned where he was asked to. The noise of the engines could be heard before the car hit the street. As they pulled into the car park emotions stirred in Kane that he thought were long forgotten. He hit the button for the window. As it went down, he could smell burning oil and the odor that only red-hot tires made.

Steven Asher watched the older man's face. He could see the fire in his eyes, smoldering ready to ignite. He knew there and then Commander Branson could race. Steven stepped out of the car, and out of sheer courtesy and respect, opened Kane's door for him. Kane acknowledged with a nod of his head, and without waiting for anyone, set a stride across the car park towards a waiting Jimmy Rogers, who was waving his arms frantically at Kane.

"Boy is that man going to take some keeping up with," murmured Steve. He looked at his old partner. "You okay, Dave? You look a little pale. Must be something you ate," and he suppressed a laugh.

"Kane drove faster than yesterday. He's crazy. Thank God we don't have to get in the racing car with him. He'd kill us," and Dave heaved a sigh as he struggled out of the car and leaned on the doorframe.

"No, he wouldn't," and Steve looked in Kane's direction. "He knows exactly what he's doing."

The Italians climbed out muttering words that sounded remarkably like they were cursing. Bruno leaned against the car, while Sergio sat down on the ground and heaved a sigh of relief.

"Mr. Rogers. Great morning. Man, wonderful day to race," and Kane stared right past him to the edge of the track.

"Kene. Right on time." He glanced at his gold watch. Jimmy figured Kane to be Mr. Punctuality. "No Mrs. Branson?" Jimmy looked around for her.

"No. Left her asleep. She didn't get much rest last night," and Kane laughed out loud. He glanced at Rogers hoping he had made the point very clear. "So where does one go to get a suit?"

Rogers bristled slightly before answering. "Straight to business, Kene. I like that in a man. Follow me. See you have your guys with you." Jimmy peered across the lot. "They can watch from the stand. You should take six of your own with you to Silverstone and some of my guys, of course, that's if you do okay today. I can only get you last place at the practice at Silverstone; the rest is up to you. Can only do that as I own Mercedes." He slapped Kane on the back.

Kane thought maybe there was an ulterior motive for letting him get a car. And that was not an option. He saw the way he looked at Kelly, or rather Jenny.

"Then let's get this show on the road and see what I remember, mate." Kane didn't like being slapped on the back by anyone, but especially not by Jimmy.

"Sure, sure. One of the guys will show you where to get suited. Helmet's with the car. I'll be waiting right here. Car's over there." He pointed across to the track.

Jimmy Rogers chewed on his cigar as he spoke. Kane looked in the direction Jimmy was pointing, and there in the gleaming sunlight sat the silver dream machine, its nose pointed towards the north. The power machine sat waiting, with its horsepower revving, and all systems waiting as the mechanics gave it one last check. Kane Branson's eyes gleamed, and he raised his hand to his eyes to shield the sun, trying to get a better look as he drank in the splendor of the car.

"To hell with the suit!" and Kane took off across the grass towards the car.

"Mr. Branson, you have to wear it. Rules. If the thing catches on fire…" yelled Jimmy Rogers.

Kane stopped, surprised at Jimmy's concern.

"Yeah, okay. You're right," and Kane turned back and headed for the changing area.

Steve was watching as they walked across the lot. "Told you. Our man is going to be one handful, and the two Italians are not worth a damn. It's you and me, Dave… and Inspector Graham."

Steve kept walking.

"I heard that in the car," replied Dave. "God, of all people to take, he picks our boss. What about Kelly?"

Dave was having trouble keeping pace with Steve, let alone Kane.

"She's going to Silverstone. How, I'm not sure. But where he goes, she goes. And words of warning, my friend, don't even smile at her in a more than a brotherly way. Not unless you don't want to live," Steve remarked seriously.

Dave blushed. At twenty-five he was still immature where women were concerned.

"I know but she's so pretty and…" he didn't finish.

"And she's Commander Branson's wife. End of story." Steve said it with finality.

By now they had reached the changing area and looked in the door for Kane.

"You ready, Mr. Branson?" yelled Steve.

Kane walked out into the light. The grey metallic skin-tight suit that Kane wore only emphasized his masculinity. It was unzipped to the waist, showing more than a fare share of skin and grey-blonde hair that sprung from his chest in defiant curls. His muscles rippled, and the suit moved with him. In his hand, he carried something with him and handed it to Steve.

"Hold this till I get back." And he slipped his gun to Steve who immediately shoved the object down the back of his own jeans.

Kane swaggered ahead of them with hair hanging from a band, and his arms resting by his side.

"Don't think anyone in their right mind would mess with him," stated Steve. "I think we are going to spend most of our time keeping people out of his way. I can't wait to get to see him race. He has a fire in his eyes just like your brother. Come on, let's go and watch. Speaking of watching, bring the other halves of the condiments with you," and Steve laughed and looked across to where his new boss was standing.

Kane neared the car, dynamite on four wheels. It had been so long since he'd even touched one of these babies. Mechanics swarmed around him and the car like bees on a honey-pot. Kane ran his hands along the car's side, and to him it was as soft as Kelly's skin. Swinging his legs over the side, he seated himself in the car. It was smaller than he remembered, or he was taller, but still he settled in nicely. A few more controls greeted his eyes than when he raced last. Kane pulled the fireproof mesh over his head and tucked his now unruly ponytail inside it. Electric blue eyes looked out as a mechanic handed Kane the helmet. Another checked the car and one checked him. Making sure the driver was safely tucked in was their job. There were suddenly more people everywhere than two minutes ago. Had he climbed in a honeycomb instead? Someone was pulling his safety harness tighter and tighter.

"Man, that's enough," and he grabbed the hand that was about to deprive him of fulfilling Kelly's wishes. "Tight enough, mate."

Kane pulled the helmet down over his head, as Jimmy Rogers approached the car and its driver.

"We'll be up in the stand. You go as fast as you want. I won't talk to you. No radio contact or anything. Not first time out. Free reign. Now go. Let's see what you are really made of, Kene Branson."

He patted Kane's helmet, then stood back. Kane revved the engine to power up the car. The soft racing shoes he wore touched lightly on the metal and that's all it took to know that the car was waiting for his command. Kane saw them all move back from the pit. Now it was his turn, as he looked ahead and saw a clear and deserted track.

"For you, Alexander!" and in a blink of an eye he left the red-hot ground standing behind him as the checkered flag dropped, and 'Branson' was gone. The group watched from the stands as a blur of silver flashed by them.

"Did you see that? Did you know he could go that fast?" yelled Dave, his curly black hair blowing in the sudden gust of wind.

"Kind of thought he might," uttered Steve.

"Your man is crazy. Si, he is crazy," echoed Bruno waving his arms in the air.

"You better hope not, my friend, cause he isn't that keen on you," retorted Steve. "Hey, I made a joke. Dave…Keen on you…Kene…oh, never mind." He gave up.

Dave was too intent on watching Kane to notice. Jimmy Rogers raised his binoculars to his eyes, and all he saw from them was a silver streak and a helmet glinting in the sun. He checked Branson's speed on the computer monitor. One hundred, a hundred and sixty, and then one-seventy. He shot past them again, his speed getting higher.

"Damn fool," muttered a now seated Jimmy. "He only needed to do one-sixty to qualify. What's he trying to prove? I have my proof."

Jimmy lowered the glasses till they hung loosely round his neck, and fished in the back pocket of his khaki colored twill pants till he found his lighter. He lit his chewed cigar, dropping bits of tobacco down the front of his Mercedes inscribed black shirt. His cheeks flushed and perspiration rolled down his face.

Steve noticed. "Seems Mr. Rogers is a little nervous of our man and his precious car."

"I'd be nervous if it was my car," whispered Dave. "Look at him go. Wowwwww." He sat down next to Jimmy.

Kane Branson was having the time of his life. And proving to himself that he hadn't lost it. Glancing down at the speedometer, he clocked one hundred and eighty miles an hour. The car handled like a dream. Some play in the steering only made the car faster. One-ninety. He figured by now Jimmy Rogers was having a heart attack. Heart attack. He should probably remember that. Wasn't so funny. He himself had already had one a few years back. He could feel the sweat rolling down his back, his hands getting clammy. Maybe it was time to slow down. One more burst then he would. He wasn't paying attention, not concentrating on the situation in hand. His thoughts had drifted to his own experience of code red in the hospital ward, his own pain as the trauma of an attack shot through his chest. Maybe he should remember that in the future. The car swerved and shuddered on the tires, and brought him abruptly back to reality.

'Concentrate, man. Do that again and Jimmy Rogers won't let you near a fucking car.'

Under control again, he launched the car into a final last fling. Kane wanted to go out on a high note and amazed himself at the control he had taking the car round the bends and...suddenly, there was a buzzing in the earpiece of the helmet.

"Okay, Kene. Bring the damn thing in. I'm convinced. You can drive the spare car. You get to go. Last position, though. You can plough your way through the ranks." Jimmy Rogers just condoned the use of the car.

The words were music to Kane's ears. Now he could go to Silverstone with a great cover and find out the truth. He slowed the car from its breath-taking pace to a mere one-twenty. He dropped gears to a decent pace and pulled in alongside the pit, the tarmac steaming beneath his red-hot tires. Before the crew got to him he unleashed the harness and jumped out of the car. Dumping the helmet in the cockpit and removing the mesh, he pulled the band from his hair and walked arrogantly across the grass towards the stands. Unzipping his suit as he walked, he cut a menacing figure in silver, his hair blowing back in the breeze and exuded a masculine strength and confidence that had made him commander. Kane Branson was never surer of himself at that minute than at any other time in his life.

They'd all seen him crossing the line, the line that divided the men from the boys.

CHAPTER 5

"Are you totally insane, Mr. Branson?" asked Jimmy Rogers standing up to meet him as Kane ran up the steps towards him.

"Absolutely. Man, that felt good."The sweat dripped down his face and he wiped it away with his leather-gloved fingers.

"Good," bubbled Jimmy. "That's what makes a good racing driver great."

Rogers chewed his cigar butt. Kane tuned to Steve.

"So, what's your opinion?" Kane asked.

"I think you're crazy like the Italian said. But if it gets us where we want, then you have to do it," replied an effervesant Steve.

Kane tried to pull the tight fitting gloves from his hands and failed. Sweat had made them cling to his palms like glue on tape. Steve leaned forward to help him.

"Kinda reminds me of something else," laughed Kane.

Steve smiled. He could see the joke, and tugged on the silver-ribbed gloves. Free from the encumbering articles, Kane lowered the zip on the suit even more. Jimmy could see flesh underneath.

"Kene, I hope you'll wear the protective suit underneath when you race? It's for your own good." Rogers seemed just a little annoyed before his voice changed to condescending. "Please, Kene?"

A bad mistake. Kane couldn't afford to get on the wrong side of Rogers.

"Sorry. Was just in a hurry. I'll wear it next time. Can I go again?" Kane looked back at the car and the track with his blood still burning fire.

"Today? You really are insane," replied Jimmy. " I guess you should. This time listen to the commands given you. Unfortunately, I can't go with you tomorrow so one of my guys can talk you around. They can go with you to Silverstone and teamsters will go, too. You have your own six people, okay? You do have six, right?" pestered Jimmy

"Course," Kane lied.

Kane had five, and Kelly. Pulling Steve to one side he whispered to him.

"You and Dave take Bruno and Sergio and give them a crash course on how to operate in a pit, though I have a feeling if Maria hired them they already know. You two know what you're doing, but if they don't look right mixing in with the Mercedes guys someone is gonna get suspicious. Jimmy knows Peter, but Peter could just be accompanying us as a friend. Chances are I will only have to drive once on the real track. That isn't the object in going, though I have to admit it was fun."

"Mr. Branson, *sir*. Next-time when you are having fun, maybe don't be so convincing that you are such a good driver. Do you know how fast you were going out there?" the blonde Englishmen asked.

Steve was trying hard to get through to Kane who stared straight at the younger man, oblivious to everyone else around.

There was a gleam in Kane's eyes. "It was like I'd gone back twenty years. All was right with the world. The only thing I was missing was Kel. You understand that, Steve? It was power."

Kane's face was pinched. He suddenly envied youth, but with youth came inexperience and it didn't include Kelly.

"I understand. But I wonder if your wife is going to?" and Steve inclined his head towards the car park.

Kane intently watched the Savoy courtesy car pull up, as a pair of jeans and long curly hair stepped out. She was wearing a usual Kelly style shirt, low and sexy and also one of the ones Kane had picked out for her. Swinging her purse over her shoulder her long, thin legs marched across the grass.

"Happiness on two legs," murmured Dave.

Steve flashed him a severe look. Jimmy also looked across to the where everyone's attentions were diverted, too.

"Your wife came to join us," stated Jimmy. "How nice."

Kane didn't hear. He was halfway across the grass. Kelly saw him coming towards her with a feeling inside of her that was unexplainable. She looked at Kane like she had never seen him before. If she thought he was attractive before now he was dynamic. His suit was open to the waist with sweat pouring down his face and onto his chest. He pushed his hair behind his ears and he walked with an air of total dominance. The tarmac shimmered behind him; steam rose from the track, highlighted only by the sun beating down on it. Kelly starred at him as she walked towards him. She wanted him there and then. No man would ever take Kane's place and she reached her arms out to him.

"Pity there are people near us," she murmured as he slid his arm around her waist.

"My thoughts exactly," and Kane brushed stray hairs from her face.

"So, how did you do? You qualify?" she looked up into his warm and loving eyes.

"Don't I always," he laughed.

"Oh yeah," and she slid her hand inside his suit. "Definitely a pity."

"How did you know where to find me?"

Kane was trying hard to concentrate. Kelly had shown up at a bad time. He needed to practice some more, and he didn't want her around to watch, especially when Rogers was on hand.

"The hotel told me where Mercedes was and they arranged for the car to bring me here. How's our friend?" and she inclined her head towards Jimmy.

"He's fine. Kelly, it may have been better for you not to..."

She put her fingers on his lips and stopped him speaking.

"I'm a big girl and I'm your wife. He can't hurt me. Jimmy Rogers is a sad man who loved my mother. I can't change that fact." She paused, changing the subject. "Can I watch you drive?"

"I guess now that you're here I have no choice. But don't get freaky on me. I just clocked a hundred and ninety miles an hour," Kane burbled.

He watched her face and Kelly hid the shock very well. She really was trying.

"That slow, huh?" she quipped.

But he felt her hand tighten on his waist and Kane laughed. Arms around each other, they walked back to the stands. Kelly let go of her husband's waist and stretched her arm towards Jimmy.

"G'day, Mr. Rogers. I hear my husband did well this morning. He's full of surprises." She felt Jimmy's clammy hand touch hers. "Thought I'd surprise him and come to watch."

"Surprise for us all. Would you like to sit with us in the stands? Kene's going to go round the track again. Says he needs the practice." Jimmy dusted off the seat for Kelly.

"Kelly," Dave interceded. "You want to sit with Steve and I?"

"Sure," she replied, and turned to Kane. "Who are *those* guys?' she asked looking at the two Italians. "Haven't I seen them somewhere before?"

"Part of my crew," Kane replied. "Friends of the Vincentia's. With Dave, Steve, those two and Peter..."

"And me..." interjected Kelly, turning to look up at her husband's face.

"Right, and you, we have enough. Rogers is sending the Mercedes crew, or rather they will be there. I guess as its car he gets to say who goes and who doesn't. He can't make it, thank God. Stay here with Steve, baby." In his mind Steve was the safest. "I'll just drink some water and I'll try racing again."

Kelly sat down with the guys in the stand shuffling round till she was halfway comfortable on the bench. She laid her overstuffed purse beside her and leaned back on the seats behind her. Steve sat next to her and Jimmy Rogers grabbed the seat the other side of her. He puffed on his fat cigar. Kelly waved the smoke away from her face, which irritated her more than Kane's cigarettes.

"Sorry, Mrs. Branson. Didn't mean to blow smoke at you. So used to smoking these things," and he pushed the cigar the other side of his mouth.

"They'll be the death of you, Mr. Rogers," she replied, and focused her attentions on her husband.

She didn't like Jimmy Rogers, and it wasn't for the obvious reason. There was something other than that that she couldn't quite put her finger on.

"You wait till you see him go. Your husband is a natural," added Jimmy.

And that's what worried her the most.

At the side of the track Kane downed a half bottle of water. The last thing he wanted to do was dehydrate and pass out at the wheel. He zipped the suit back up, pulled the mesh over his head, and climbed into the car. The hand came down again and cranked the harness tight. Kane grimaced. With the helmet in place, the mechanics made sure that Kane could both hear and speak to the control. He pulled the leather gloves on and gripped the steering wheel.

"Okay, Kene... be ready...watch for the flag, Kene. Don't over rev the car...keep your foot ready...watch, Kene, watch..." yelled Jimmy into the headpiece in the Mercedes car.

Kane's eyes watched for the flag. He watched, he waited, it dropped, he heard the word *GO*... and he was gone.

Kelly stared at the track. Was that really Kane, that silver flash of car? She realized that Jimmy was watching her.

"Your husband is good. Maybe he should take this up fulltime. He could have raced for our company, and would have built up a nice little career for himself by now on the track. Only thing against him at this point is his age. Pity he's not thirty years younger. But he's good. Not like Vincentia, but at least I'll have another car on the track. Always like to have two."

"You always have two?" asked Steve turning to look at Jimmy.

"Always. My other driver is Michael Ryder. He was in third position on the pole. With Vincentia out that puts him in second position." He puffed again.

"You sound very sure that Mr. Vincentia is out for good," stated Steve.

"Not for good, but out of this race. Spoke to the hospital this morning. No chance. The drivers know the risks when they get in that car."

Rogers held the cigar up to his face, decided he'd had enough and stubbed it out under his black brogue shoes.

Kelly shuddered.

"Cold, little lady?" Jimmy asked.

"No, just scared," she replied.

"For your husband? Nothing is going to happen to Kene."

Jimmy Rogers was sure. Too sure. And none of them missed it.

Kane listened to the earpiece. This was something new for him. He was used to doing his own thing and in this age you didn't. Most of the way round they'd given him instructions. Do this; watch that, till he wondered who was driving the fucking car. His hands were on the wheel, but he wasn't in control. Some jumped up little jerk back in the stand was. Once again he reached one-ninety. And again he was in control of the situation. Why should he listen in the earpiece? He could do just as well without them. But that wasn't the game and he mumbled to himself.

"You say something, Kene?" came a voice through the helmet.

'Do they hear everything?' "No nothing," he replied.

As he looked through the visor his vision became blurred. Raindrops splattered on the car and a new sprinkling of water on the track made a great deal of difference. Immediately the road became slippery. Kane still had on dry tires and not wet weather, and on the slick road he slowed down immediately. Big mistake. He couldn't do that on the track and pushed the speed back up to one-ninety.

"Very good, Mr. Branson. Very good indeed. We're impressed. Bring that baby home," the English voice came again.

From the stands Kelly watched a man she thought she knew. The one she didn't know was racing round the track. He confused her, and he also terrified her. Her fingernails dug into her hand and left indents in her palm, her knuckles turned white. She'd watched him gather speed and race like some maniac. Some maniac that was going to get himself killed in the process of trying to help his friend. Kelly felt a hand on her shoulder, and she felt herself cringe beneath it.

"Your husband is going to do just fine, Mrs. Branson. He's got what it takes and I assure you nothing is going to happen to him. The man has a talent. You know I have seen him in magazines. But somehow I don't think it was connected to racing. He ever do any modeling or something like that?"

'Maybe for the Australian Police Times front cover, special edition,' she thought. "Not that I know," and she tactfully slid out from under his hand. "How can you be so sure he won't get hurt? Racing is a dangerous game."

"He's driving one of the safest cars in the business," replied Jimmy arrogantly.

"Alexander was also. He thought he was safe and look what happened to him," Kelly retorted.

"These things happen. Alexander was unlucky. He'll be fine. Meanwhile, Kene will take the Mercedes car." He looked down to the pits and to his men.

Kane screeched to a halt and climbed out of Roger's precious car.

It was raining harder with a storm that seemed to come from nowhere settling over the track. The sky darkened, yet it was only early afternoon. Kane threw his helmet to one of the guys and ran for cover under the tarpaulin, darting up the stairs to where the group was gathered. Kelly was the first to greet him as always. His suit was soaked and hung skin-tight to his body. He tugged at the zip to pull it down, but the wet driving gloves prevented that. Kelly helped him pull them off, one at a time, and she tossed them on the bench.

"Not used to wet weather like this. Man, let's hope that the track is dry in the next few days." He looked down at Kelly. "You okay, baby?"

He'd tried to ignore the look on her face. "Something bothering you, darling?"

"Just not used to seeing…" and she stopped. Of course, she would be used to seeing him race like that back in Australia. He was Kene Branson. "To seeing you race in the rain. Always dry back home." She covered it well.

Kane pulled her to him and encircled her with his arms and she nestled into his protective arms.

"Think we'll call it a day, Mr. Rogers. Kelly and I need to go collect a few things, and I should talk to my guys here this evening. How many more days practice do I get?"

"Only the practice laps at Silverstone. That's it. No time. My guys will look after you. Such a pity I can't come with you. Tomorrow you and the car will go up there. I can send transportation for you in…" Jimmy didn't finish the sentence.

"I have my own car. We'll make our own way up there, so just give me the instructions on where we have to go. I've already booked Kel and I into a hotel. May as well still stay there. Some place called the Devere. Sounds nice." Kane watched for a reaction.

"That's because it's one of the best around the track." He viewed Kane with a suspicious look. "Very expensive hotel. Surprised you can..er, going to stay there." Then again, he'd seen Kane shopping in Harrods.

"I race as a sideline and I teach racing for money. Be surprised how much you can make back in OZ doing that," replied Kane. He was quick with his thoughts. Rogers must not be suspicious. "And I have another line of work." Now he was pressing his luck. "I'm a part-time security guard for some important folk."

"A bouncer?" He looked Kane up and down. "That I believe. I wouldn't want to mess with you. Then you should be able to handle anything that comes your way."

"No, Mr. Rogers, you wouldn't want to mess with me," replied Kane forcefully. He took hold of his wife's hand. "If that's all, we'll be on our way. Kind of hungry and I need to get out of these wet things."

"Of course." Jimmy Rogers extended his hand to Kane. "Good luck. I don't expect you to win, but I'm sure you'll give a good account of yourself for Mercedes. My blokes will keep me posted. I'm sorry to miss the race. Give my best to Vincentia, and tell him he still races for me. Goodbye, Kene. Kelly," and he walked heavily down the stairs and away from the stands.

"Wonder why he's not going to be there," whispered Steve.

"Very good question. One we should find out. Something isn't right. His top driver is in a crash, he let's a rookie take the other car. Something is very wrong here. Dave, ask your boss to check him out real good. Jimmy Rogers isn't all that he seems to be." He turned to Kelly. "I'll go change and then we'll go eat."

Kelly whispered to him.

"I mean all of us." Kane viewed the two Italians. "Even you two," and slapped the tall Italian on the back.

Sergio and Bruno had been extremely quiet throughout all of the proceedings. Kane figured they were reporting everything back to their boss, and he didn't mean Maria. He needed their help, but he also had to keep one eye on them and didn't put them past sabotaging someone, especially him.

"I didn't know they had McDonalds over here," stated Kelly, as tomato ketchup dripped from her precariously balanced hamburger. "Just like being in the States."

"They get everywhere, darling, which is where that sauce is going to be in about two seconds from now," observed Kane.

Kane slid a napkin under her hands to stop the dripping-red puree from running onto her jeans. Didn't matter if it hit the floor. That part of the establishment seemed very comfortable with things spilling on it.

"If you keep eating like that, we'll be buying you larger clothes. Speaking of clothes, we need to pick up some more gear." Kane turned to the other table. "You guys nearly finished? This lot's costing me a fortune. Good job there is some prize money at the end of this."

The hamburger shot out of Kelly's bun and dropped into the plate of grease.

"Prize money? Kane, this isn't for real. This is just a job. You're not gonna race for real… are you? Tell me you don't mean that. Kane?" Kelly looked up at him as he rose from the table and the bright red stool he had been sitting on. "Kane?"

He smiled at her. And she knew. He was racing for real, and she felt her stomach turn over. Kane finished his hotdog in two bites.

Steve saw the looks between Kelly and Kane, and he knew it spelled trouble. Kane was being more than macho, more than a cop. He was being crazy.

"Kane, that's a pretty dangerous game, even for the best of drivers," Steve boldly commented.

"Your point?" retorted Kane, the electric blue eyes switched on.

Steve withered under the gaze, and made a desperate attempt at recovery.

"We can't have you killing yourself on English turf. In your own country, that's different..." 'Shit,' thought Steve. 'That was tactless in front of his wife.'

"Humph..." and Kane laughed.

He realized what Steve was saying, but he also knew to get to where he wanted to go he had to play for real. And this was for real.

"Gonna go smoke. I'll wait for you all outside," and Kane left through the large glass doors with the big red M on them.

Kelly was speechless. She picked up her carton of fries and took off after her husband. Dave started to follow and Steve grabbed his arm.

"Give them a minute," and he pulled his partner back on the seat.

Kelly found Kane outside. "Are you serious, Kane?" yelled Kelly.

"Anyone ever told you how your eyes glow when you're angry, Butterfly?" laughed Kane.

"Stop it, Kane. This is one time when that won't work. You weren't joking this time were you? I thought I knew all your tricks. Even your best friend isn't worth dying for. You can find out who's behind this without risking your damn life." She paused. "Are you even listening to me," and she tugged on his shirt.

"Yeah, me and half of London. You know what I'm doing, baby. You know. You always know. Can I have one of your fries?" he joked, and tried to steal some from her carton.

"Go f..."

"Kelly! That's no way for a lady to speak. And you are a lady."

Kane slid his arm around her and whispered in her ear. His eyes creased and she nodded very slightly. As they walked towards the parked Mercedes, a black truck turned into the street. Its windows were dark and its wheels large and menacing. The over revving engine made Kane turn slightly just in time to see the glint of the grey steel of a gun reflected in the shop window. He pushed Kelly to the ground, her fries shooting up in the air like fireworks. Kane pulled his gun from the back of his jeans, crouched down, stretched his arms straight in front of him, and with hands encircling the handle of his gun, took aim.

The bullet from the passing vehicle missed his head by inches and buried itself in a tree. Kane fired, hitting the back window of the truck, shattering it into a zillion pieces. The truck sped away down a side street, its tires screeching as it turned the corner. Window-shoppers ducked behind anything they could find and the screaming of women and children filled his ears. All they could think of was terrorists.

Kelly was still on the ground when Steve reached her. Dave was behind him and the rest of the group on their heels.

"You okay?" Steve helped Kelly up.

"I'm fine. Is Kane okay?" and she picked up her open purse, grabbing the contents from the streets of London. Lipstick, passport, change and gun had all spewed out when she hit the deck. "Is he?" she repeated far more loudly.

Kane still held the gun, its barrel smoking. He was mumbling.

"Kane, you…" Steve screamed at him.

"Get the fucking number down. GON880. You got it?"

He pulled pad and pen from his jeans pocket. "Got it. You okay…" replied Steve.

"Course I'm okay, Steve. They weren't trying to kill me. That was just a warning. At that range, if it was meant, I'd be dead. Ask your boss if you can carry, would you?"

Kane tucked the gun down the back of his jeans. He saw the trembling and nosy people around them. He reached for Kelly's hand, finding she was shaking fiercely.

"Okay, folks. Shows over. Just the good old Australian way. Just a joke," and he laughed. Kane turned to Steve. "Open the car door and get Kelly in the front. You sit by the window."

Steve did as he was told. Kane looked at Steve, and in his mind the plan was forming more intensely than before. Steve could pass for him at a push. He glanced at the Mercedes, making sure Kelly was safely in the front seat. Kane grabbed Bruno's arm and ushered him at a not so leisurely a pace round the corner, into a secluded alley behind the stores.

"Okay, Mr. Bruno. Was that one of your guys or not? Straight answer or my fist is going to connect to your face. Comprenday?" and Kane stood menacingly in front of the Italian, fist in line with Bruno's nose. "Was it? Was that my warning to tow the line with your friends?"

Bruno backed up as far as he could go, right into the wall. His eyes were piercing and his nostrils flared.

"*Commander Branson,* if we wanted you dead, then you would be dead." His thick accent shone through.

"*Commander*? You bastard. How long have you known?" and Kane grabbed for Bruno's collar, bringing himself eye to eye with the Italian.

"There is no need for this, Commander. We are not who we said. We showed you false papers. Sergio and I work for the Italian government, not the Mafia, as you thought. We were told to work with you. You assumed we were from the wrong side of the Sicilian tracks and, we let you think that for cover. Like you, sir, we don't want our identity declared public knowledge. I am Captain Bruno Van Camp, Italian Secret Police, just like you are AFP. So now you know." He was quiet.

"You can prove this?" Kane questioned.

"Of course. Your friend Maria Vincentia knows us. We have been trying to protect her husband, I admit, not successfully. When the Vincentias called you to come on the vacation and meet with them, it seemed like a prime opportunity for all of us to work together. But you, Mr. Branson, are a one-man-band and this was the only we could think of to go with you. It was Maria's idea. Good, no?" he continued.

"Good, no is right. I was about to break your nose." Kane let go of the man's lapels. "Suppose I don't believe you?"

"You believe me, and you can check with Inspector Graham."

"He knows, too? Were Kelly and I the only ones that didn't know? Did Steve and Dave know?" Kane queried.

"No, they did not. Inspector Graham felt it better that they did not know. Now it is up to you. You decide. This is your operation. You know more about Alexander and about racing than any of us." Bruno straightened his lapels.

Kane stepped back. He did believe him and hadn't he had his suspicions all along? Pulling his cigarettes from his pocket, he shook the pack onto his hand. One dropped out, and he put it between his lips, while Bruno Van Camp offered him a light. Kane accepted it graciously.

"Well, Commander? Do we stay undercover, or do we go public and ruin everything?" he waited and watched the Australian.

Kane puffed hard on the weed and blew smoke through his nose. Bruno was right. It would blow their cover. But the question remained of who shot at him. Only so many people knew where they were. Van Camp watched him.

"I know what you are thinking. Who pulled the trigger? The same person that wants Mercedes' drivers scared …or dead. The same people that sabotaged Alexander's car, and will stop at nothing to get you, and Mercedes. That was a warning. Next time you may not be so lucky. We will all protect you as much as we can, but maybe best that your wife does not know." His Oxford English was perfect, only complimented by his Italian accent.

"How the fuck can't she know? She was standing right there. These bastards aren't going to stop at one shot, 'specially as I fired back. How many racing drivers carry guns?" He answered his own question. "Except maybe crazy eccentric Australian ones. Okay, it's a deal. One last thing. You and Steve are to look after Kelly at any cost, and I mean any cost. Her life is not up for grabs," and he put his hand out to Bruno.

Van Camp shook it vigorously.

"We will look out for her. On that you have my word, and we will also try and find out who pulled the trigger. You are going to tell the two Englishmen?" he asked.

"I'll let Graham do that, if he feels he should. Man, who would have thought this? All I wanted was a bloody vacation with my wife. Instead I get to race round some track called Silverstone, work with M15 and the Italian police. This will be one for the grandchildren…if I live that long."

As he finished the sentence Dave appeared round the corner.

"Everything alright, boss?" and he looked cautiously around him.

Kane slapped Dave on the back.

"Everything is just beginning to be fine. You find that bullet yet?" asked Kane.

"Yes, sir. It was sprouting from a tree branch about six inches from where you were standing. We called in the registration number for the truck. Stolen as usual. Your wife is really upset and is asking where you are." Dave finished his sentence.

"Son, that's not the first time I've been shot at and it won't be the last. When you and Steve get back to headquarters tonight listen well to your Inspector. Tomorrow, Detective Goodman is another day. And if you'll both excuse me, I have to go say something to Kelly."

Kane left a bemused young cop, and a veteran IPA, standing in the alley. There still was time for them all to blend together. Now he knew why Graham had jumped at the plan to go to Silverstone at dinner. And he knew now Kelly had to be kept out of this. This was industrial espionage and attempted murder at first pole position

CHAPTER 6

"Okay, Kelly, that's enough with the silent routine. You haven't spoken directly to me since McDonalds. This is beginning to be an annoying habit and one I won't tolerate from you." The silence was deafening. Kane tried a different approach. "Kelly, we're both cops. We know when we have to do our job…"

Kelly turned to face Kane. "Our job? I thought we were on vacation? Not solving England's crimes." She paused. "I've been thinking. You go on to Silverstone. I'll stay here."

Kelly sat down on the sprawling, luxurious bed in their suite and pouted while packages of clothes surrounded her. A short, sharp trip to the stores, on the way back to their hotel, had enlarged their wardrobe immensely, plus suitcases to hold their new apparel.

"What?" Kane stopped from his task of pulling out the paper stuffing from the cases.

"You heard me, or has all that engine noise gone to your brain? I'm not going with you. I won't watch you die," and she turned away, tears welling up in her eyes.

"You are going, and that's that. So start putting the clothes in the case!" He picked up some pants and threw them across the bed to her, while Kelly turned away from him. "We're leaving first thing in the morning. Steve and Bruno will drive with us. The others will go with Mercedes' men and the racing car." He looked towards her. "Are you listening to me? You don't think I'd leave you here. Jimmy Rogers is still back here and probably some gun happy bloke just waiting to separate us all. So get packing and I'm not gonna repeat myself. Do I make myself clear?" Kane yelled at her.

"Perfectly, Commander Branson."

Kelly composed herself and started packing the suitcases with military precision. Kane sat down in the plush velvet chair and looked at his wife.

He hadn't meant it to come out like that, and he knew he sounded like some over-bearing commando, exactly what he didn't want to convey.

Kelly knew he was watching her. She zipped up the one case and left room in the other for the rest of their things. She tossed the now discarded Harrods bags onto the floor and kicked them with her feet. Slowly, she slid out of her jeans, pulled the t-shirt over her head and purposely pulled one of Kane's shirts on. Leaving a couple of buttons undone, she tossed her hair over the collar of the shirt.

"Damn hair is always in my way," she mumbled.

"You say something?" Kane asked, never taking his eyes off her.

"Nope," and she pulled the silk sheets back and climbed into bed, and stared straight in the direction of the wall.

It was all Kane could do not to laugh, but to do that would undermine his wife's stand against the position she was taking. He pulled his boots off, dropping them with a thud on the floor, and lay down on the bed, fully dressed. Kelly knew he hadn't had time to take his clothes off, and she half turned towards him to see what he was doing.

"What you doin'?"

"No need to undress. Nothing is gonna happen tonight, darling, except sleep" and he closed his eyes.

She'd played on his level and lost. She turned back towards the wall and stared at the flocked wallpaper with tears streaming down her face. This was Kelly. Tough little Kelly Walker-Branson that never cried. Kane could hear her and was tempted to put his arms round her and tell her it was going to be okay...he hoped. But this time he couldn't guarantee it. With these thoughts in mind he drifted into an uncomfortable sleep.

Kane woke with a start, and to the sound of the shower running. He swung off the bed, pulled off his shirt, and unzipped his jeans. The thought of joining her in the water spurred him on, and he hurriedly moved towards the bathroom door. The water stopped running and from out of the shower stall Kelly emerged, like a moth to the flame. With a fluffy white towel wrapped around her body, and one round her hair, she entered the bedroom.

"Kelly, I'm sorry about last night." His voice was soft as he moved forward to hold her.

"It's okay. You were right. I have to go with you, and if I go, I go in the pits." Kelly was more than calm and moved on by him.

She unnerved him. Kelly not wanting him to hold her?

"Kel, we went over that. There is no way you're gonna look like some guy…"

"No?" and she pulled the towel from her hair, dropping it to the floor.

Gone were the curly locks that Kane loved to run his hands through. In their place was short, spiky hair, which Kane stared at horrified.

"What the fuck did you do? It's a wig, right? Kelly, tell me you didn't cut your hair off, baby."

"Can't lie, Commander. Agents don't lie. It's in the rubbish bin in the bathroom. Now I look like a guy. In the protective suit no one will ever know the difference," and she brushed passed him.

He grabbed her arm and he held on tight, so tightly that he hurt her.

"Why, Kelly? Because of last night? That it?" he yelled.

"No, Kane, because you wouldn't let me into your plans this time. Everyone seemed to know except me. You're trying to protect me, and I took an oath to protect and serve, just like you. And just because you're the one we have to protect, you're shutting me out. Someone drew on you last night. Next time they could hit you, and I can't live without you…" Now she broke down. "I can't, Kane…" She almost collapsed on him.

He caught her in his arms. "Oh, darling, I'm so sorry. It was not my intention to shut you out. I figured the less you knew the better."

He stared at her hair and in some kind of weird way it suited her. Kane touched it. It was soft and short…very short and made her eyes seem larger and her lips fuller. His other hand gently removed the towel from around her body.

"Darling, whatever you do, you are never gonna be a guy," and Kane picked her up and carried her back into the shower.

"You got both cases out there?" Kane yelled to the bellhop.

"Yes, sir," came the reply from the corridor outside the suite.

"Okay, Kel, let's go." Kane grabbed his jacket and turned to look at his wife.

She was wearing leather jeans, leather jacket, boots and not much else.

"God, Kelly, you're gonna shock those English guys to death. Thought you were trying to look like a guy? Do you know how sexy you look? Pity Jimmy Rogers can't see you now. You don't look anything like your… fuck!"

"It's okay. That was half the plan not to look like her anymore." She twirled around for him. "So you're impressed, huh?" She glanced at the front of his tight black jeans. "I see you are. And if I may say, Kene Branson, Australian racing driver...you don't look so bad yourself."

Kane wore jeans. He also wore a black leather jacket open to the waist with his hair hanging down, and facial hair preserved from several days. That alone turned Kelly on.

The luggage arrived in the lobby before the Branson's. Kelly stepped out of the elevator first, followed closely by her husband. Kane tipped the elevator guy and that prompted him to remember he still owed Steve money. They walked across the lobby to where Steve and Bruno waited. Salt and pepper were very much shaken and very visibly stirred. Kelly held onto Kane's hand. Even with high-heeled boots, Kane towered over Kelly.

"Good morning, to both of you. It is Kelly, right?" Steve squinted his eyes in mock gesture.

"Good morning, Steve. I decided to look like one of the guys. Look's good huh? I should have done this years' ago," she laughed smoothing down her jacket.

"So, you are going to do the same, Commander?" Steve whispered to Kane. "And Kelly...you are never going to look like one of the guys!" and he shook his head.

A look to Kelly from Kane, and a playful arm lock from Kane around Steve's throat, gave him his answer.

"Car outside?" asked Kane glancing around.

"Ready when you two are. They're putting the luggage in now," came the Englishman's reply.

"Then, man, let's do this." And Kane heaved a big sigh.

Kelly dozed in the warmth of the car and her leather outfit. Steve wondered just how she could accomplish sleep the way her husband was driving. Obviously she trusted him all the way. The journey was only three hours or so, but the traffic slowed them down on the M20 for some time. Impatiently, Kane sat in the line of vehicles. Ten miles an hour was not his speed.

"So," whispered Kane, "you guys tell your wives you'd be away for a few days?" Kane adjusted the rear view mirror so he could get a better view of the people in the back.

"How did you know I was married, Commander?" 'Stupid, Bruno. He's

AFP. Of course he knows.' "Don't answer that. I don't believe I asked you."

Kelly woke at the sound of voices.

"We nearly there yet?" she said blinking her eyes, and then staring out of the steamy windows to get a better view of where they were.

"No, baby. Stuck in this damn English traffic. You okay?" and Kane rested his hand on her leg.

"I'm hot," Kelly replied, shuffling in her seat.

"Yeah, baby, you sure are!" muttered Kane, and moved his hand farther up her leg, feeling the soft leather beneath his hand.

The Australian's forthright comments didn't faze Steve anymore. And Italians, it seemed, were even more used to them.

"When is your boss driving up?" Kane asked Steve. "I called him this morning and his line was busy for ever." His hand lingered on Kelly's leather pants

"He said he would meet you at the Devere, in fact, that's where we all are meeting up. Apparently, Mr. Rogers arranged for us all to stay there." Steve had been thinking about that fact.

"All of you?" he exclaimed. "What the hell prompted that? Teamsters and mechanics don't normally stay at the same hotel with the drivers, not that it's not a great idea, just unusual. Or, are things done differently over here?" asked Kane.

"No, sir. It's unusual. But then this whole thing is getting weird. I believe Mr. Rogers upgraded you to a suite, and we poor mechanics get single rooms. But it's still strange." Steve leaned over the leather seat. "Something else. How are you going to explain Kelly sleeping in your room and then being a guy at the track?"

"No one will see the person that goes to the track. She'll be dressed like a guy and wear a cap. When she's out with me, she'll be Mrs. Branson. No problem." Kane had thought that out.

"Can we stop and get a drink or something? Don't you guys want one?" Kelly was nodding her head up and down to them in mock gesture.

"We're almost there, Kel. According to the co-pilot in the back, it's just another couple of miles. See, look, a signpost...Silverstone," and her husband pointed to the side of the road.

Kelly's blood ran cold. That was the last thing she wanted to see.

"And over there is another signpost... to the Devere. Look at the driveway, baby."

Kane turned the car off the road and into the Devere's grounds. They were opulent as was the hotel. Large Victorian lights heralded the way down the long tarmac driveway. Each side of it large scented bushes greeted the weary traveler. The house loomed into sight, majestic, historic and expensive, with ivy seemingly clinging to every wall. As they approached the car park, it buzzed with the rich and the famous. Apparently Kane wasn't the only one that thought this was a good hotel.

Kane pulled the Mercedes up at the hotel entrance. Immediately the valets were at the car, scrambling to be the first ones at the doors. They all climbed out as the doors opened and they stepped onto the gravel. Several women standing just outside the doorway turned to look at Kane. Kelly saw it.

Kane took in his surroundings. This would be a hard place for anyone to shoot at him, with too many people to witness the event. He immediately felt comfortable with the situation. The luggage had been brought out of the car and now sat on the cart waiting. Kane collected his group and entered the hotel foyer.

It was impressive. Crystal chandeliers, Victorian décor, and the all the trappings of old England beckoned the patron into the majestic hotel.

"Very nice, very nice indeed," whispered Steve to Kelly. "Your husband knows how to pick hotels. My wife would kill to stay in a place like this. You are very lucky, Kelly."

"I am? Yes, I am. Except you aren't going out on some track to race are you? But like you said, I am lucky," she replied and walked with bigger strides to catch up to Kane.

Kane smelled her perfume and reached his hand out to her. She slid her cold and tiny hand in his large and sprawling hand.

"May I help you, sir?" the blonde desk clerk inquired.

"Kene Branson with Mercedes. I think there should be…"

"Of course, Mr. Branson. If you would be so kind as to sign the register, the bellboys will take your luggage to your suite. Your keys, sir, and the rest of your party have rooms in the annex," the desk clerk replied.

'Well, they would,' thought Kane. "Thank you. Can we get room service?"

"Anything you want, sir. Mr. Rogers sent word that you were to have *anything* you desire," and the blonde person smiled at him.

"Well, isn't that just dandy. Man, think this is gonna be just perfect here. Nice place," Kane looked at the clerk's badge pinned on to her thirty-six sized chest, "er, Judy," and Kane kicked his boot on the lobby floor, well aware the clerk had just made a pass at him.

"I'm here to be of help, for *anything* you want, at any time of the day, or evening," reiterated size 36.

Kelly stepped out from behind Kane.

"Thank you, Judy. My husband and I will remember that should *we* need anything," and Kelly smiled, while slipping her arm around her husband's waist.

Kane laughed to himself. Kelly was jealous of the pass the clerk had made at him. He didn't know why. Kelly could outshine anyone in the foyer. But she was playing in a man's world of racing, and she had elected to go the final mile.

The Branson's suite was magnificent. Black and white beams for the ceiling, flock wallpaper, plush thick carpets, mahogany furniture and a four-poster bed that would have befit the Queen of England. The suitcases sat in the corner of the room, ready and waiting, and the room came equipped with a cart of food that was enough to feed an army.

"So what you blokes think?" Kane asked as he sat down on the red velvet couch. He went to prop his snakeskin-booted feet on the expensive looking table and thought better of it. " Help yourself to the buffet." Kane looked at the cart full of food. Pastries, juices, coffee, fresh fruit, sandwiches, caviar… caviar? He wondered how much this really was going to cost. "Kelly?"

Kelly was lost in the bedroom. She fingered the posts of the bed and smoothed down the cream silk sheets. Wandering around the bedroom, she came across lavender-filled pillows in the drawers and embroidered towels on the dresser. Leaving the spacious room she opened a door. She peered in cautiously and discovered a bathroom which came equipped with gold handled taps and wall-to-wall mirrors. Huge, fluffy white towels seemed to spew from every nook and cranny. Then Kelly caught sight of the view from the windows. A balcony stretched from the bathroom right round to the bedroom windows, and underneath the balcony was a whole host of ivy and honeysuckle growing up the wall. The fragrance through the open window was like nothing she ever smelled before. She stepped out and moved around to the other window.

"Kelly?" shouted Kane. "Excuse me, gentlemen." And Kane left Steve and Bruno.

"In here," and she sat down on the window ledge and removed her jacket. Leather today was a mistake. She was hot. A nice cool shower would go down really well.

"Hey, baby, you okay? You look a little flushed. Told you that leather may be too hot…I know what it's doing to me!" and Kane laughed playfully with her. He leaned on the doorframe and watched her with some amusement.

"Look at the view from here. You can see right across the gardens." She peered out from the balcony and across the gardens.

Kane walked across the room and looked for himself. "Yeah, you can almost see the track," and he stopped.

Kane sat down on a chair near the window.

"I have to do this, Kel. Alexander would do it for me. And speaking of Alex, we should go to the hospital and see him this afternoon. They brought room service for us. Bruno and Steve have started on the food. Come on; let's go join them before there isn't any left."

He took hold of her hand and led her into the main room, knowing exactly what she was thinking. Kelly let herself be led away…

The food smelled good and Kane picked up a ham sandwich. Fresh tomatoes and lettuce made the sandwich juicy, and Kane tucked in with relish. Sandwich in hand, he sat down on the couch, and this time propped his boots on the table.

"Come on, Kel, eat up, then we can get to the hospital. Maria gave me the address and I'm sure the desk clerk can tell us the best route." 'Mistake…' he thought. "Or, Steve here can map up a route. You bring your laptop with you, man?"

"Don't go anywhere without it. You never know when you might need info, 'specially in this line of work." Steve leaned back on the plush cream couch. "Wish my house looked like this, even one room would do."

"Our house in Sydney doesn't look like this, Steve. First time Kane has ever brought me anywhere like this. Speaking of Sydney, can I call home from here? Would love to talk to the family. I miss the baby and Star. And what's this?" Kelly picked up some caviar in a spoon and peered at it like it would jump out and bite her.

"I was wondering when you were going to mention the kids. Surprised you hadn't called them earlier. And that's called caviar…"

Kelly fingered it and then tasted it. "Yuck, it's disgusting…" and she spat it out into a napkin. "What is made of?"

"Fish eggs," replied Bruno munching into his with great enjoyment.

"Oh, my god…yuck!" Kelly wanted to vomit.

Kane poured some freshly squeezed orange juice and handed it across the table to her. She sat on the opposite cream couch next to Steve, who was hunched in the corner eating like his life depended on it.

"I did call them already, from London. I called on your cell," and she bit into a crispy croissant instead. "This tastes much better. Can I make the call before we leave? Is there time?"

"Sure, baby, right over…"

As Kane spoke, the phone rang. No one, except the desk clerk, knew what room they were in, as the rest of the crew hadn't arrived yet.

"You want me to get it, sir?" Bruno was closest to the ringing phone.

"No. I will," Kane replied.

Dropping his sandwich onto the plate, he reached across the couch to the nearby table for the phone.

"Kene Branson." He remembered to answer correctly.

The line hissed and crackled. There was a long silence, then a click.

"Wrong suite," and Kane hung up the phone.

But he knew better and looked across at Steve.

"Call the kids on the cell, Kelly," and Kane pulled it from his boot and handed it to her. "Call from the bedroom, and give Star my love. Then we should get going." Kane waited till Kelly shut the door behind her. "Think the problem followed us here. There was someone on the end, someone who was breathing real hard. From now on, if you guys are in here, answer the phone. Think it may be better that Kelly does stay with us. There is some bastard out there that really doesn't want me to race a Mercedes car…and maybe race period."

Steve nodded.

"By the way, any news on the car and driver from yesterday, Steve?" Kane followed up.

"Not much to go on yet. Car was of course, reported stolen." Steve spoke though his dish of caviar. He wasn't going to pass up this opportunity.

"Same in every country," replied Kane. "They'll cover their tracks really well. No one wants a shooting traced back to them."

Kane picked his sandwich back up from the plate and finished it, just as Kelly came hurtling back through the door.

"Okay, ready. There was no one home, so I left a message. I'll call back later." Kelly grabbed another croissant and hastily drank down the rest of the juice. "Really ready now."

"Your wife like this, Steve?" asked Kane.

"Absolutely nothing like that," Steve replied, as he watched Kelly slide back into her leather jacket.

"I'm ready. Look at you blokes hanging around. Trust men never to be ready," and a precocious Kelly smiled at her husband. "I thought Italians were punctual," and glanced across at the stalwart Bruno.

"We are," and Bruno shot a disparaging look at Kane.

"Okay. I get the picture. Let's go," and Kane picked up the keys and closed the suite door behind him.

Inside the car, Kane climbed into the driver's seat. Kelly climbed in beside him, and buckled up. The two cops, of such opposite nationalities, occupied the back seat. Kane turned the keys over in the ignition, and they sped away, with tires screeching at his usual speed down the long drive, out through the side roads, arriving at the motorway after some instructions from Steve.

"Kane, you aren't on the track yet, and besides you don't want to kill the two people in the backseat," Kelly laughed.

"Guess not," and he slowed down, much to the appreciation of the backseat drivers.

But Kane wasn't slowing down because of what Kelly said. The car wasn't handling right. There was too much play in the steering and something didn't feel right. Kane pulled over from the fast line, steering the car across three lanes.

"I said don't kill them… not all of us," joked Kelly. Then she saw the look on Kane's face. "What's wrong, baby?"

He didn't have time to answer. The left front tire on his side blew. Immediately the car swerved and lurched into the surrounding traffic. Car horns sounded from every direction. Only Kelly's seat belt stopped her from careering into Kane. She screamed and grabbed hold of the armrest.

"Hang on, all of you," yelled Kane.

In the side mirrors he could see the traffic behind him. He tried to bring the car back under control, and pull it back towards the hard shoulder. A passing truck with horn blaring grazed the side of the Mercedes as it tried to swerve out of the way. Kane turned the steering wheel one way, and then the other, till finally the car moved to the side of the road. Steve realized had Kane not been such a good driver they may have died in that instant. The Mercedes came to a shuddering halt, and Kane pulled the keys from the ignition. For a moment he sat with his hands resting on the steering wheel and tried to come to terms with what had just happened. He stretched his arm out to Kelly and she grabbed his hand. Bruno climbed shakily out of the car and bent down by the crumpled heap of tire. Kane saw him cross himself and look up to heaven. There, but for the grace of God, they may have ended up. Steve pulled his cell phone and was about to call the police. As he dialed 999, a police car, with lights blazing and sirens blaring pulled in behind the sagging Mercedes. Steve, with badge in hand, jumped out of the car and ran towards the officers.

"You okay, Kelly?" Kane's voice was shaky. He clutched Kelly's hand.

"I thought we were going to die. I closed my eyes and I could see the kids in front of me," she cried.

"I wouldn't let that happen, darling." Kane tried to reassure her.

He released his seat belt and then hers, pulling her to him, and she cried on his shoulder. Gently, he let go of her and carefully climbed out of the car, making his door creak as he did so. There was a long, black gash down the side from the passing truck.

"Fuck. So much for this getting back in one piece," and Kane kicked at the solid tire.

Kane moved around the front of the car and opened Kelly's door. "Come on, Kel. Get out. Safer outside the car than in. It..." Kane didn't finish.

He looked at Bruno, who was holding something in his fingers. It was a bullet lodged in a piece of the burning rubber.

"Is this what you were about to look for, Commander?" asked the Italian.

Kane looked down at the bullet. Someone just didn't want Kane not to race, but they wanted him out permanently, and they didn't care who else got in the way. Kane took the offending object from Bruno's fingers. Maybe they weren't so safe out of the car after all.

"Yeah, something just like that. Man, someone has it in for Mercedes and, obviously, me. Only this time they put my wife in the line of fire. And that I won't tolerate."

Kelly climbed out and leaned against the car, sliding her fingers gently into Kane's hand. They were cold and clammy, and Kane clenched his fist around her small fingers. His jaw was set and now the shock had worn off, and he was angry. In the palm of his other hand he still held the bullet.

"Mr. Branson?" the uniformed young policeman asked.

Kane slipped the bullet into his jacket pocket. He didn't want some local bobby confiscating his piece of evidence.

"Yeah. That's me," he stated in his thick Australian accent.

"Detective Asher says he was escorting you to the hospital when one of the tires blew on the car. Everyone all right?" and the police officer looked at Kelly and the Italian.

"We're all fine, officer. My wife's just a little shaken, that's all. Car wasn't so lucky. Truck hit my side. Not his fault. I was going to visit..."

"Alexander Vincentia. Your escort told me. And you, Mr. Branson, are racing in his place. Just let my partner move the traffic on past you and we'll get you on your way. We'll get a towing service for your car. I've radioed for backup, and we'll take you safely to the hospital. Unless you'd rather go back to your hotel?"

Kane thought Steve had covered it all pretty well.

"We'll go to the hospital. I need to see my friend. Can you get the Mercedes brought to the hospital when the tire is fixed?" asked Kane.

"Yes. You sure you're all okay? The lady looks upset."

The policeman peered into Kelly's face. Kane thought he looked awfully young, and then reminded himself that meant he was getting older.

"Really, we're okay. If you could take my wife and I on, then the two guys can follow. Would that be okay, officer?" replied Kane. He needed to get them away from that location. Suddenly, he felt they were a prime target. "Can we sit in the squad car and wait? She'd be better out of the sun," and Kane inclined his head towards the car. 'Sun? What fucking sun this time of evening?' Kane thought.

"Of course, sir. Ma'am, right this way," and the policeman escorted the pair to his parked car, complete with flashing lights.

The bunched up traffic was moving a little more freely again. The other cop was waving traffic on past the accident. Steve stood by the police car, and peered in at Kane.

"No accident, right? Bruno told me about the bullet. You have it?" Steve asked.

" I have it. No accident, Steve. Not at all. You meet us inside the hospital. I'm sure these guys know where St. Johns Hospital is. Get there as quickly as you can. Someone doesn't want me to live, let alone talk to Alexander." A thought flashed through his mind. How safe was his friend in the hospital? " Think I'll call ahead and make sure that Vincentia has protection. And maybe someone can meet us there. I have my piece just in case."

"And I have mine," mumbled Kelly. She was beginning to recover from the shock. "Kane, who are these guys? Why are they after us?"

'Us,' thought Kane. Kelly had made a good point.

"Don't know, baby, but we'll find out," and he put his arm around her shoulders.

Kane pulled the cell from his boot, flipped it open and dialed the number for the hospital.

"Maria Vincentia please." There was a pause. "No, I'm not a relative. Put me through to Alexander Vincentia's room… NOW." He waited. "What do you mean, he's not there and no one can take calls." He listened and he closed the phone, his face turning ashen.

Kelly saw his face. "Kane, what's wrong? Kane?" she screamed, "What's happened?" and she tugged on his jacket.

Steve leaned down on the door and put his head inside the open car window. Bruno walked to the car and stood behind Steve, his face inquiring.

"Commander Branson, what's happened?" asked Bruno.

Kane's face was of stone. His features taut. Kelly looked from Steve to Kane. Kane Branson looked at the time on his watch. He took a deep breath and, in a slow and deliberate manner, he murmured words he, nor any of them, would ever forget.

"Alexander Vincentia died thirty minutes ago."

CHAPTER 7

Kane didn't stop to thank the policemen that drove him and Kelly to the hospital. With huge strides he took off down the stone steps that led to the front of the old building. St Johns was ancient, even by English standards, with its brick walls surrounded by tall grass. Kane pushed the huge glass door open and entered the lobby. Kelly quickened her steps behind him and followed him straight to the front desk.

"Need to see someone in charge around here. NOW!" and he banged his fists on the registration desk, more out of frustration than anger. He'd lost his best friend.

"Kane?" a soft voice whispered behind him.

Maria Vincentia stepped out of a side room and into the light. She pulled the shades from her eyes, revealing a tearstained face. Her long, red hair hung down her back and Maria looked like someone who wanted to die.

"Kane. I..." she tried to speak to him.

Kane rushed to her and took Maria in his arms, as she clung desperately to him, with her face pinched and drawn. Her hands shook on his back as Kane's strong arms encircled her slender body. She needed him. He was her husband's friend.

"Maria," he whispered. "What happened? How did Alex die?" The words choked in his throat. "Where is he?"

She released her hand from his back and pointed to the room she had come from. Maria glanced at the girl with Kane. The young woman stood motionless, watching as Kane went through hell, along with the distraught woman he was holding. Maria tried to compose herself. Kane gently let her go and turned to Kelly. He stretched his hand to his wife who took hold of the fingers he offered her.

"Maria, this is my wife, Kelly."

Kane pulled Kelly into the picture. The last thing he wanted was to shut her out now. He'd done that enough lately and he needed the warmth that he knew she could offer. Kelly moved forward and stretched her free hand to Maria. The older woman didn't look shocked at Kane's choice; in fact she would have been surprised if the woman had not looked like a Kelly.

"Mrs. Vincentia, I am so sorry about your husband. I…" Kelly took hold of Maria's hand.

"Kelly, zee name is Maria. And zank you. Would you come wit me?" her voice was directed to Kane, even though her hand still held Kelly's.

"Is Alexander in that room or did they move him?" asked Kane. He glanced up, hoping to see him walk out of the door.

Maria shook. "Alexander is still there. You would like to see him, yes?" She paused. "Kane, he…well, you will zee."

Kane opened the door for them all and the little group entered the room. Clinical white and sterile walls surrounded them. Kane closed the door behind them and stared at the bed, moving in slow motion to the side of it and pulled back the sheet. In front of his eyes was a man he did not recognize. Alexander was burned beyond recognition. Kane stared at the person lying there and then his eyes shifted back to Maria. Her eyes swam with tears sending gigantic drops trickling down her cheeks. Kane knew she had loved Alexander very much. Kane put his hands on Vincentia's shoulders wanting to shake him back to life. He wanted to wake him. He wanted to… and Kane pressed his face on his friend's, and then he cried.

Kelly was staggered, and suppressed the cry with her hand on her mouth. She had never seen Kane cry…never.

Kane Branson could not completely understand that his friend was dead. He held Vincentia's head and shoulders in his arms and whispered softly in the ear of a charcoaled face. It was no wonder the man had died. Maria had not told Kane that Alexander was this badly burned. How he had survived to date was a miracle. Kane raised his head, and his tear stained face looked at Maria.

"You never said he was this bad… you never said. I would have come sooner . There we were going to dinner and buying clothes. I, we…" His tone was almost angry.

Maria moved to Kane's side and touched his arm. "I did not want you to know. I hoped zat he would recover. I hoped he would live…"

Kane gently laid Vincentia back down on the bed and pulled the sheet back over the man that had been his friend. He took the man's wife in his arms, and Maria Vincentia cried till she could cry no more. Kane held her tightly and buried his face in her flaming red hair.

Kelly backed away from them till she leaned back on the door, feeling she was intruding on their grief. This was part of her husband's past life, and she was an outsider. Kelly pushed the door open and stepped outside, flopping down on the sofa opposite Vincentia's room. She'd noted the police on duty as they came in. Kelly noticed most things. She'd seen dead people before, but never one like that and now she wanted to be sick. And Kane was going to race? That she could not come to terms with, just like Kane could not come to terms with his friend's death.

"Hey, you okay?" came a gentle tone.

Kelly looked up.

Steve looked down at her. "Kelly, where's Kane?" He crouched down beside her and rested his hand on the arm of the couch.

She pointed towards the room facing her and Steve made a move towards the door.

"Don't go in there…not yet. They need space, and Kane needs some time with her."

Steve retraced his steps and sat down on the patchwork green couch. He crossed his legs and rested his arm behind Kelly.

"So, you went in?" and inclined his head towards the door.

She nodded.

"You wish you hadn't, right?" asked a concerned Steve.

"Yep," and Kelly pulled her leather jacket up around her face. She stifled the tears that welled up inside her. "Should learn I can't share all his lives."

Now Steve knew why she was so upset.

Bruno plummeted through the doors and down the lobby to where Kelly and Steve sat. He glanced around the entranceway. He, too, noticed all the police in the hallway, but no Commander Branson. He figured he was in the room opposite, and hovered by the couch waiting for some tidbits of what was going on in the room.

"I spoke to Inspector Graham. He and your partner are on their way here. Sergio will not be joining us. He has a virus and is confined to London, so we are one man short, but we will have Roger's crew with us." Bruno hesitated and looked at the closed door. "Is the Com…is Kene still going to race?"

"More than ever," answered Kane's wife.

Kelly watched the hands slowly move round on the clock in the waiting room. Steve fetched them all coffee, twice over. They waited patiently for Kane and Maria to emerge, while the sky turned a darker shade of grey, and night descended on the worst day of Kane Branson's life.

Floodlights lit up the parking lot as Inspector Graham and Dave strode across the tarmac. They entered by the main doors and saw the three people on the couch. Peter Graham coughed discreetly. Kelly had fallen asleep and had fallen against Steve's arm, which led to him being her pillow. Steve had pulled her jacket tightly around her, and rested back on the arm of the couch. When he heard the cough, he looked up at his boss.

"She's been asleep awhile," Steve whispered. "Kane is still with Maria. Apparently he's taken it very hard…" Steve's words very interrupted.

The door from Vincentia's room opened and Maria and Kane stepped out. They both wore shades and Maria clutched at her purse strings. Maria's long hair hung round her face in stark contrast to Kane, whose hair was pulled tightly back in a ponytail, and he wore a look of defiance about him. His leather jacket was zipped ready for the English night air and Kane had his one arm around Maria's shoulders. When he saw Peter Graham, he ushered Maria towards him. Kelly stirred at the noise in the lobby.

"You want to pay your respects to Alexander? I should warn you it will be a shock when you see him." He paused. "Maybe you should do it at a later date." Kane looked at Kelly, then back to Peter. "You want to help me with Maria? She shouldn't be alone right now. She can come back with us for tonight. Right, Kel?"

Kelly was only half awake. "Um, yeah, guess so," she replied. She looked surprised that she was leaning against Steve, moved and gathered her thoughts together. "Course she can." Kelly smiled at her. She didn't know Maria and was surprised at her own thoughts of resentment towards her. Kelly rebuked herself.

"Zat is very kind of you, Kane," and Maria slipped her hands around Kane's arm.

Kelly noticed. Bruno stirred from the back of the group and made his presence known.

"Mrs. Vincentia, I am sorry about your husband. Our government sends its condolences to you. They will make all provisions for your husband to be flown back to Italy. You need not worry about anything. You rest for a day or two while all the arrangements are made. Documents and papers will be in order, too." He looked at Kane. "You are still going to race, sir?" asked a seemingly concerned Bruno

"Yes, more than ever, mate. It means a whole lot more now." Kane didn't look in Kelly's direction. He had a feeling right now she was not a happy woman. "I just hope that you can give me some kind of protection, and better than this afternoon." He looked around. "No Sergio?" Kane asked.

From his pocket Kane produced the bullet and handed it to Peter.

"See what you can find out about this, would you? Was no fuckin' burst tire. Someone shot it out," Kane said rather loudly, not really caring who heard.

Kelly stood upright and pulled her purse with her. That was it. Enough was enough. "Excuse me," and she brushed passed them all and walked away with clinking heels down the corridor.

"Kelly, wait," shouted Kane, letting go of Maria.

No response. She kept walking, her boots making quite a noise on the hard floor.

"Kelly… I said wait!"

Everyone turned to look at the departing Kelly, and saw only a swinging door through which she had departed.

"I'll be back!" remarked Kane as he, too, took off down the corridor.

Kelly walked a few paces from the door. Kane was right behind her, his long legs catching up to her very quickly.

"What the fuck are you doing, Kelly?"

Kane reached her and grabbed her shoulders.

"I can't do this. I can't watch you die! And I can't watch you with…" she stopped. She knew she was saying things she would regret.

"Doing what? Giving consolation to Maria? Or racing? You knew I was gonna race, baby. That's why we came on up here," and he touched her chin with his finger tips.

"You had a bullet in your hand. A bullet, Kane! I thought the tire blew out. That's twice now. Someone doesn't want you to race. Take the hint. Or are you so obsessed that you can't see it?" Kelly yelled at him, and then turned away from him.

"See what? What the hell are you talking about?" Kane yelled back at her. "And don't turn away from me like that!"

People were now beginning to stare at the two figures standing under the lamplight. Kane turned Kelly around and physically moved her beside a wall.

"He was my best friend, Kelly and I just lost him. How the fuck do you think I feel? You ever lost your best friend?" Kane asked.

"I just did," and Kelly pulled out of his grip and she leaned back on the cold brick wall.

"What?" Kane pulled the shades off and peered at her.

"Said I just did." Kelly pouted.

"Heard what you said. What did you mean?" He stuffed the shades in his jacket pocket.

"Answer me one question," she looked him in the eyes, her head tilted upwards. Kane was just a breath away from her.

"Okay, what?"

"You ever slept with Maria?" Kelly surprised herself at having the guts to follow through with her question.

Kane was stunned and it showed. His expression was one of total disbelief that Kelly had worked it out. He also couldn't lie to his wife.

"Yes," he stared her straight in the face. "But Kelly that was over thirty years ago. She was just a kid…" He stopped.

"You still slept with her and that gives you a bond. And she knows it."

"Knows what, baby?" He didn't understand, he really didn't.

"Knows how to pull your strings," she replied, a stillness about her.

"Her husband just died. My best friend. Doesn't that give her just a little right?" Kane questioned.

"It gives you a right. Not her. I love you, Kane Branson, with all my heart and my being. Without you, I would die. I just want you to know that. I'll wait out here for you. Maybe Dave can come and stay with me while you sort things out."

There was a look on Kelly's face that frightened Kane.

"Kelly. Don't do this. Not now, not ever. Come back inside and wait with me, please?" Pleading did not come easy to Kane. "Please, darling? I need you."

"So does Maria. Now go. I'll be here, waiting. I'll always be waiting for you."

Kelly swung her purse over her leather jacket and walked to a nearby bench. Kane watched her go. Why now? Why had Kelly figured it out? Maria meant nothing more than a friend to him now, just a brief fling one summer when none of them were married. Maria was alone and Alexander had left for Brisbane. Sage Jay was also out of town. Circumstances had thrown them together. Two or three nights, that was all. Kane had never thought anything of it, but it had taken but a blink of an eye for Kelly to see what he could not. Kane pulled his cigarettes and lighter from his jeans. He tipped the packet and slid one out. Flicking open the lighter, he lit the cigarette, put it to his mouth and inhaled deeply, crossing to the bench at the same time. He sat down on the stark wood, inhaled deeply, and then handed her the cigarette. She took it from him and took one drag before handing it back to her husband. When her hand touched his she let her fingers linger. Her eyes met his and the look pierced his soul. The words echoed in his head. 'I won't watch you die.'

Kane dropped the cigarette to the ground and stamped it out under his boot. He stood up and stretched his arm out to her, his strong hand reaching for hers. Kelly took hold of his fingers and she grasped tight hold.

They walked back in to the hospital together…hand in hand.

"Peter, I think maybe Maria should be in her own hotel with police protection. What do you think?" asked Kane.

"Agreed. Think that may be better for everyone." Peter glanced at Kelly. "She okay?"

"Think Kelly can answer that better than me." Kane turned to her.

"Everything's okay, Peter. I just can't stand the sight of used bullets. You gonna take that with you?" and Kelly gestured to the one sitting in his hand.

"I'll send it back down to MI5. See what they find out. Kane…be careful. This is getting out of hand. There's still time, you can always pull out. They've already got Alexander."

"Yeah, they did. Man, if I could I would and maybe…" Kane hesitated.

"Maybe nothing. You're gonna race, Kene Branson," and Kelly reached up and threw her arms around Kane's neck.

Her eyes closed and she fought back the tears. She clung to her husband and he to her.

"Some woman you've got there, my friend," stated Peter.

"Yeah, man, I know that," he whispered, his hands resting on Kelly's back. 'And tonight I nearly lost her. That can never happen again,' Kane thought.

The little group watched, especially Maria. And Bruno also watched Maria with interest. Peter spoke up.

"Dave, you and Steve go back with the Bransons. Bruno, you and I will take Maria back to her hotel and stay with her." He turned to Kane. "We'll meet in the morning before you go to the track. Some paperwork you probably have to do and the Mercedes people will want to talk with you..."

"Yeah, I'm sure they will. I wouldn't be surprised at seeing Jimmy Rogers now." Kane said it loudly.

Bruno saw Maria flinch.

Something wasn't right. It had come in handy that Sergio had a virus. It had given someone a reason to keep their special agent back in London. Kane turned his thoughts and attentions to Maria, but he still kept hold of Kelly.

"You'll be fine with Peter and Bruno. Kelly and I will be at the other end of the phone if you need us. I do need to get some sleep and I'm expected to be on the track tomorrow. I know it's just to practice, but I need some kind of position. Day after tomorrow is for real. I'll do justice by Alexander. I'll find out who sabotaged the car."

Now Kane had said it out loud...sabotage.

"I know you will, Kane. You haf always been my husband's friend. And mine," replied Maria.

Kane leaned over and kissed Maria's cheek. As he did, his hand tightened on Kelly's arm.

"Maria, Kane is right. If you need us. We'll be there," added Kelly. '*We'll*, is the right word,' Kelly thought.

"Zank you," and Maria turned to Peter.

Steve drove the now repaired and safely deposited Mercedes back to the hotel. Kane and Kelly sat in the back seat, with Kelly leaning against him. It had been a long and strange day.

"Tired, darling?" Kane asked, hugging her to him.

"Yeah, just a little. You?" she replied.

"For some reason I am." He paused. "Kelly, I can't stop thinking about Alexander. He just...well, he looked so bad. All the times I've seen death and I wasn't prepared for that. It just didn't seem possible. He was too young to die..." Kane couldn't finish the sentence.

"Kane, it's okay to feel like that. Really it is. I know he was like your brother."

"He was, Kel. He was the only brother I ever knew." His arm tightened around her shoulders.

"I know, baby. I know," she whispered. She wasn't exactly sure how he felt towards Alexander, as she had never been that fortunate to have a friend like that.

It was pitch dark along the lanes to the hotel until the Devere loomed into sight. It was beautiful by night and instantly reminded Kelly of something out of a dream, only this dream had turned into a nightmare. When they stopped the car, the doorman opened the door and the Bransons stepped out.

Steve handed over the car keys and they all moved out on to the gravel. Inside the hotel, their suite awaited them. In the lobby Kane assured the English salt and pepper they would be fine for the night, but apparently not enough. Not until they escorted Kelly and Kane to the rooms would they be happy, so Kane gave in graciously.

"You know the room number. You hear anything, sir, you call us. Doesn't matter what time. Dave keeps me awake with his snoring anyway," Steve laughed. "You call us, okay?" Steve commented far more seriously.

"Yeah, we'll call," and Kane opened the suite door.

Steve stopped him. "Maybe we should just check the rooms before we go," and he slipped past Kane and into the majestic suite.

Steve covered the rooms in two minutes flat. He checked the windows, the bathroom and beyond. It was clean and he returned to the door.

"Goodnight, sir and you too, Kelly. Get some rest, and sir, I'm sorry about your friend," added Steve.

"Yeah, me too," replied a very serious Kane.

Kelly collapsed on the bed with sheer exhaustion. This was too much of a day. She rose up and pulled her jacket off, wriggled out of her pants and lay back down on the bed. Underneath she wore a black lace g-string and a black camisole. She could hear Kane in the other room, and wondered what was taking him so long?

He sat down on the couch and pulled off his boots. His jacket lay strewn on the floor, along with the belt from his jeans. Then he turned around. There was a bottle of Irish whiskey sitting conveniently in the drinks cabinet. Kane hadn't noticed it earlier that day. Standing up, he moved to the bottle and relieved it from its hiding place. Picking up the bottle, he unscrewed the top and poured some into a nearby glass, gulping it down in one go. It tasted good. Long time since he had tasted such good whiskey. One became two. He took the bottle back to the couch with him and set it down on the table. He rolled the glass round in his fingers and held it up to the light. As he did so he caught sight of Kelly framed in the doorway. He started with her feet and his eyes moved up her legs. They hesitated on the black lace underwear, and then carried on their journey up to her breasts. He could see their outline through the cameo top. One strap hung down her arm seductively, while she leaned against the frame for effect. One finger gently caressed her freshly painted lips, while another seductively slid into her mouth.

Kane set the glass down firmly on the table. He picked up the bottle and carefully screwed the top back on. That joined the glass. Kane stood up and moved across the room, stepping out of his jeans as he went. He flipped the light switch off and stood in front of Kelly, towering over her. Without saying a word, he picked her up in his arms, his face near to hers. She could smell the whiskey on his breath as his mouth brushed against hers. Then his lips came down harder on her mouth. She was falling, falling back onto the bed. The pillows scattered everywhere.

In the light from the bedside lamp she could see Kane's features. They were strong and determined. She reached up and pulled the band from his hair letting it fall onto his muscular shoulders and resting there. He said nothing. Kelly ran her fingers up his chest to his mouth. Her thumb slipped inside his lips. Kane leaned low across her and his hand slowly slid up Kelly's leg till he reached the g-string. He removed it without her even knowing. His fingers caressed the hidden moistness. Kelly moaned gently while his mouth came down on hers and he kissed her with whiskey breath until she could hardly breathe. His mouth carried on down kissing her neck and further. She arched her back, and her head tipped backwards, her eyes tightly shut. Kane kissed the butterfly on her breast, and he felt her nipple harden beneath his tongue. Her hands clung to his arms and she could feel the power in him. It only enhanced the sexual tension between them. She let go of his arm and reached down for him. She murmured with pleasure knowing she still had this effect on him. He pulled her hand free and thrust himself inside her. Safe and secure, he pulled Kelly upwards and she clung to him, her legs around his back. Kelly cried out loud and the bed creaked beneath them. He clasped her face in his hands, and he had a look in his eyes like Kelly had never seen. A look she would never forget.

Kane was in total control of Kelly's emotions and he knew it. He had his wife exactly where he wanted her. He had a power that she only could bring out in him. Two of a kind, they came together, and Kelly fell forward on Kane's chest. He rocked her gently in his arms, backwards and forwards till she quieted her breathing.

Kelly fell asleep with Kane still locked to her. Gently he laid her on the sheets and Kane watched her sleeping. He watched her breasts rise and fall in time to her heartbeat while sleep would not come to him. It was six AM by the bedside clock. Time to start another nightmare day. The only solace of yesterday was Kelly.

Kane tried not to wake his wife. He climbed out of bed and made for the shower, glancing back at her. She turned in her sleep and her hands clung to his pillow, all the time murmuring his name. Kane watched her and then stepped inside and closed the bathroom door behind him.

The water was warm on his body and he squirted a ton of liquid soap onto him, then ducking his head under the shower. Kane stayed in the water a while thinking about making love to Kelly. Maybe he'd go back out and wake her, pick her up and bring her back in the shower. He liked that idea. He turned the handle on the tap and the water ceased running. Kane wrapped a towel around his waist and stepped out of the shower, letting his hair drop back behind him.

Kane opened the door to the other room and it was the last thing he remembered with any clarity. It felt like an iron bar on the back of his head, and he felt like his eye balls were going to pop out. He hit the ground doing forty. From the view from the floor he could make out two men holding Kelly. She was screaming loudly and then they put something on her face. She fought hard against them, but she wasn't strong enough. And when the needle sunk into her arm they had her, and she was out cold. One of them was pulling clothes on her, while the third man was pulling him by his arms. He was being dragged into the bedroom. He saw them carry Kelly out of the door and he saw the white bear being pulled out of the suitcase along with some clothes. At least that's what he thought he saw. A little white bear on the pillow where Kelly's face should have been. And then Kane Branson was kicked in the side of his head and he knew no more.

CHAPTER 8

"Commander Branson, Kane...for God's sake wake up," begged Steve.

Steve and Dave dragged Kane up from the floor with their hands under his shoulders. He was a two hundred pound odd dead weight in their arms. They held him against the bed and Kane tried with some difficulty to focus. The first thing he saw was the clock, which read eight AM, making two hours he had lost. The next thing that came into focus was the white bear on the bed. Kane shook his head and it hurt. The pain was excruciating, and as he tried to stand. He was unsteady on his feet.

"Kane, sit down before you fall down," and Steve sat him on the end of the bed. He grabbed one of the Devere's custom robes and slid it around Kane's back.

"Ke...lly. They took Kelly," Kane's speech was slurred, and he held his hand to his head.

"We know. There was a note on the bear. I already called Inspector Graham." Steve looked at Kane's face. "You okay? You want to get a doctor..."

"No!" interrupted Kane. "No, damn doctor." He tried to stand, and fell back on the bed. "Fucking hell. What's going on? Why did they take Kelly?" Kane held his head in his hands.

Dave fetched a wet cloth from the bedroom and handed it to him. Kane stuck it on the back of his head, where he found a huge lump. The side of his head hurt, too, and he remembered the kick from the boot and he knew he owed someone the same enjoyment later on.

"They? How many were there? Can you remember what you saw?" prompted Steve.

Dave pulled a note pad from his back pocket. As he did, there was a knock at the door. Setting the notebook down, Dave went out into the main room and peered through the spy hole, then opened the door.

"Good morning, Inspector. Kane's in the bedroom..." Dave didn't finish.

Peter Graham brushed passed him and straight through to Kane.

"Kane, what the hell happened? Let me look at you." Peter looked at the lump on the back of Kane's scull and the bruise on the side of his face "You need a doctor..."

"Like I told them. No doctor." Kane wrapped the robe around him and tied the belt. "How did you know there was anything wrong?" The thought just occurred to him and he looked at Peter.

"Someone called Steve's room about half an hour ago. Steve called me and they came up to you only to find the suite door open. Said they found this note pinned on the bear."

"Let me see!" and Kane snatched the note. It read, 'cross the line.'

"And there won't be any finger prints because they wore gloves. All three of them," muttered Kane.

Dave was writing down everything that Kane said.

"They drugged her, Peter. I lay by that fucking bathroom door while they drugged my wife. And then they put some clothes on her and carried her out wrapped in a blanket. Why didn't someone see them? Why? Why did they take Kelly, Peter?" Kane's voice was loud and uncontrollable and he thumped the bed.

"Kane, I'm not sure. They..." Peter stammered.

"You're not sure?" he yelled. "What kind of fucking police force is this? You don't carry guns..." He remembered Kelly's gun. He stood up shakily and moved to the dresser, opening the top draw. The gun was still there. Chances were they didn't know they had an AFP agent. "So, why you all standing here? Go find her..." Kane gestured with his hands.

"Not that easy. No one saw anything and there is no trace of her outside. You are the only witness," replied a somewhat confused Peter Graham.

"Now isn't that very convenient. I need a drink." Drink. That made Kane think. " I had a drink last night."

They followed him out of the spacious bedroom, mainly in case he fell over. On the table in the lounge the bottle still stood, but the glass had gone. Kane creased his brow. On the glass were his fingerprints. He stared at Peter.

"They came for me, didn't they? It wasn't Kelly they were after. I was in the shower. She woke up and cried out and they had to silence her. They hit me and she wouldn't shut up, so they couldn't leave a witness. I'm right, aren't I? It was me they were after." Kane was still shaky.

"Yes. It looks that way. The room next to yours was conveniently empty this morning. There was no one to hear her cry. You said you were in the shower? Not asleep?"

"No, Kel and I had not slept much. We made love most of the night. She finally fell asleep and I got up and showered. I was going back to get her... well, the rest is history. She cried out to warn me and I couldn't hear her because of the water. They changed plans mid course. Came for me, and left with her. They couldn't take both of us." Kane sat down on the couch pushing last nights discarded clothes aside. The look on his face was unmistakable terror.

"Kane...what? What is it?" asked Peter.

"They took my gun," and Kane's face was ashen. "They're gonna set me up. And they're gonna kill Kelly if I don't do what they ask. They are gonna kill her with my own gun." Kane stood up and stared at Peter. "You better find those bastards before I do or English law or not, I won't be responsible for my actions. And you two get out of my sight and get ready for the track. We are gonna go practice and win."

The dynamic English duo of Steve and Dave fled out of the door.

"What?" asked Peter.

"I have to. That's what they want me to do," stated Kane.

"The note only says cross the line," argued Peter.

"Exactly. The winning line. It doesn't say don't race. There are two sides here, Peter. One side wants me to go on and the other doesn't. The people that killed Alexander don't want me here and the other does."

"But you just said that the guys changed plans. If they were going to take you..." Then the penny dropped. They were taking him to make sure he did race and win. " Oh, my God." Peter turned and grabbed the phone.

He dialed the number for his hotel. "At last. Bruno get Maria out of there. We all stay together till this race is over. One of your fellow countrymen kidnapped Kelly."

Kane went back into the bathroom and looked through the mirror. Everywhere he could see Kelly even her perfume lingered in the air and it taunted him. Where would they take her? How would they treat her? Kelly was tough, but it was a long time since she'd been exposed to drugs, a drug that was meant for him. Maybe a drug to make him do what they wanted, maybe sodium pentothal, God, he hoped not. Even tough little Kelly would tell them who she was.

Kane fingered the lump on his head. It was still bloody and he tried to wash the dried blood away. His hair would hide the bruise now growing on his face and head. He fingered the stubble on his face. From his wash bag he produced a razor. Soap and water took care of the rest. It lathered on his face and Kane shaved off his facial hair. A man many years younger looked back. From the closet he pulled the tightest jeans he could find and a black shirt to match. He looked in the mirror. A great looking guy stared back. All you could see was a bruise, and that he could have got from racing. He smiled. And underneath the façade, he was dying.

Kane walked out to greet the others. Maria and Bruno had joined Peter, and the group stood talking in the other room. He could hear them clearly from the bedroom. As Kane passed the bed, he cringed. How easy it would be to give in and do what the one side wanted. He wanted Kelly back. Pausing at the dresser, he procured Kelly's gun stuffing it down the back of his jeans, and headed for the door before he changed his mind. He could just go out there, find them his way and shoot the bastards. And maybe get himself killed trying. Let Peter handle it… for now.

If was the Mafia as he suspected that had Kelly, she would be safe for now. He'd omitted to tell Peter anything about the three men. As the one walked away he'd recognized them. If it was whom he thought then they already knew she was AFP. Someone was playing with a double-sided coin. And it wasn't these three that he worried about killing Kelly. They had his gun, but it wasn't going to be used on Kelly. Someone knew who the Branson's were, knew how they played the game. They hadn't come for him, but for Kelly and she was their insurance policy. Kane had fed Peter Graham a whole bunch of red herrings. He just wished they hadn't hit him so hard and focusing was still an issue. It was Jimmy Rogers he worried about the most. If ever he found out exactly who Kelly was then her life really was in jeopardy. Kane still couldn't figure out why Jimmy Rogers didn't want him to race? To go to the extent of having someone shoot the tires out was extreme even for a man like Rogers. And why had he offered Kene Branson the job in the first place, unless it was to keep him in view? And Kane was Vincentia's friend. All this ran through his mind as he opened the bedroom door.

Maria saw him first. Her eyes gleamed and then it was gone. Kane saw it. So Marie was in on it, too. But on which side?

"Kane, I am so zorry about Kelly," she lied. She couldn't have cared less that Kelly was gone. "Peter here will find her. She's a tough little girl."

"She has to be tough to keep up with me. At least she'll have all last night to think about." Kane watched for reactions.

It was obvious what Kane meant. Maria twitched. This time Kane noticed. He didn't believe he hadn't seen it last night. Kelly had. Maria certainly had overcome her grief awful fast. Attired in a black dress, one that showed Kane her figure to perfection, Maria watched him.

"Maria," Kane leaned down and kissed her cheek, and extended his hand to Bruno Van Camp.

"Commander, we are sorry that they took your wife. Inspector Graham explained what happened," responded Bruno.

Inspector Graham had told him what Kane Branson wanted him to know.

"Thank you. Kelly is tough. She will be safe as long as I do what they want and for now that means race. By the way, you never said where Sergio was?"

"He's back in London. My partner has some kind of virus," replied Bruno to Kane.

"Sure he has," muttered Kane under his breathe. 'And he's gonna have a bigger one if he harms my wife,' he thought.

Bruno couldn't help think that Kane was awfully calm. But then he didn't know the Commander very well. Kane wasn't calm; he was arrogantly confident and extremely angry. This was his masquerade.

"What's keeping your guys, Peter? I need to get out of this suite and down to the track." Kane glanced back at the bedroom. He wanted Kelly.

His thoughts were disturbed as the two bundles from Britain burst back through the door.

"Bout time," snapped Kane. "If I can be ready with what's going on in my life you two can be." Kane swung his jacket across his shoulders and picked up the car keys. "Your men going to look for clues in the bedroom?" Kane asked sarcastically, knowing full well there wasn't one left. Everyone there had touched the evidence.

"They'll go over every inch with a fine toothcomb. Security will be at your door when you get back..." insisted Peter.

"Bit late, pal..." and Kane disappeared through the open door.

This was the only way that Kane knew to deal with the situation by being arrogant and defensive. He needed the exercise and took the stairs two at a time, then Kane strode across the floor to reception. He was testing the waters to see how much the hotel knew.

"Good morning, Mr. Branson. Is everything fine with your suite, sir?" asked the precocious Judy with the thirty-six inch chest.

No one knew a thing. "Everything is just fine," he lied.

Kane swaggered across the floor. Judy peered from behind the cashier's sign on the counter to watch his butt in the tightest jeans she ever saw. Kelly would have been proud of him.

Kelly.

In the back of the dark blue van Kelly lay unconscious. The three men had clear instructions not to hurt her, very clear on how to treat her, and where to take her.

The crowds were huge even for the practice laps at Silverstone. Kane's Mercedes, with Steve and Dave on board, wove through the traffic. Peter Graham's black car, carrying Maria and Bruno, lost them once or twice on the road. As Kane drove his vision blurred more than once and it bothered him. He shook his head and his eyes came back into focus. Steve saw him do it. He wasn't about to say anything at that point in time.

Kane pulled into the lot marked for drivers keeping the engine revving. Kane's window slid down.

"Kene Branson driving for Jimmy Rogers and Mercedes," he hesitated, "In place of Vincentia."

"Right this way, sir. Mr. Roger's crew is over in that corner of the garages. Park over there if you would, sir," the uniformed attendant yelled above the noise of people and high-powered engines.

Kane turned the wheel, and while driving across the lot his vision blurred again. This time he stopped the car and Steve spoke up.

"Kane, you can't race like that. You'll kill yourself. I'll tell Inspec..."

Kane turned in his seat belt and grabbed Steve by the shirt. "You'll do no such fucking thing. You want to kill my wife? Remember, I told you anything happened to her I'd kill you?" The anger on Kane's face was unpredictable rage. "I'll be fine."

Steve drew back from Kane. "Okay, okay. I won't say a word. But..."

"No buts. I can manage one round. I'll stay at the back. Steve, I'm sorry. It's just not knowing where Kelly is. You two in this car are the only ones

I trust. And I mean the only ones." He sat back in the seat and undid the seatbelt, still blinking his eyes.

"Are you kidding? What about Inspector Graham? You don't think he has anything to do with this...do you?" Dave's astonishment was apparent. He leaned across the seats to be able to see Kane's reactions clearer.

Kane didn't answer. He opened the car door and climbed out, slamming the door behind him. They got their answer. As he walked towards the garage, an attendant in a blue uniform stepped out.

"You're ID, sir?" the small obnoxious looking man asked.

"What ID? The guy back at the gate didn't stop us. Name's Kene Branson. Racing for Mercedes." Kane was more than irritated.

"Still need to see your ID." The portly attendant was enjoying his job.

Kane felt like punching him out and thought seriously about it. As he was contemplating it, he smelled the aroma only emitted by Cuban cigars

"He doesn't need ID. He's who he says he is and he's racing for me."

Jimmy Rogers emerged from the garage into Kane's full view, chewing the end of his cigar as he smoked. The light grey suit he wore only made him look fatter. Kane clenched his fist by his side, figuring how easy it would be to deck him right there in front of everyone. What a coincidence he should be there at that minute. No coincidence. Not with a friend in MI5.

Jimmy Rogers extended his fat little hand. "Kene, glad you could join us." The cigar moved with every word he said and gold dripped from his fingers as he removed the cigar from his mouth. Jimmy didn't give the appearance that he knew anything was wrong.

"Mr. Rogers...surprised to see you here. Thought you had something else to do?" said Kane sarcastically.

"I did. But after I got the call that my main driver had died, I came straight here. I talked to Maria by phone. Told her we would pay all the expenses and anything she needed," Rogers replied rather coldly.

'Now wasn't that interesting? The government and Mercedes paying for things.' And Maria hadn't mentioned it, not to him anyway. 'And who had called Jimmy Rogers?' thought Kane.

"Guys nice to see, too." Jimmy spluttered, while positively shoving the cigar back into his mouth.

The rest of Kane's little group had joined him and stood behind the only man that they also were sure of at this point of time. Kane glanced over his shoulder and also noted that Peter was to one side of him, along with Maria and Bruno.

"Inspector Graham. Wasn't expecting you," added Rogers.

'Bet you weren't,' thought Kane. "Right" Kane smiled.

"We're one short in the team, so I offered my services. Any objection?" asked Peter.

"Course not. You can help out. But my guys will be with Kene here." Jimmy slapped Kane on the back.

Now Kane was confused. Either they were both damn good actors or, they were both telling the truth. And Maria had been with Peter since last night, before Kelly's abduction. Maybe Jimmy Rogers didn't know... yet. And Kane didn't like being touched... especially by Jimmy Rogers.

"Maria, I am so sorry about Alexander. As I told you on the phone, you have Mercedes' condolences. Is there anything you need? Anything at all?" Rogers practically drooled on her.

"My husband back would be nice," and she wiped her eyes with her painted red-nailed fingers.

"Aside from that?" Jimmy asked.

"Nozzing," she replied, "nozzing zat you can give me."

Jimmy looked a little taken aback. He didn't understand that comment and tried a different approach. "No Kelly?" Jimmy peered around the bunch.

Jimmy wasn't that good of an actor was he?

Peter shot a sideward glance at Kane. Peter went to speak, and Kane nodded his head very slightly from side to side.

"No. She wasn't feeling good. Well, I guess I had better go get suited. Steve, Dave why don't you guys come with me. Which door?" Kane turned his attentions back to Jimmy.

"Straight through there." Jimmy pointed to a door on the opposite side of the garage. "This attendant will show you and your guys the way. Talk to you in the pits, Mr. Branson."

"That you will. Oh, that you will." Kane turned and walked across the garage floor.

Maria watched him go. She tossed her flaming red hair back behind her ears, and smoothed down her black dress. Maria Vincentia was known at the track and she still had to keep up appearances. She had been the wife of one of the most influential Formula One racing car drivers that ever lived. Now, he was gone and she was just plain, but very rich, Maria

Vincentia. It was then the loud speaker from the commentary box burst into life.

"Last night the world lost one of its finest drivers. Alexander Vincentia died after his car crashed in practice. Number 9 will never be the same again. Let's all rise and have a minutes silence for number 9, Alexander Vincentia, and our condolences to Mrs. Vincentia." The commentator finished speaking.

The crowd was silent and then they cheered, for that's what Vincentia would have wanted.

The commentator continued. "Along with Michael Ryder in number 6, racing in car number 21 is Mercedes replacement, Australian Kene Branson. Kene takes last position in the qualifying race today here at Silverstone. So, in pole position is John Camery driving number 3 for Ferrari. Behind him on the grid comes…." And the commentators voice faded into the background.

"You are feeling well, Mrs. Vincentia?" asked Bruno.

"Fine. I am really zee fine, however I would like to go back to zee hotel. Would you take with me please?" Maria asked, her tone quiet.

"You don't want to watch the race?" Bruno questioned. He wanted to stay near Kane for several reasons.

"I don't want to zee him die," she whispered and hung her head.

"Maybe it's too much for her. Bruno maybe she should go back. I'll stay with Kane," Peter interjected. "Jimmy Rogers said I could stay. I'll stay with Kane. You go back with Maria. I'll be fine. I'll just potter around. Keep an eye on things here." He'd find somewhere to go in the pits.

In the changing room Kane pulled the suit from the hanger. The fireproof suit hung behind it. This time Kane would wear it. He stretched his hand out to the hanger to grab that too, and missed it by several inches.

"He can't drive like that," whispered Dave. "Kane can't see straight."

"You going to tell him that?" replied Steve. "You that brave, or that stupid?"

They were pulling their own similar color suits on some feet away from Kane.

"He's going to get killed. What good will that do Kelly?" repeated Dave.

"Kane won't get killed. He'll just do enough to qualify. That will give us an excuse to hang around here and really see what's going on. Someone sabotaged Vincentia's car. Someone has Kelly. The link is Kane. Someone wanted to get him here and Kane knows that. They have him where they want him. The note said 'cross the line'. One part wants him to, one doesn't. But crossing the line could have a double meaning."

"Very good, Steven Asher. You're gonna make a damn fine cop," whispered Kane in Steve's ear.

So busy were the two guys in conversation they didn't see Kane standing right behind them, their backs turned to him.

"Kane, we were..." uttered Steve.

"I know what you were saying. I heard you. Trained ear, you know. Can one of you help me with this thing? Stupid fireproof thing that does up the back. Kelly would..." Kane stopped.

Kane was taking the situation much harder than they all realized. As they zipped him into it, Kane looked around him. The place was like a beehive. Each driver had his own crew, and each crew had his own location in the garage. Some of Kane's crew hung out by Michael Ryder's patch. The looks towards Kane could have been much kinder. Michael Ryder himself even hung back. Some team spirit. Kane could hear whisperings across the garage. They echoed in the cavernous room of the changing area.

"Wonderful. Three lots of enemies in one day. And they are supposed to be on my side!" Kane mumbled.

"Regular Mister Popularity," added Steve finishing zipping the back of the mesh suit for Kane. "They're watching you liked you killed Mr. Vincentia so you could take his place."

Kane turned almost taking Steve's hand with the zip.

"What did you say?" Kane's eyes burned fiercely.

"I said you could take his place..." Steve never finished his sentence.

"Yeah, man. You did. Maybe that's it. Maybe I'm supposed to be in his place. I'm the rookie driver with no chance of winning. Mr. Popularity and Mr. Dispensable and an Australian to boot. Commentator made sure everyone knew that. Alexander was one popular guy. I guess I have something to prove to them here. Do me a favor guys. Make sure they put the tires back on the car properly," Kane laughed. But it was a laugh that held a genuine fear. Perhaps Steve had seen what he had missed.

Dave handed Kane the silver-gray suit with countless emblems on it, including his old friend's tire company. Kane stepped into it and zipped up the front, flipping his blonde hair outside the material. Stepping into the shoes he felt a thousand eyes on him. He glanced up and most of them turned away. That was it. They resented him because of Alexander. Now he really had to race to prove to them here he could do it. The note only said 'cross the line'. Nothing about winning.

Kane picked his gloves up from the wooden bench and felt something hard in them. He shook the glove and out dropped Kelly's brand new ring. Kane stared at it.

"What is it? Kane, what's in your..." Steve pushed the hair from his eyes and looked harder. "Kelly's?"

"Yeah. It's Kelly's!"

Kane stashed his clothes in the given locker. Discretely he handed Steve Kelly's gun. "I never asked you, Steve? Can you shoot?"

"To kill, sir. To kill," replied Steven Asher.

"Good. Then let's get this show on the road." He took the chain from round his neck, undid it and slipped the chain through the diamond ring. He replaced the chain, zipped up the suit and snapped the top shut.

With giant and arrogant strides, Kane followed the other drivers out into the arena to do battle. His silver-gray suit shone in the morning sun and his blonde hair flowed behind him. The men may not have liked him, but the women certainly did this hot new hunk from Australia.

"And coming out now is number 21, Kene Branson," the commentator announced.

The shrieks of delight hailed Kene Branson to the cars. His eyes darted too and fro.

"He's looking for Kelly," Steve moved by Dave's side. "Kane thinks she's here, but not with whom she's with, and if she's not here, I'm sure they have her watching."

Inside Steve, there was sadness for Kane, but for himself one of sheer delight at getting to be at Silverstone.

In front of them stood the silver-gray Mercedes flying machine, its sleek body reminding him of Kelly's. The car beckoned Kane, calling his name and he experienced adrenalin flowing inside him like a rushing river. The tarmac gleamed in the sun and fresh steam rose from the pavements. All around the crowds cheered for their favorite teams. Hotdog smells filled the air on this unusually hot English July day. Ferrari red cars took pole positions. McLaren white and black, and then Williams' blue and white cars fell in line behind them.

Kane strode to the car, the audience's full appreciation ringing in his ears and he needed that right now. Someone had to be on his side and

Kane raised his arm acknowledging the crowd. Kane reached the ready and waiting car. Whether they liked him or not they were paid to do a job for Mercedes. Kane climbed in and as he did so, beckoned to Steve and the younger man leaned down into the cockpit.

"Steve, remember. Watch my back. You two blokes are all I've got."

Steve nodded, and stepped back.

Mercedes crew surrounded the car. Kane pulled the mesh over his head and tucked his hair in tightly. He took the helmet the mechanic handed him and stuck his head inside. Adjusting the earpiece he could hear words.

"You go out there, Kene, and just do your best. That's all we can ask. Don't worry about winning or anything stupid like that. And don't get in your teammate's way. Just drive. We'll talk you round. Pace yourself. You only need one-ninety and you're in. That's all we need you to do. A good speed." Jimmy Rogers finished speaking.

'A good speed. I'll give you a fuckin' good speed, mate.'

"Yes, Mr. Rogers, sir," Kane replied as he pulled on the matching grey leather gloves.

He placed his hands on the wheel, put his foot on the pedal and Kane could feel the power beneath his foot. The car revved. In slow motion Kane turned his head and he stared straight at Steve and smiled. His vision blurred again and he blinked his eyes.

Steve saw it.

"Wait…" and Steve's English accent was drowned out by the roar of engines.

He banged on the top of Kane's helmet and then Steve saw the flag rise. The cars dropped down on dry weather wheels, and the mechanics moved away with all the gear.

"Ready, Gentleman," the commentator's voice boomed.

Engines roared and drowned out even Kane's thoughts. Kane raised a thumb to Steve, then like a caged animal waiting to be unleashed, he watched and waited.

The flag dropped and with tires rolling, Kene Branson was gone.

CHAPTER 9

Kane heard nothing now except the engine's roar. He was aware of cars alongside of him and a mess of cars in front. Racing on his own was one thing; racing with a bunch of professionals was very different. He steadied the wheel in his grasp glancing down at the speedometer. Only one-fifty mph. He needed to increase the speed, and pushed his foot down harder, with the car responding instantly. One-seventy. Kane watched the gage climb, feeling the car vibrate beneath the seat. Passing one of the lagging Ferrari's in his path doing one-eighty he'd done it on a real lap. Just then a Williams' car shot by him making Kane a little upset and he went after it. The driver fought back. Neck and neck. Kane was dangerous, and passed the Williams' car on the turn, causing a screeching noise from the earpiece.

"Kene!" yelled Jimmy down the microphone.

No response.

"I know you can hear me, damn it! Don't do that again unless you don't want to drive that car. Kene, you hear me?"

"You told me to race. I'm racing. Something wrong with this earpiece. Can't hear everything you said. You said race faster?" Kane yelled back, feigning ignorance.

"No! Stay at that speed. You're a lap behind. Michael Ryder is right there with you. Let him pass. Don't block him. Kene! You're blocking him. Let him go!" Jimmy Rogers was not a happy man.

"Block him you said? Okay!" replied Kane.

And Kane pulled right in front of his teammate's car.

"Get out of the way!" screamed Jimmy Rogers.

"You son-of-a-bitch, Branson. Get out of my way! Damn you, man. Move it!" yelled Ryder.

This time Kane dully obliged his teammate.

One-ninety mph. Kane screamed round the bends weaving between the cars. His harness tightened as his body exuded strength. He was enjoying this and Kelly would hug…

"Shit! Kelly won't even know…" and he lost the momentum.

Kane slowed instinctively and Ryder passed him. He had to concentrate, powering down again, and this time he hit two hundred miles an hour. He was still a lap behind with twelve laps left. Suddenly, his vision blurred and he saw double. He went to wipe his eyes and hit the visor instead. He blinked his eyes and two more cars slipped by him. When he looked again he was approaching the curve. Kane turned the wheel sharply and regained the control he thought he had lost with the car handling like a dream.

"Kene, pull in the pits. Now!" demanded the Mercedes boss. "NOW, Kene!"

"What the hell for?" came his arrogant reply

"For one thing, fuel. Don't you read dials in Australia?" yelled Jimmy.

The tank was reading near empty.

"Fuck!" but he'd cleared two hundred and ten miles an hour.

Seeing the mechanics waiting, Kane screeched to a halt in front of them. Jacking up the car, they changed the tires at the same time pumping gas through the line. His visor washed clean, Kane could see again, and saw Steve banging on the side of the car. He was distracted by the ear piece once more bursting into life.

"You ever do that again, Kene, and you're out of this place and my car! You understand me?" Jimmy Rogers yelled down the earpiece.

"Yes," replied Kane submissively.

"Kene, you okay in there?" screamed Steve in the visor face.

Kane nodded.

Ten seconds.

"Too fucking slow," muttered Kane pounding his fists on the steering wheel.

Time to go. The mechanics stood back… all clear. Kane pulled out of the pits with screeching tires, and back on the track, narrowly missing Ferrari's leading car. He pulled in behind it.

"Get in its stream! Stay there and go with it," yelled Jimmy.

They passed the pits next lap doing two-hundred mph. Kane was still a lap behind, but the other cars had to pit. Without warning the earpiece burst into life again, but this time it wasn't the same signal and it sure the hell wasn't the same voice. The earpiece crackled and hissed

"Kane, baby...can you hear me...I'm safe. Cross the line for me," and the soft and controlled feminine voice was gone.

"What the crap was that? Some interference on the lines there. You still with us, Kene?" Jimmy yelled.

Kane's voice was shaky. "Yeah, I'm okay."

How had they intercepted Jimmy Rogers' line? Kane would know Kelly's voice anywhere. She was alive and she was okay. That's all that mattered. Fuck Jimmy Rogers. Kane accelerated like his life depended on it and he pulled out of the stream. It was a tough call, for now he was on his own. Kane pushed hard, still half a lap behind. He needed a position on the pole. This was for Vincentia and for Kelly. Jimmy didn't want him to get any pole position. Rogers wanted him at the back. He wanted Mercedes to lose the race. Jimmy was throwing the race. Why? If he was, then Michael Ryder was in serious trouble. He had to warn him. Something was gonna happen to Ryder's car just like it had to Alexander's car, maybe not in practice, but definitely in the race tomorrow afternoon. A race that would be seen by millions all over the world, watching while Ryder's car would be deemed out of the race. Mercedes gave Kane no chance of winning. Someone was paying a handsome price for Mercedes to lose. Was it Mafia backed? He thought not. It was someone else. Kane came back to reality and the staccato like questions left his brain. The only thing he had to concentrate on now was that position. It was do or die time. He had to win the race and he couldn't do that from back of the line. The crowd watched, as the rookie pounded ahead and the predominantly British crowd went wild, standing in their seats and cheering the rookie on.

Two laps left and Kane was catching them fast taking chances he knew were stupid. He stopped listening to Jimmy Rogers' ravings down the earpiece way back. All he concentrated on was staying alive and crossing the line. He could see Ryder's car in front of him, all the time knowing he had to get alongside of him. When he did Kane, glanced to his side and saw Ryder's front right tire. It seemed smaller than the other three and was losing pressure fast.

Kane yelled into the mouthpiece. "Ryder's tire is gonna blow!"

There was no response.

"You hear me? Your blue-eyed boy's tire is on its way out." Kane listened. Nothing. "Fuck!"

Kane stayed along side Michael. For a second he let one hand leave the wheel and motioned with his glove to the tire. Ryder ignored him and lunged forward with the car, stepping on the gas. Michael Ryder accelerated to a ridiculous speed. If the tire blew now he was dead. One lap left. Camery and the Williams' camp were way out in front. Ferrari's number one driver, Sandini, followed him. Somehow Michael Ryder and Kane were in third and fourth place leaving Kane to wonder how the hell it happened. Kane saw the checkered flag, and he also saw Ryder's tire getting lower. Ryder was shortly going to have a hard time controlling the car. It was then Kane made the decision and bumped Ryder's car very slightly. Instantly as their wheels locked together, Kane took his foot from the gas. His car slowed immediately and took the other car with it, sending them careering across the line and over the grass that bordered both sides of the track. The cars spun around, still locked together, till Ryder's car hit the balustrade taking the brunt of the impact. Kane fell forward in the harness which did not give under his weight and he felt his ribs crack. The cars came to a grinding halt and the flag went down as they, too, had literally crossed the line.

Through the haze of exhaust fumes and smoke, Kane could hear the sirens, and could see Michael Ryder emerge from the car. The man removed his silver helmet and threw it on the ground. The anger on the younger man's face was indescribable. He pulled the mesh off his curly black hair and tossed that, too, on the ground, then turned in Kane's direction. With a lot of effort Kane released the constricting harness, climbed out of the car removed his helmet, and stood clutching his chest.

As Ryder reached Kane, he was screaming at his teammate. "What the fuck did you think you were doing?" and without any further ado Michael Ryder's fist connected to Kane's jaw.

Kane went down on the dry ground, while the crowd hesitated in anticipation of the kill.

"Saving your life, man. Look at your wheel? The right front tire. Go look before you hit me again."

Michael walked back closer to his wreck of a car and leaned towards the front end. The tire was in shreds. Kane's wheel was locked into the back tire, not the front. Ryder crossed himself. This man had indeed saved his life. Another few seconds and that tire would have meant his death.

Michael strode back to Kane and away from the stench of smoldering oil and reached down with stretched hand to Kane. Kane took hold and pulled himself up. Once more he hugged his chest.

"How the hell did you know? I would be dead now, just like Alex..." Michael froze.

The crowd was quiet as the sirens got louder. Then they stopped.

Kane dropped his arm down by his side. If Jimmy thought he was hurt that would put an end to his racing career right there.

"You okay? God, I'm sorry I punched you. What the hell is going on here?" Thirty-three year old Michael Ryder looked like a steam train had hit him. "I can only thank you. My car is out, though. They'll never fix that by tomorrow. Yours maybe. Shit, all these months of waiting. I had a shot at one of the places on the podium. Gone, just like that." The man looked exasperated and waved his arms in the air as he spoke.

"At least you have your life. More than your old teammate." Kane dropped his voice.

"Yeah, thanks to you. Are you hurt? Where?" the younger man asked.

"It's nothing, man." Kane rubbed his face. "You Americans can throw a punch."

"Sorry about that. Let's get away from these cars," and the young Michael Ryder led Kane away.

He winced in pain. Kane knew one rib was cracked, maybe two or three. The paramedics arrived and Kane waved them away while crews shot foam on the cars. Number 21 cooled immediately, but Ryder's car was not so lucky. The side that hit the balustrade had smashed the front of the car. The alignment had gone, plus the suspension was shot. The left wheel buckled under the car with tie rod damage, and smoke billowed out from the side. How Ryder got out without a scratch was a miracle. The crowd watched the whole proceedings nervously, not even a ripple of applause for the winner.

When the lap car picked them up, Kane climbed in first. Again, he felt the pain in his chest, but this time remembered not to hold his chest. Michael climbed in beside him and sat down and turned to the other man.

"You and Alexander were very close. I...," Ryder hesitated, "I am sorry we were so rude to you this morning. It will not happen again. It was just that you were taking our friend's place and Vincentia was a good man. But then you know that." Michael was truly sorry he had done what he did and the man beside him had just saved his life. He offered him his hand. "Thank you."

"Was nothing, mate. You'd have done the same for me." That Kane wasn't sure about, but he shook the offered hand anyway.

"I have no car. Mercedes won't fix it in time and you have the spare. Maybe..."

"Maybe they'll give it you?" Should he risk telling the young man? "Doubt it. They don't want you to race. You were supposed to be injured in a crash so they won't give you my car." Kane could see the look of disbelief on the other man's face.

"If you don't believe me watch when we get back to the pits." Kane could say no more.

He wasn't sure how much Ryder would believe. When the car stopped the pair disembarked, with Michael and Kane walking into the pit side by side. The mechanics were on Ryder like bees to honey. Steve and Dave made their way through the honey pot till they reached Kane.

"Do you know what you did out there, sir? You could have been killed," rebuked Steve. He glared at Kane, not his usual attitude towards his new boss.

"If I hadn't done it that man over there wouldn't be breathing right now. His tire was so low..." Kane stopped speaking and almost doubled over. The pain in his chest suddenly increased ten fold.

Steve grabbed Kane by the shoulders.

"What's wrong? Kane, what is it?"

"Get me out of here...now," pleaded Kane, his eyes full of pain.

"*Mister Branson*... a word." Jimmy Rogers appeared.

"Steve, get me out of here. My ribs..." Too late. "You wanted me, Mr. Rogers?" and Kane's brave exterior was back. "All I did was save a man's life when his tire blew."

"It did?" Jimmy Rogers did a good job of looking surprised. "Then I guess I should be thanking you." He put his hand out to Kane.

Kane reciprocated the gesture and felt his own skin crawl as he touched a soft and clammy hand.

Michael Ryder pushed his mechanics aside. "Kene, don't go. I want to thank you." He pushed through the crowds to stand next to his teammate. Ryder may have been young, but he was as powerfully built as Kane. He bear hugged him and Kane thought he was going to black out as pain shot though his body. He looked at Steve with the hopes that he would rescue him.

"Mr. Branson needs to go back to the hotel. Kelly isn't feeling well," Steve said and took Kane by the arm.

"Kelly? She's okay, right? I thought she'd be here cheering you on today.

She will be here tomorrow, right?" asked the fat little man that had the power in his fingers to make or break a driver. He hovered around his drivers like a bluebottle about to settle on one of them.

"Hope so, but right now she needs me. I have to go." Kane blinked and fought to keep upright.

"Kelly? She's your wife?" asked Michael.

"Yeah." Every word Kane uttered was torture.

"Maybe I could buy you guys dinner tonight? To say thank you in the very English way." Ryder was trying desperately to make amends for earlier and also he wanted to talk in private to Kane.

Kane looked again at Steve. His electric eyes were pleading.

"And there's paperwork, Kene. You have to fill out paperwork for the race tomorrow, and we need to talk about what just happened." Rogers hovered like a fly on shit.

It was like Rogers knew to keep him there and Kane didn't want to discuss it right now.

Kane took a breath and spoke. "I'll come back later today."

He turned and, not waiting for the others, made for the lockers. Steve ran after him while Dave carried on talking to Jimmy Rogers, trying to distract him from following Kane. He was first into the changing area and sat down hard on the bench clutching his chest.

"Get this fucking suit off me and get me into my own clothes," moaned Kane. "I feel claustrophobic in here."

"Kane, you have to go to the hospital. If you have cracked ribs…" Steve whispered as he helped Kane.

"I've had them before and I'll have them again. I just need…," the pain was excruciating. "Just need to get them bandaged. You can do that. Need to rest." Kane was struggling.

Kane unzipped the suit while Steve pulled it down him. Kane was in a hurry and climbed into his jeans without waiting for help. Pulling on his shirt, he picked up his boots in his hand and set out barefoot to the lot. Steve hastily tugged his suit off, and his street clothes on, and beat a hasty exit after Kane.

Kane reached the car first, found it was locked and remembered Steve had the keys. There was no one there. Not Maria, Bruno or Peter. He was thinking that was strange when Steve caught up to him.

"Where is everyone?" Kane was breathing hard.

"Apparently Bruno took Maria back to the hotel. Funny that, and then the Inspector disappeared. We didn't have time to go look for him. Dave and I needed to be where you could see us." He looked hard at Kane. "Is the pain bad?" and Steve reached for the door handle.

"Fucking stupid question. Harness too tight. Hit his car. Snapped my ribs. Get bandages. Open the fucking door."

Steve turned the key in the lock and pulled the door open. He looked back for his partner who was nowhere in sight. Kane climbed in, lay down on the back seat of the Mercedes, stretching out as best he could. Steve knew he had to get Kane some relief if there was anyway he was going to be able to race tomorrow. He climbed in the front seat of the car and it was then he heard Kane whisper.

"I heard Kelly's voice."

"Where?" Steve turned to look at Kane.

"In the helmet," Kane replied.

Steve looked doubtful. "You took a nasty blow, Kane…"

"You think I dreamed it? Or I'm going senile? They broke though Rogers' line," Kane raised his voice, and it hurt.

"God damn, where's Dave?" He mumbled looking out of the window. But Dave didn't come out. "He'll have to get his own ride back to the hotel. You need attention." Steve turned to look at Kane again.

Kane's eyes were closed.

"Kane? Kane!" yelled Steve. He reached over the seat and shook the man's shoulder.

"You trying to kill me? Not dead, if that's what you're thinking. Just go!"

Steve pulled out the lot doing the 'Branson' speed. Kane was impressed. They weaved in and out of the traffic and made it back to the Devere in thirty minutes. The Mercedes screeched to a halt outside the entrance. Steve climbed out and opened the back door of the car and tried to help Kane to sit up.

"I can get out on my own and walk across the lobby. No one must suspect that anything is wrong. If Jimmy finds out he'll have a perfect excuse to get rid of me." Kane struggled from the car, but walked with determined steps from the car to the hotel.

Kane made it across the lobby to the stairs. Judy was keeping her usual vigil at reception and Kane knew she'd notice if he was acting strangely. She watched him walk, and she was satisfied.

Kane reached the suite, and handed Steve the key to the room, who turned it in the lock. Kane almost fell through the door and collapsed on the nearest couch, pain searing through his ribcage.

"And you're gonna race tomorrow in the British Grand prix? Let's take a look," and Steve bent down and kneeled beside Kane on the floor.

"So you're a doctor now then, Steve?" But Kane knew Steve was right and tried to pull his T-shirt over his head. It took him a few minutes to succeed.

Steve saw him wince with pain as Kane leaned back on the couch and closed his eyes.

"How's your vision?" Steve leaned over him.

"What?" Kane frowned.

"I said…"

"I know what you said. Since when has my vision been in question? It was a little blurred. It's fine now," Kane lied most convincingly.

"Since you saw double after that blow on the head. I saw you blink and shake your head, both Dave and I did. Now this? How many things have to go wrong before you don't race again?" Steve sat on the end of the mahogany table.

"You know fucking well I have to race. Kelly's well-being rides on it. If I cross that line I get her back." This time Kane propped his feet on the table…expensive or not.

"And if you race, what will she have to come back to? They're going to kill you, Kane. You do know that don't you?" Steve was trying to make the man in front of him see sense.

"Yeah. I figured it out the same as you obviously have." Kane paused, trying to get some relief. "Jimmy Rogers doesn't want his team to win. Someone is betting on him heavily to lose. You and Dave need to check on the odds on the teams. Any bookie can give you that information. And where is Dave? And better still where is my *old friend* Peter Graham?"

"Good questions, …especially my boss. Do you really think he's involved?" asked Steve.

"We're driving a Mercedes car that Peter loaned us. Quite a coincidence don't you think? A brand new car? They pay Inspectors that well in England? I think your boss and my old friend may just have had a sideline in dealing in faulty tires. And where is the security on the hotel room that your boss promised. You see it? Someone's been in here, done his job and left. Left us alone, that is. Another coincidence?" Kane undid the top button of his jeans which offered some relief to his ribcage. "You'll find bandages in the first aid kit in the bathroom. Seems every racing driver's room should have one. There is everything in this place. No fucking wonder it costs so much. I wanted Kelly to have some nice places to remember England by. I failed there." He paused and waited for Steve to return from the bathroom.

Steve hesitated, holding bandages and pins in his hands

"What the hell are you waiting for? Wrap them round me. They have to be tight. My ribs are used to getting broken one way or another. Elastic bandages would have been better, but the cotton ones will have to do for today. Maybe later we can pick some different kind."

Kane struggled and sat upright on the couch.

"What if the ribs have done any damage inside you?" asked the concerned young cop, and gingerly he put his hand on Kane's rib cage.

His fingers moved across the Australian's skin. Steve felt for the cracked ribs, counting far more than one as he moved across Kane's chest. He saw Kane's fist clench tight on the arm of the couch.

"You have at least four cracks…"

"Yeah, I know. I felt everyone when you pushed on them. Where did you learn that little art? The English 'how to inflict pain' school?" quipped Kane.

"Sorry. It has to hurt like hell and you never made a sound," complimented Steve.

"What are you? A mother hen? Son, when you have been on one hundred missions for the AFP you learn to live with pain. Now, just do it!" demanded Kane.

Steve started wrapping and pulled the bandage as tight as he dare. He saw Kane's hand clench tighter, but still he made no sound. His fist turned white and his other hand had a death grip on the mahogany table.

Steve finished the bandaging and put a safety pin in the last piece of the cotton. Kane leaned back on the couch and closed his eyes for a brief second.

"Feel any better?" Steve's eyes were full of concern.

"Sure. Only hurts now when I breathe." Kane clutched the bandage. "I wish…"

Kane was interrupted by a knock at the suite door.

"Hopefully, Dave." Steve crossed the room.

"Hopefully, but check first. And give me back my wife's gun," added Kane. He stretched out his death-grip hand.

"I don't have Kelly's gun. You said to put it in the locker room. In the locker..."

"Fucking hell! Then it's still in there. I thought you picked it up. Guess I was more out of it than I thought. We have to get it back. A gun sitting in a locker is gonna raise some eyebrows. A standard .38 AFP gun is gonna raise even more."

Steve peered through the spy hole. It was Dave, but he had someone with him.

"It's Dave, but Michael Ryder is with him," whispered Steve.

"Oh, Christ." Kane pulled the T-shirt back on. "Let them in. You don't mention this," and he motioned to his chest. "And you don't mention Kelly. She's in the bedroom sleeping."

"This time of day?" asked Steve.

"This time of day," Kane replied firmly.

Steve could still not get over the calmness of Kane towards Kelly's abduction. If he had known him better he would have known that he was not calm at all, only sporting a deep volatile anger that was seeping towards the surface. Steve couldn't imagine how he'd feel if it was his wife, and opened the door for their guests.

"Bout time, Dave," Steve whispered. He turned to Michael. "Mr. Ryder. What an unexpected pleasure. Come in." He opened the door wider and let the guest in.

"Wow, even my suite isn't this good," and Ryder let out a soft whistle. "I can't afford this. What doesn't this suite have? Bar, mahogany everything," Michael glanced around. "Mr. Rogers must be paying you awfully well."

"Mr. Rogers isn't paying me at all. This is coming out of my pocket," replied Kane.

"Some pocket." Ryder sat down on the plush couch and ran his hand along the seat. "I wanted to thank you again for saving my life. And also to tell you you were right. They won't let me have your car." He was looking at the other door. "Eh, mind if I use your bathroom. I came straight here with your bloke."

Kane leaned forward on the couch and looked at Steve. "My wife is sleeping in the bedroom...oh, fuck. You're gonna find out soon enough. You have to go right through the room to get to the bathroom. And when you come back there are a few things I'd like to discuss with you."

Michael Ryder didn't even blink an eye, got up and opened the door to the bedroom. Kane thought that a little odd. He pulled out his cigarettes and slid one out. He was just about to put the cigarette to his lips.

"Kane, don't think that's such a good idea, not right now," said Steve.

Kane looked up. "You my keeper now? Man, you English are worse than Americans. If I wanna smoke, I'll smoke." He placed the tip in his mouth, flicked open the lighter and lit up the cigarette. Immediately he coughed and clutched his ribs. "Okay," he muttered, "So you were right," and squashed the cigarette out in the tray.

Dave looked at Kane like he didn't believe this man. Was he superhuman? He thought maybe he was.

Michael came back into the room as Dave moved himself to the window and hovered there. Steve sat down on a hard-backed mahogany chair watching the proceedings with some interest. Michael, who was staring at Kane, was obviously there for more than using the bathroom to pee.

"Mr. Branson, what's wrong? I knew you were hurt. Maybe there are some things I'd like to discuss with you. Like why you lied about your wife? Why did I hear a woman's voice over my headset today? And why did Mr. Rogers not let me, the obvious choice, take the spare car? But mostly, why was there a .38 in your locker? And what the hell is going on around this place?"

And Michael Ryder pulled Kelly's gun from the back of his jeans.

CHAPTER 10

"How the hell did you get that?" Standing up, Kane pointed at the gun, and moved to take it from Michael.

Michael pulled his arm back. "Not so fast, Mr. Branson. Or should I say Kane? That's what the woman called you. Was that your wife? When they broke into your line it cut into mine. Normally each car is separate so I knew something was wrong, but I hadn't a clue what. I knew it wasn't a regular line either." He seemed a little unsteady with the weapon and he made Kane nervous.

"Michael, would you not wave that around like that? It's loaded!" This time Kane got the gun from him. But as he stretched for the gun he felt excruciating pain in his chest. Kane clutched his ribs and fell back down on the couch.

Steve flopped down beside him and stuffed a pillow behind Kane's back for support.

"You should see a doctor. Four cracked ribs are not to be trifled with." Steve looked to Michael for help. "He can't race like that. The harness will cut into him. Would you tell him, please?"

"If Jimmy Rogers sees him in that shape you won't have to worry. He won't let him near his precious car and then he'll have all his wishes. He has to race. Kane's our last hope." Michael said the last sentence with feeling.

"Excuse me. I'm still here. And what do you mean …last hope? Do you know something about Alexander? Was he being blackmailed?" Kane chanced it.

"You knew about that?" Michael sat down opposite Kane. "Yes, he was. He told me only a few days before the last practice. Someone wanted him to throw the race. He wouldn't do it and he paid for it with his life. Rogers was all over him the last time I saw them together. Jimmy knew he had friends coming in, just not that you were a driver, and some driver at that. The same day as my teammate crashed, I started getting phone calls at the suite. Then the line would go dead."

"We had a couple here," interjected Kane.

Michael acknowledged the fact and continued. "They never say anything, just all times of the night, like they want to keep me awake."

"They do," added Kane. "Make sure you are on edge. Any of the mechanics know about this? Or better still, have you mentioned it to Jimmy?"

"One or two of the guys that I have known for years. I did not tell Mr. Rogers. Some little voice said not to. Seems I was right. Then today when they saw you, they, like me, thought Jimmy Rogers had brought you in. They resented you." Michael sounded somewhat apologetic.

"He did bring me in, but because he thought I couldn't run with you guys. He thought I was some deadbeat guy from the outback. Must have made his day when he met me. He thinks I'm Kene Branson, a relative of mine who races down under. But as you know, my name is Kane Branson." Kane looked into the man's face. Michael Ryder was on the up and up. Kane laid the gun on the table. "As you so rightly pointed out that's a.38 and it's a standard firearm for the Australian Federal Police. Alexander and I grew up together in OZ. He became a racing driver and I became a cop. I'm Commander Branson, undercover agent with the Australian Federal Police, really here on vacation until this. The voice on the line was my wife, Kelly. She was abducted from the bedroom while I showered. She is also an AFP agent, and she's someone's insurance policy to make sure that I cross the line tomorrow. I think I know who is behind it, but it's gonna take a lot of proving. You game to help?" the Australian asked.

"Very much so. I thought a lot of Alexander. So you know Maria then?"

Kane thought that an odd question.

"Yes, I *know* her. Why?" Kane dropped his head a little. He said the word *know* with more meaning than was called for.

"She was always on his case. Poor guy couldn't do anything right for her. Alexander was talking about quitting racing. I was out back of the garage one day and heard them arguing. She was saying that she wanted him to carry on racing, then they would have all the money they would ever need. Well she has it now. His insurance policy must be worth a fortune. You knew her long?"

"Yeah. I knew her long..." and his voice tailed off. Suddenly, sleeping with her sprang into his mind. She had wanted him, but as he thought back Kane remembered that she was always after the guy that she thought would make the most money. Now her meal ticket was gone, but she was a very rich widow. Things were starting to fall into place. Kane looked up to see the guys staring at him. He'd given away what he meant without even realizing it. He cleared his throat and continued. "By the way, where did she go to this afternoon? The last I saw of her was with Bruno and Peter."

"Bruno and Peter?" asked Michael. "Who are they?" He shrugged his shoulders.

Kane had started so he figured he might as well finish.

"Bruno is Italian police and was here to look out for Alexander. Seems he failed. Peter is Inspector Graham of MI5. These two blokes boss," and Kane inclined his head at the two other guys in the room. "The blonde that thinks he's a mother hen is Steve. And you met Dave. They both are cops."

Things started to fall into place for Michael. "That's why you were talking to Mr. Rogers and why you escorted me back here. You are protecting your man."

"It didn't start out like that. Our *man* here conveniently got himself picked up by your Mr. Rogers in Harrods quite by chance. We came as mechanics, and somehow ended up being bodyguards. Someone took a shot at Kane in London, blew out the tire on the car we were driving in, and then they took Kelly, Mrs. Branson. And now it seems that Inspector Graham has gone AWOL. He didn't go back with Bruno or Maria."

"How did you find out Peter isn't with Maria?" asked Kane.

"Dave called Bruno," replied Steve.

"That's what you two were whispering about a few minutes ago. Was Maria there?" asked Kane.

"Yes. She was there. You think we should tell Bruno to make sure she stays with him?" asked Steve.

"Might be a good idea. Firstly, we don't know who is on which side. We are one person missing, and the only real thing we know is that Jimmy Rogers is mixed up in this somehow. I don't think that he has Kelly. That's the only thing I'm real sure about. He wants me to lose, not win. The people that have Kel want me to cross the line. I don't think I can do it, not now. But you could."

Steve followed Kane' eyes. He was looking at Michael.

"Mr. Branson, I can't take that car out. How would I pass for you? Even suited I don't look like you. And I don't want the responsibility of not winning and not getting your wife back…"

"You'll win. You have a better chance than I would. But first we have some things to go sort out." Kane stood up and moved to the window staring out. Where was Peter?

"There is still daylight left. Why don't we go look for Inspector Graham?"

"Just our boss? Don't you want to look for your wife?" Steve couldn't help but ask.

Kane turned from the window. "Drop it, Detective Asher. You are doing a better job of unnerving me than the people holding her are. I need to be able to think clearly. Not having Kelly here is clouding my judgment. Kelly and I have a special bond, one that none of you can understand. I know she is safe. If she wasn't, I would feel it. And right now she is safe. All we have to do is win the race." Kane paused. He glanced at the other driver. "I do know your Mr. Rogers is not playing a very nice game, but he doesn't have Kelly. Sergio was one of the guys that took Kelly. Either the Italian government wants retribution or some other body of Italian men does. That's why we have to win. Rogers double-crossed someone down the line. I want to go back and look at the tires on the cars." Kane moved to the bar and poured himself one drink. He downed the whiskey and replaced the bottle on the bar. He rotated the glass in his hands. Why had they taken the glass with his fingerprints on it? The thought kept going around in his head. His gun, his fingerprints and his wife. Sergio knew exactly who he was and who Kelly was. Kidnapping an Australian Federal agent was not a smart move in any language. What if they hadn't kidnapped her for ransom? What if Kelly was working with them? "Fuck!"

"Excuse me?" asked Steve.

"Kelly may not be there against her will. Maybe they asked her to work with them?" Kane appeared to be animated.

"What? That's crazy," replied an astonished Dave.

"Is it? Think about it. You heard her, Michael? Did she sound like she was panicking over the line?"

"Well, no, she didn't. Actually she was calm, thinking about it. Kane, may I ask a question?" Michael was a little hesitant. "You don't have to answer it if you don't want to."

"Ask." Kane knew the question before Michael asked.

"Is your wife...well, is she younger than you by some chance?" Michael Ryder looked a little afraid that he had brought up the question to the god of war.

"Kelly is in her twenties. We have two children; one is a baby of six months. I rescued Kelly from her father, who had a nice little drug cartel going. Kel turned state's evidence. We married in a drug kingpin's front garden at Malibu, and seven months later she gave birth to our first child, Star. Kelly joined the AFP, trained under me and went with me on my one-hundredth mission, and also lost our baby in Hong Kong. After that she and I had another child, Kene. We are very happily married and I'd like another couple of kids. That answer your question, mate?"

Michael was beetroot red. There wasn't a hole big enough for him to crawl in.

"Adequately."

Steve suppressed a smile. That description sounded like it would fit Kane and Kelly Branson's description to perfection. Steve coughed simply to alter the direction the conversation had taken.

"But Bruno said that Sergio had a virus and was back in London, didn't he?" asked Steve.

"He said that, Steve. Sergio also is Italian Police. Even they have crooked cops just like any other force. They weren't exactly doing a great job of protecting Alexander. But then neither is my good friend doing a wonderful job of protecting us. I'm still looking for that protection Peter promised us. So I think we should go do some checking of our own. Michael, you and I can go to the car without being stopped, right? I mean will they let us get near them without being suspect?" asked Kane.

"Guess so. I've never been stopped, but then I've never wanted to go back after a race and check out tires. You think that's the key factor?" Michael looked at Kane curiously.

"I think it would be a good place to start. It seems to be the link. The tire was shot out on our car en route to the hospital, yours blew, well almost, and I bet if we could take a look at the report about Vincentia's car we'd find it had something to do with tires." Kane was thinking out loud.

Steve could almost see the light go on in Kane's head.

"Who would have the records of the crash? Would the police have them or would the track still have it?" asked Kane. He was pulling his jacket on at the same time by slipping one arm into the sleeve and then he tried the next. He stopped finding he couldn't do it.

Steve moved towards him and Kane pulled back from him.

"I have to do it. I have to be able to get suited up tomorrow to go out to the pits, at least before Michael takes over." Kane pursued in his task.

They could clearly see the pain that Kane was experiencing.

"Takes over? I'm going to take over? How the heck are we going to manage that?" Michaels' eyes widened.

"You'll see," laughed Kane.

"Don't question him, Mr. Ryder. He's Commander Branson…he can do anything!" joked Steve. But it wasn't so much of a joke as he was suggesting.

Kane tossed the car keys to Dave. "You drive. You're the safest one amongst us…" he didn't finish.

His cell phone rang, and Kane dug down into his boot to get it. Michael looked astonished.

"Told you. He's Kane Branson!" laughed Steve.

Kane flipped open the cell and listened. The line crackled and hissed and he paused to listen to the voice. Kane answered in fluent Italian. No one seemed surprised. A smile spread across Kane's face. Only two people in England had his number and this was one of them. Kane listened intently.

"Baby, have they hurt you?" Kane waited for the reply. "Fed you to death? Well, that's okay. Just play along with them, Kel, and before they cut you off, I love you…" and the line went dead.

"Kelly?" asked Steve.

"Yeah, man. Love of my life. She's okay, so far. Then again, if Sergio lets anything happen to her, I'll kill him where he stands, with or without a gun. I just told him that, and I meant it."

Of that they all had no doubt.

"Why are they still holding her? I mean you know who it is?" Michael commented.

"I know it's Sergio, not who the party is. He wasn't as condescending as to tell me that. But she's okay and that's what counts. Without them knowing, Kelly gave me information that only she and I would understand. Let's go," and Kane ushered them all out of the suite door.

Kelly knew she had succeeded in telling Kane what he needed to know. Sergio escorted her back into the bedroom of the manor house and locked the door behind her. When they had first arrived Kelly was still groggy from the knock out drug. She couldn't remember much after Kane and she had had that wild night. She smiled to herself and once again when she thought of making love to Kane, felt that surge between her legs. She lay back on the bed and closed her eyes. Wearing Kane's shirt, she snuggled in the material and could smell his aftershave on there, which gave her some kind of comfort. He'd find her of that she had no doubt. She was the Italian's insurance policy. Kane had to cross the line and even win… against all odds. She was safe until he lost, but he wouldn't. He was Kane and Kane never failed. She thought about what was happening. They had meant to take her, not Kane, and he had interrupted them. Kelly heard the door unlock. She swung her legs over the side of the bed and sat up on the side. Long tan legs that hung barefoot. She pulled Kane's shirt tightly around her and yanked her short shorts down her legs as far as they would go. That's all the clothes they wrapped around her. The room was stuffy and that's all the clothes she needed.

"Afternoon tea, Mrs. Branson." The butler put a tray on the bedside table. " Please let me know if this isn't what you want. We have other kinds of foods here."

"And where would here be, mate?"

"Same answer as lunch time. I can't tell you that. I hope the room is to your liking. You will only be here tonight until your husband races again tomorrow. If he crosses the line, you will be free to go…"

"And if he doesn't?" she asked as she raised the cloth on the breadbasket.

"That's not my place to discuss the options. Sir only…" and he stopped.

"Sir? Which Sir? Sir who?" Kelly had noticed the rich scent of cologne in the room. And she couldn't quite place it. But she knew she had smelled it once before in the last few days. She was right.

"I cannot discuss that with you. Sergio will be back later. He will tell you more. Meanwhile enjoy your meal. Dinner will be at eight. There is a button on the wall if you need anything. And as you probably know the phone does not work." The distinguished gentleman with graying hair dismissed himself from the room.

"And what if he doesn't come through for you all?" muttered Kelly. "Too much food on this tray. Enough to feed an army." She left the untouched tray on the table.

Still Kelly smelled the cologne. There was nothing else to do. Explore the room maybe. She used the bathroom when she got there mainly to be sick in. She couldn't take drugs anymore, but Kelly had to admit that her hosts seemed very concerned about her welfare. The closets. Maybe they would give her some clue. She opened one of the glass doors. Empty. Nothing. Not even a pair of shoes. She opened the other door. Inside was the most beautiful red Japanese style dress she had seen. Kelly pulled it out. The slits on the side ran up almost too high. She fingered the material feeling the satin. Still no shoes. She thought that strange. They had made sure she couldn't walk anywhere. Walk, maybe not but climb? She returned the dress to the closet. Kelly went to the windows and tried to open one. Locked up tighter than hell! She tried to pry them open with her fingers. It didn't work. Outside was a courtyard. Climbing one flight down to it would have been easy for Kelly, especially with all that ivy clinging to the walls.

"Shit, now what?" she muttered.

Kelly sat back down on the bed. She wanted Kane. She missed him. Only a day away from him and she missed him. Tomorrow he would race. Tomorrow he could be dead. She nestled into the pillow, and tough little Kelly Branson cried.

Kane stopped walking in the lobby. Somehow he felt Kelly's pain. It must not affect him, not now. He had to get back to Silverstone and check a few things out. He started walking again, as Steve caught up, and walked alongside him.

"You felt something, didn't you?" he asked.

"Yeah, man. I felt Kelly."

"How do you do that, Kane?" Steve asked.

"Something that we adopted when I first met her. She was only twenty-one. I was supposed to protect her and bring her out of her father's compound as a key witness. Her father and his little band of merry drug dealers murdered my first wife." Kane paused for this statement to sink in to Steve. "I went to the drug compound to destroy her father, and to do that I took what he cherished the most, I took his daughter to bed. Kelly was a hooker and a drug addict. Only didn't turn out like I planned. I had feelings for the kid. Those feelings deepened very quickly and she, well she fell in love with me. The rest is history. You heard me tell Michael. Kelly and I are like one. There are things I have done for Kelly that you don't want to know about. Not quite on the right side of the law. And she almost gave her life for me, twice. The one time, she lost our baby. But still Kelly didn't quit. She has guts and determination like you would not believe. That's why I am puzzled that I have this feeling right now."

"Perhaps it's you she is scared for," remarked Steve.

"Very astute, and I think you may be right. Steve, if anything happens to me, you get her back to Australia and to my kids. Dan Lord is married to my daughter; he'll know what to do."

"I thought your daughter was four?" Steve was confused.

"I have another daughter older than Kelly, a grandchild, the baby, and I have Sam."

"Your oldest son?" questioned Steve, hoping he was keeping up with the Branson family tree.

"Yeah."

Steve didn't push it. If Kane wanted to tell him he would. He felt that Commander Branson had confided so much. Steve realized that this man was certainly not just Crocodile Dundee with long hair. The four men continued walking to the door. Outside the hotel it was busy as one car after another streamed passed the doors. This time Kane nor Michael could escape neither the press nor the fans. Kane's heroics of the afternoon had now made front-page news. The place was crawling with press and, until confronted with this situation, hadn't even thought of this angle.

"Oh shit! No one mentioned this. Try and cut through them," shouted Kane to Michael.

"You think this is bad, you wait till tomorrow. The Grand Prix draws so many people you won't be able to move. Go around to the valet. They are used to getting the drivers out of these situations." Michael moved in front of Kane as if to protect him.

"Mr. Branson? Mr. Branson, what happened today out on the track? You saved Michael's life," asked the man with the microphone which was now shoved in Kane's face.

"Can you give us a story, Mr. Branson?" yelled a female reporter from the back.

"I have nothing to say at this point, except that I am glad I was of help today. That's it." Kane carried on walking and didn't really care who was in his way.

"Michael," the same obnoxious reporter yelled. "What have you to say about today?"

"Same as K...Kene. Nothing."

"Was it an accident? We heard at the track maybe it wasn't an accident. Is that true, Mr. Ryder?" bellowed a cry from the back row.

"It was an accident. That's all I can say at this point. We are on our way back to the track to see our boss. I'm sure Mr. Rogers will make a statement to the press." Michael carried on walking and pushed though the crowd.

"But Mr. Ryder, you must have some thoughts about this. You just lost your other teammate. How do you feel? And will you be taking the Mercedes car tomorrow?" Questions from all corners and microphones in one's face were becoming tedious.

"I said no more comments, and if you ask again I'm going to punch you out." Michael replied angrily, his fist clenched by his side.

"And I thought only Australians spoke to the press like that. Couldn't have put it better myself. Your English press is relentless," and Kane pushed on and made it to the waiting car.

Michael climbed in and slammed the door shut behind him. "Relentless bastards. You should have seen them when Alexander crashed. Like vultures waiting to descend on the carcass."

Kane was escorted to the opposite site of the car, and was quick to get inside. He lay back on the seat doing his best not to look like he was in pain. But his chest hurt and he was tired. His vision seemed normal again, and he was thinking ahead. If he went into the pits tomorrow, and then got back out before the race, no one would know it wasn't him. Michael would have a much better chance at winning than he would. Get Kelly back; get the sons-of-bitches that had messed up their vacation and even the score for Alexander. That left Maria. She was tied in to this. He just wasn't sure how. He wondered what Kelly was thinking? Which person had her? Who was Sergio working for?

Kelly didn't hear the key turn in the lock as she dozed on the bed. This indeed was a long day. As the figure stood in the doorframe watching her, they wiped the sweat from their brow. Moving to the closet, the figure pulled the dress from the hanger and laid it on the bed next to Kelly. They smoothed the material down and on the top put a string of pearls. The person was satisfied that Kelly's husband did not suspect them. The Oscar performance of the last few days would have convinced him and letting Kane see Sergio would have thrown him a curve. The obvious choice for kidnapping would be someone of Italian design. Sergio had told Kelly what to say and how to say it. She was safe but for all the wrong reasons. The person knew that Kelly thought she was in the hands of the mob. And telling Kane to cross the line was in total contradiction to the reality of the situation. Once Kane crossed that line he was a dead man, and he would definitely never see Kelly again. A plane standing by at a private airstrip would see to that.

Before they left the room, the intruder turned on the television, and then stood silently watching her sleeping for a moment. Quietly they let themselves back out of the room and locked the door. Now let the red herrings swim where they may.

Kelly awoke to the low sound of the noise. Only the TV lighted the room as she reached for the bedside lamp. Turning it on, the dress and pearls caught her eyes. Kelly picked them up and clutched both items in her hands. She stared in horror at the pearls, and then she caught sight of the TV screen. Jumping off the bed, Kelly rushed to the controls and turned up the volume.

"And after the near fatal crash in practice today, Michael Ryder's number 6 car has been confirmed as out of the race tomorrow. Australian newcomer Kene Branson will race in the spare Mercedes car. Car number 21 will be the only one running for the team. All eyes will be on this Australian. If today was an example of his driving ability, John Camery had better watch his back tomorrow. But none-the-less a sad day for Mercedes with the death of Alexander Vincentia, and now the accident to Michael Ryder. If it had not been for his teammate, Ryder would not be alive."

The pictures of the crash flashed across the screen. Kelly could see Kane and Michael standing by the cars. She could see the wreck and her heart missed a beat. The bulletin flashed to the pits and to Kane's face. Kelly knew that look. She knew he was in pain. For a second she saw him holding his chest and all she could think about was his heart. The bulletin jumped to the hotel and to the abrupt and impromptu press conference at the Devere. Kane did not look happy. Kelly watched intently as he made the statements, and then pushed his way through the crowds. The cameras followed the men to the car. She could see her husband, Michael, Dave and Steve. She couldn't see Peter Graham or Jimmy Rogers.

Once more she was aware of the cologne smell again, only this time it was much stronger. The first day she smelled it, Kelly hadn't paid much attention to it. But now it was different. Someone had been in the room where she was sleeping. Someone wearing expensive cologne, who liked pearls and liked her. The pearls tumbled from her hands as realization set in.

"Oh my god, Kane. Get me out of here now!" Kelly screamed.

CHAPTER 11

"Damn the press. Knock them down if you have to. We need to get back to the track. And we need to find Peter." Suddenly there seemed to be urgency for Kane. His little voice was telling him that there was something wrong with Kelly. "Put your foot down, Dave. I didn't give you those keys so you could go slowly."

"Sir, there are people in the way…" Protested Dave.

"Run the fuckers over," Kane was very blunt.

It was obvious to everyone in the car that Kane was suddenly anxious. Kane felt the band of his jeans and realized it was empty. In his haste he'd left Kelly's gun behind. He remembered laying it on the table and that's where it stayed. At least it wasn't stuffed in the locker at the track.

Dave pushed on through the crowds. The road out to the track was equally as busy. Kane didn't speak, just sat staring at the glass in the windows like he wished it would shatter. Michael wanted to speak, looked at Kane's face, then changed his mind.

Kane pulled the cigarettes from his pocket and lit one up. He pressed the button on the door and the window shot down, at least insuring now it wouldn't shatter. Kane was thinking. He was glad to hear from Kelly. He also knew she could hold her own, but hearing from her had distracted him, and now she was all he could think about. He wanted her out of this, somewhere safe, preferably in a glass box where no one could ever hurt her. He smiled. Kane realized that Michael was watching him. He also realized he that was the oldest man in the car. Injured and no gun. Should he go back for the gun? His thoughts were disturbed.

"Here, boss," Steve ventured.

"Yeah, I can see that," muttered Kane.

This was a darker side of Kane that the two English cops hadn't seen before. They exchanged glances with each other.

It was getting dusk as they pulled into the car park, but floodlights lit up the track, making it almost like daylight again. Amongst all the noise and commotion the Mercedes stopped in the appropriate place, with all the guys in the car peering at the happenings. The Grand Prix was the highlight of the year and the cars were so highly tuned and conditioned that the mechanics would be there way into the night. Kane waited for no one, and even injured, stepped out of the car striding across the lot. Michael took off after him.

"So, where do you want to go first? To find Mr. Rogers, or to the track?" Michael was trying to keep pace.

"*Rogers* will be at the track," and Kane kept on walking.

His strides increased and he reached the track just ahead of Michael. The first person he saw was Jimmy Rogers.

"Kene, how nice of you to drop by. I'm glad to see you," and Jimmy slapped Kane on the back.

Kane winced. "Yeah, I bet you are. I'm racing tomorrow, right?"

"Course you are. Michael Ryder is out. Car won't be fixed in time. You get to drive, Kene. Good job you turned up when you did. I'm just about to go give a press conference. You want to join me?" Jimmy seemed a little agitated. He sported the Mercedes gray sweatshirt and still had a cigar sticking out of his mouth, dropping ash everywhere.

"Yeah, and so does Michael!" replied an arrogant Kane.

"I do? What do I want to do?" asked a very surprised Michael.

"We're going with Mr. Rogers to his press conference. Think we might find it interesting, and so might the TV crew," responded Kane.

"You're going to say something, aren't you, Kane? What are you going to say?" asked Michael with a certain deliberation.

"It's what I am not going to say, mate, that will count. And where's the guys? I need them to go and look through paperwork. *Mr. Rogers* made a big deal about me signing some papers for tomorrow. Chances are that the rest of the team paperwork is here somewhere. Doesn't the manger have a trailer or something?" Kane was looking around for such as that.

"Usually. But Jimmy Rogers has a house near here," replied Michael.

"Really? How near?" Kane tucked the thought away. That would explain the number on his cell phone from Kelly. Clever little thing, his Kelly. He could call it back or have it traced.

"About ten miles from here. I thought you knew that. He rents it out sometimes. You know, Kane, I was thinking if Mercedes isn't doing that well lately with Jimmy Rogers in charge, why let him stay at the helm?

Unless he's being threatened, too. Maybe someone is hanging something over his head. But it still doesn't explain why he wants to lose, unless the same someone is betting heavily for us all to die. If you win..." Michael's brain was working overtime.

"Then I get Kelly back, and I'd upset the whole betting field. I asked the guys to find out what the odds were on Mercedes. They're 100 to1 against. Someone really wants us not to win. We're rank outsiders. Now if I thought that was because of me racing, I'd believe it. But it's not. Those odds were before the accident today," explained Kane.

Jimmy Rogers was out of earshot and mixing with the press.

"When we've done this, you and I are going fishin'," whispered Kane.

"Fishing?" asked Michael.

"Yeah, didn't you pull tires out of the river when you were a kid?" joked Kane.

"Oh, I see," replied Michael.

And Kane hoped to God he did.

"Ladies and Gentleman of the press." Jimmy coughed and spluttered still chewing on his cigar. He had to stand on the bottom set of seats to make himself seen. "As you know, car number 6 is out of the Grand Prix. So number 21 goes in its place."

"Mr. Rogers? Is it true that Kene Branson will be driving it and Michael Ryder is out?" shouted a gray haired reporter from the front line.

"If that's what the TV said then I guess it must be true," laughed Jimmy nervously.

"Isn't that a strange move?" yelled the same reporter.

"Not really," replied Jimmy. "He actually registered a better speed than Michael Ryder today. And we only have the best interests of Mercedes at heart," he lied.

Kane seized his opportunity, stepped up on the seats next to Jimmy and started talking to the reporters.

"If I may add to that, I think Michael should race also, but we have to go on Mr. Rogers here's say so. Man, I hate taking a teammate's place, but I will pull out all the stops to win that race. I will drive like I have never driven before. Mercedes will be proud of me and I will honor the name of Mercedes... and Alexander Vincentia."

"Mr. Branson? Is it true that you came to England to visit Alexander? You and your wife? She'll be here tomorrow, won't she?" and the man in the front row shoved the microphone in Kane's face.

"Kelly. Her name's Kelly, and yes she'll be here watching like she's watching now." Kane turned directly into the camera lens. "Hi, baby. Sorry you're not feeling well. I'll see you in just a little while. Be ready for me, Baby. Winning… well, you know what winning does to me… Love you, baby."

Jimmy Rogers shook. That wasn't planned.

Steve slipped the reporter a twenty-pound note and sidled away into the mass of people. Mission accomplished.

Kelly sat on the end of the bed and watched the screen. She heard Kane's words very clearly. He was telling her he would get her out before the race and to make sure she was ready. Kane would have the number traced back to the house. Sergio had been sloppy in letting her dial. But then Kelly had figured Sergio wasn't the smartest of men and that may be to their advantage. What she couldn't understand was why he was in clear view all the time. And if Jimmy Rogers was holding her to stop Kane winning, why had she been told to tell her husband to cross the line? Now she was confused. She looked at the dress on the bed. The dress and the pearls smelled of Jimmy Rogers. But Jimmy was on the screen. No matter how close the house was to Silverstone, he couldn't be there and here. Someone was aiding and abetting. But who? The dress was the key. The pearls were Jimmy's idea. But the dress?

Kelly pulled her clothes off and slipped the red satin over her head. It was too long for her and someone taller than her had worn it. It trailed on the floor as she made her way back to the food tray. She found an English butter knife, not very sharp, but a knife none-the-less and made a tear in the satin. That's all she needed. The material ripped under her fingers and the bottom of the dress lay on the floor. Now it wasn't what her captive wanted. It was a Kelly style dress, short and sexy. In the bathroom she found soap. She wet her hands and lathered up the foamy soap and slicked it through her hair. Kelly looked in the mirror. She looked more like a sixteen-year-old punk rocker instead of the sophisticated woman her host wanted her to be. Satisfied, Kelly pushed the button on the wall.

"You all right, Mr. Rogers?" asked Kane, and slapped Jimmy on the back. "You look a little white there. By the way, I hear you have a house close by. You never mentioned that before."

"I didn't? Well, I do. Not that it's any of your business." Jimmy stepped down from the seating and walked a few paces, the press still trying to get their pound of flesh. "But I'm not staying there right now. Rented it out. Some guy offered a great deal of money to stay there this week..."

"And you couldn't turn that down, could you? Especially when you need money!" Kane was enjoying this cat and mouse game.

"How do you know that?" Jimmy was becoming more agitated.

"Well, you must do, what with your wife spending so much money in Harrods. You remember the other day when you bumped into Kelly and I. Quite a coincidence that. I mean what were the chances of it happening? And then again at the hotel, for dinner with Peter Graham. Quite a coincidence," Kane mused.

"What are you implying, Kene?" asked Jimmy shakily.

"Just that your wife spends a lot of money. Where as mine hardly spends any," and the seed was sown. "You know, I'm actually grateful for the chance to race tomorrow. Like a dream come true for me. A dream come true. Pity it had to be in such circumstances though, with Alexander's death. You keep records on the cars here, Mr. Rogers?" Now Kane was playing with fire. Mr. Rogers became more defensive.

"Do I what?" Jimmy dropped the cigar in the dirt.

"Well, I thought I could look at the accident reports. I don't want to make the same mistake with this car. I mean, all these things with tires..." Kane didn't finish.

"What things? Only Michael's car had a blown tire. Alexander's car didn't have..." and Jimmy stopped speaking. He looked at Kene in the light. He was asking too many questions. Who was he? All he knew was what Kene had told him. "I have seen you somewhere before. I asked Kelly if you had been in a magazine. That's not where I've seen you. It sure wasn't any racing magazine. Last trip I made to Australia was a few months ago. You were on TV." The light came on in Jimmy Rogers' head. "You're a friend of Inspector Graham's. You're a..." Jimmy stopped, his eyes wide with fear.

"Bravo, Mr. Rogers. Why don't you tell the whole fucking world? Let's walk over to the side here away from this crowd." Kane forcibly ushered Jimmy to the garage.

Jimmy Rogers looked relieved to be away from the reporters.

"Is there somewhere we can talk?" asked Kane.

"Right into that room, the one we are using as Mercedes temporary office. I guess I have some explaining to do and I think you do, too."

They stepped inside the room followed by Michael Ryder, who sat down on the end of the hard wooden bench. Racing pictures adorned the walls, Vincentia's amongst them. A row of silver metal file cabinets stood in the corner.

"After you, Mr. Rogers," stated Kane, and sat down on the table edge.

"Aren't you going to tell me your real name?" asked Jimmy.

"It's Branson, but Commander Kane Branson, Australian Federal Police, and my wife is also a special agent. And perhaps you would be good enough to tell me where you have her hidden?" Kane was polite.

"Kelly? I don't have Kelly. You said she was sick and I believed you. Then again, I believed you about lots of things. One being a racing driver. But I don't have Kelly." Jimmy was nervous and it showed. He glanced towards a seated Michael.

Without any warning Kane leaned down to Jimmy and pulled him towards him by the Mercedes gray sweatshirt. He held onto him tightly.

"I'll ask you one more time. Nicely. Where is Kelly?"

"I don't have her!" Jimmy protested.

"You're lying, and I don't like people that lie." Now Kane was getting angry. His face only confirmed his feelings.

Kane dropped Jimmy onto a hard backed chair. The sudden movement of lifting Jimmy was too much and the pain shot through Kane's chest. He tried to suppress the pain. Michael saw it.

"I don't think you should lie to Commander Branson, *Mister Rogers*. He packs a gun," Michael added.

Jimmy looked more than terrified. "You carry a gun here in England?"

Michael bought Kane the time he needed to breathe.

"Yeah." And Kane sat down on the bench alongside Michael.

"I don't have your wife…really I don't. I would never harm her. Never," stammered Jimmy, sweat beginning to trickle down his face.

"Really." Kane pulled the cell from his boot. Jimmy stared. "Then you won't mind if I call back the number that is on my cell. Kelly called from it today. See Kelly isn't any ordinary woman. She thought to let her captors think she was calling the hotel, where the call couldn't be traced. Instead, she called my cell where the number still sits. So, we'll call it."

"Go ahead. I'd like to know where she is, too. Why would I take her?" asked a very perspiring Jimmy.

"Cause Jenny was her mother and you had a thing for her mother," as he spoke, Kane reached in Rogers' shirt and pulled the locket from around Jimmy's neck. Kane ripped it hard and the chain snapped.

Michael looked astonished at the goings on. It was too much to take in.

"You think I should go get the guys?" asked Michael tentatively

"Yeah, great idea. Maybe I can convince our friend here to let you race tomorrow, instead of me. And while you're gone, perhaps I'll find out who *Mister Rogers'* partners are."

When Kane pulled the cell from his boot, Jimmy Rogers froze. He thought it was a gun.

"Made you nervous did it? Its just a fucking phone," and Kane flipped it open.

The last call in was local. He dialed it and waited.

"Michael can't race tomorrow. We have to lose. You have to race, cop or not," screamed Jimmy and he tried to grab Kane's arm.

"Why? Why do we have to lose?" asked Kane, his temper shortening.

The line crackled. "Rogers residence." Kane hung up the cell.

Michael only got outside the room when Steve and Dave caught up with him.

"You look nervous, Michael. What's wrong?" asked Steve.

"Your boss is in there scaring the daylights out of Jimmy Rogers. He says he doesn't have Kelly."

"Does Kane believe him?" asked Steve.

They all heard the crash of tables, and turned for the door. Steve was the first one through it, and inside the door a not-so pretty sight greeted him. Kane had a frantic Jimmy Rogers pinned to the wall by his shoulders.

"I didn't even know she was gone. I wouldn't take Jenny..." screamed Jimmy.

Kane's eyes creased in anger, and he released his grasp on the man. Jimmy didn't know.

"How can I be sure of that? You want me to lose the race? Why? You being blackmailed? That it? By whom? You have debts or something, or are you just trying to hide a skeleton?" Kane regained composure.

"I was told to make the cars lose. I am being blackmailed. Always just a voice on the phone. Then things started happening with the cars. Little things at first, like tools were going missing, stuff like that. Then things got bigger, like faults appearing on the car. Alexander wasn't supposed to die. They wouldn't let me come up here, and told me to keep away. Then

I bumped into you. I figured you couldn't be that good if you were racing at this late age. I didn't bank on you being so damn good. I really thought you could lose. Then the plans were changed. Some bloke rents my house, and takes this big interest in you. Sergio and Bruno were looking out for Alexander. He wasn't supposed to die," and Jimmy sat down on the bench, buried his face in his hands and wept.

Michael intervened. "But you were all over him the other day. The day before he crashed. I saw you."

Jimmy looked up. "You saw me trying to stop him racing. I knew something was going to happen. Maria wanted him to race. She never wanted him to quit. She wanted more money. Well, she got it, didn't she. He died for her."

Two people with the same story.

Kane stepped back. If Jimmy didn't have Kelly, then who did? Who was Sergio's real boss? He and Bruno were working for Maria. Only Sergio wasn't. A crooked cop. Not unusual. Two crooked cops? Maybe. He needed to know where Maria was right now. Something he couldn't verify. No one could. And Peter…where was he?

Kane stood a few feet from Jimmy. "So, where's your house? Think we should take a trip there." He grabbed Jimmy up by the shirt till he was standing. "Mister Rogers here is gonna show us his home. Right?"

"The gentleman is there, but he isn't just going to let us in. The house has a huge security system and manpower that goes with it, and he paid a lot of money for that privilege. Deal was done through my real estate agent and I really need the money. You know that. I owe a lot of gambling debts. Betting is big business over here, Mr. Branson, and I bet heavily." Jimmy Rogers rambled on confessing his dirty deeds.

"Yeah, I can see that. Hundred to one against Mercedes winning. And believe me that's all going to change. You see, I am very wealthy and I'm gonna bet on myself to win." Kane let go of Jimmy and headed towards the door.

Jimmy looked surprised that Kane knew about betting and he began to sweat. "I thought I might make a pound or two and pay back some debts. Get them off my back a little. They were good odds if you lost… but if you win?"

"Get who off your back? Who? Who off your back?" Kane yelled turning back towards Jimmy. "And you're Mercedes. They have loads of money," badgered Kane.

"Mercedes does. I don't have that much money. Not now. That's why I rent the house out. I told you that they took care of my little indiscretions and me. Bumping into you and Kelly at Harrods was both a joy and a tragedy. I knew Alexander's friends were coming. Not who they were. But someone knew. Someone also knew before me that you could drive, not just how well. You were planted here on purpose. But there is always a price to pay for ones indiscretions, isn't there, Mr. Branson? Told you a voice on the phone is the only contact. Wasn't till the other day did I recognize the one voice." Jimmy hesitated. Was Kane buying this?

"One? How many are there?" Kane was surprised at this statement.

"Two or three. When you all came to the company in London, I recognized the man you call Sergio…" blurted Jimmy.

"He's with Kelly. That's who answered the phone. No wonder he didn't speak much round you and didn't want to come to the track. Adopted a sudden virus. But I wonder if his partner is aware of it? I keep wondering that. Is Bruno in it with him? That doesn't alter the fact that we need to go to the house and find out who this guy is. This your phone number?" and Kane showed Jimmy the number on his cell.

"Yes. That's the main line in the study. Who called you from there?" asked the little man.

"Kelly." Kane moved towards the cabinets and tried the latch. They were locked. "Keys," Kane demanded and slid the phone back into his boot.

Jimmy fished in his pockets and produced a set of keys.

"The long thin one," Jimmy said nervously.

Kane put the key in the lock and it turned. He opened the drawer and flicked through the files, only to find Vincentia's file was missing.

"Anyone else have keys to these drawers?" asked Kane as his boot connected with the bottom of the cabinet.

Jimmy flinched. "One or two people. If you're looking for your friend's file, Inspector Graham came and got it earlier. Just before you arrived actually." Jimmy was sweating profusely now.

"How interesting." Kane looked at the dynamic duo. "You two know anything about that?"

"Absolutely nothing, sir," they replied in unison.

Kane sat down on the bench. "Mr. Rogers, there is something you and I have to discuss. Something I think you have already suspected." Kane was calm, quite the reverse to the moments before. "When you met Kelly, you called her Jenny and you did it again a few moments ago. You know something that we both suspect, a thing so huge that it's gonna tear Kelly apart."

Kane looked around the room. Michael Ryder stood by the door looking astonished at everything that was going on. But Kane had saved his life and he owed him. Jimmy Rogers had tried to take it. Michael would back Kane all the way. Steve and Dave leaned against the window. Steve was no longer surprised by anything. He was learning from Kane things he could never learn from his boss. Dave was young and hopefully would make it. But he was still there for Kane. Kane cleared his throat and his chest hurt like hell. But Rogers must not see it. He believed Jimmy, but he couldn't trust him. For a price Jimmy Rogers would do anything. Even down to selling his soul and anyone else's that got in the way, and he had tried to get rid of Michael Ryder.

"You and I both suspect, no I'll change that, we both know that Kelly is Jenny's daughter." Kane opened his hand and the locket. The picture stared out. "This picture you have proves that. What we both suspect is that you, Mr. Rogers…" he paused, "you, Jimmy Rogers are Kelly's father. And you had the tire shot at on the motorway. You tried to kill me and your very own daughter," and Kane stood up and dropped the locket to the floor. He pushed Jimmy Rogers to the wall so fast that no one had chance to stop him. "And I, *Mister Rogers*, I am gonna kill you, you fuckin' son-of-a-bitch."

CHAPTER 12

It took all three men to pull Kane from Jimmy Rogers, as his death grip tightened round the man's neck.

"Kane!" screamed Steve. "Commander, he's no good to us dead! We need him to get us into the house and he has to be seen tomorrow at the track. Kane, for gods sake let him go!" and Steve tugged hard on Kane's muscular arms.

Still Kane clung to Jimmy's neck. It wouldn't be the first time that Kane had killed with his bare hands and probably not the last. But they were right Jimmy was no good to them dead. He looked into the choking man's face and watched Jimmy turning blue. How Kane wanted to finish it right there and then. It was so tempting. It wasn't the three men tugging on him that made him stop, but the searing pains in his chest. He almost blacked out and that alone made him drop his hold on Jimmy. Kane blinked. Was it his ribs? Kane backed off under the men's grasp, and as Jimmy's feet dropped to the floor, his back slid down the wall. Jimmy grasped his throat. Michael still held a death grip on Kane as he didn't trust him enough to let him go.

Kane tried to pull away from Michael, but he had him firmly in his grasp. Steve stood between Kane and Jimmy, as Dave began tidying up the furniture. The tables and benches were in total disarray after the destruction Kane had wrought.

"Take your hands off me," Kane's voice was slow and determined and very menacing.

"Not till you calm down," replied Michael, exhausting all his strength in holding Kane. But still he held him.

"The son-of-a-bitch tried to kill you! The bastard sabotaged your car. Remember, man, if it wasn't for me you'd be dead," yelled Kane.

"I know that. But if he's Kelly's father?" replied Michael objectively and slackened his grip just slightly.

"Wouldn't be the first time I've killed one of Kelly's fathers," muttered Kane.

That was a heavy statement and no one commented. The men swapped glances with each other. And also no one helped Jimmy Rogers to stand.

"I didn't shoot at your car. That wasn't me!" Jimmy's voice was raspy from the pressure of Kane's hands.

Kane lunged forward again. This time Michael and Steve caught him before he could do any lasting damage.

"You know, *Mister Rogers*, you better start telling the truth or we may just have to let Commander Branson finish what he started," replied Steve to the statement.

Jimmy Rogers backed off.

"Let's step outside a moment, Kane. I'm sure your bloke here can watch Mr. Rogers a moment." Michael had sensed that something was wrong with Kane.

"You changed sides awful quickly, Michael," hissed Jimmy.

Michael ignored the comment and ushered Kane through the now open door. Steve followed the two men outside into the darkening night leaving only Dave with Jimmy.

"For a man with four cracked ribs, you really have some strength. I could hardly hold you." Michael slackened his grasp.

"Normally you wouldn't but…" and Kane pulled free.

"I know that. Are you okay?" asked a concerned Michael.

"Yeah. Hurts. That's all." Kane was uncomfortable.

"Your chest… or your heart?" asked Michael.

Had Michael guessed? Kane viewed him suspiciously.

"My chest." Kane nursed his ribs and tried to ease the pain by pulling on the bandages.

Michael frowned. "I meant the pain from finding out who Jimmy is."

"I know what you meant," lied Kane.

Steve leaned on the door while pushing his blonde hair from his eyes. He was seeing Kane in a different light. Here was a man with a temper, especially when he was going after something he wanted, and Steve wondered what Kane meant when he said he had killed one of Kelly's fathers. He thought maybe Peter Graham knew that. And Peter Graham had the file on Vincentia. And where was he?

Kane breathed heavily as his chest hurt mercilessly. Shades of his past history flashed through his mind and he turned away from the other men. He must not show any weakness, not now, not ever. He beckoned Michael to him.

"Okay, so we need Rogers if only to get into his estate. We could go marching up to the door on our own. Depends how much manpower they have there, and Jimmy may still not be able to get us in. His house or not. Some bloke's paid for privacy and that's what he expects, even if he does have my wife." Kane turned to Steve. "Go get him. Best if I stay just a little away from him. But I warn you both now if he fucks up…he's dead, and this time, Michael Ryder, you wont be able to stop me."

"I worked that out for myself, Commander." And Michael was sure Kane meant it.

Dave stepped out through the door with a beaten Jimmy Rogers in tow. Jimmy looked straight at Kane and Kane turned away.

"I didn't try to shoot the car. If it's true, why would I try and kill my own daughter?" Jimmy uttered.

Dave led Jimmy by the arm to the car. "One word out of you and I'll get Kane over here."

Steve turned to Kane. "He does have a point? And how did he find out in such a short space of time?"

"A very good question. Your boss maybe? He had access to everything, even to the dining room at the Savoy. He knew Kelly was upset at dinner. Jimmy probably called Peter the moment he left Harrods and told him he had met up with us," Kane paused. "I've known Peter since my teens. Why would he do this to me and to Alexander? He's not short of money. MI5 pays well, doesn't it?"

Steve nodded.

"He didn't send you to help me, he sent you to watch me, and you unwittingly reported straight back to him," Kane uttered.

"You think he'll be at Rogers' house?" Steve asked.

"Don't know. And Peter's not the puppeteer, only the puppet. Someone else is pulling the strings. One thing for sure, Peter didn't want us to see those records. Why?" And Kane walked away towards the car.

Steve stood scratching his head. "Another good question," and he followed Kane, a habit he was becoming used to.

When they reached the car, Dave and Jimmy were already seated inside the front. Kane climbed in the back along with Steve and Michael. He leaned back on the leather upholstery and felt that tightness in his chest again… one he couldn't quite explain. Anxiety he hoped. He closed his eyes and thought of Kelly.

When Kelly pushed the button on the wall it took only a few minutes for the butler to appear. Unlocking the door, he stepped into the room and looked Kelly up and down.

"Not quite what they had in mind for dinner but I am sure one of the gentlemen will approve. Come with me," the butler stated.

"No shoes, me' lord," mocked Kelly looking down at her wiggling toes.

"You won't need shoes where you are going, Mrs. Branson," came the reply.

"And that would be?" asked Kelly.

"Just down the carpeted stairway and turn right into the dining room." The butler ushered her from the room.

"How do you know I won't bolt for the front door?" Kelly asked with big blue eyes rolling in her head.

"Not much point, madam. The door is locked and there are men on the other side. If you wish to try, go ahead."

And the butler watched her walk down the landing to the stairway. He took a long look at the tan legs that stretched up to the short red dress. Her hips swayed as she walked and her cute little backside was tempting. The butler wasn't surprised that one of his bosses wanted a Kelly model.

Kelly descended the stairs far enough that she could see the solid oak door ahead of her. The butler was right. It wouldn't do her much good right now. She needed to find out who was holding her captive and somehow let Kane know. As she walked towards the door her mind drifted to Kane. She wondered how he was. When she'd seen him on the TV he'd looked tired and that reminded her of last night. She smiled. But she'd also seen him grab his chest. Was he injured in the crash? He'd told her he loved her and to be ready. She was always ready… for him. Again she felt that thrill. Several voices brought her back to reality.

"Kane is going to be very surprised, is he not?"

A man's voice, one she had never heard before, echoed through to the hallway. She reached the door and stood listening, her ear pressed up against the paneled wood frame. Then she heard another voice, one she definitely knew. She turned quickly in the hallway and knocked an expensive vase that was standing on a high table, dangerously close to her.

She caught it as rocked too and fro, but the noise was enough to alert the inhabitants of the dining room. The doors opened wide in front of her.

He stood there, tall, dark and extremely handsome and he stepped forward to greet her. Looking at Kelly from head to toe, a slick smile spread across his face and he nodded his head up and down.

"Good evening, Mrs. Branson." The man laughed. "Trust Kane to pick someone zee just like you. He always had zee great taste in women and zat has not changed. Come in, pleaze. We are waiting to dine. And you are zee guest of honor."

Suddenly Kelly could smell that cologne again. She looked into the room and her eyes widened in disbelief. Except for this one man, her dinner companions were all people that she already knew.

"How much further is this fucking place? The call was local. We seem to have been on the road for miles." Kane leaned over the seat. "*Mister Rogers*, you sure you are taking us to your house and not on some wild goose chase? Cause if you are, man, you're dead."

Jimmy shook. "I *am* taking you there. It's up that lane. See the lights at the end of the road? There is a long driveway. Used to be a favorite place to be. Now I hate it." Jimmy shuddered.

Dave drove the car up to the gates and switched off the headlights.

"Bloody imposing building. Much cost a fortune for electricity. Front of the damn house is lit up like Hollywood. So do your thing, get them to let us in and remember, I'm right behind your seat. Pull anything and you'll live to regret it." Kane jabbed his fingers in the back of the seat. "Or not live, as the case might be."

Jimmy jumped, thinking it was a gun in his back. Dave hit the buttons for the windows as two men stepped out of the shadows, both carrying guns. Dark suits and Italian. Now wasn't that a surprise to Kane!

Rogers leaned out of his window.

"I wish to get into my house. I need some documents from the study," said Jimmy trying to sound confident.

"And you might be?" asked one of the guards peering into the Mercedes.

"Name is Jimmy Rogers." Rogers reached for his wallet and his driver's license.

The guard stuck his pistol through the open window and into Jimmy Rogers' face. The proceedings kind of amused Kane and he half snickered at the situation. If Jimmy Rogers hadn't wet his pants yet, he had now. And if not for the fact that Kelly was in the house, Kane would have gotten out of the car and single handedly removed the two goons from their posts. But now was not a good time for anyone to see Kane, and he lay back in the shadows of the car. This was Rogers' house and he should be able to get them in.

"Who you have in zee car wit you?" The goon's command of the English language was adequate, as was his knowledge of frightening people with guns.

Kane noted the fact. He also noted that his party didn't have much chance of getting in through the front door. He whispered to Michael, who then leaned over and spoke in Dave's ear. Steve's face peered at the proceedings from the back window of the car.

"Mr. Rogers can get his things tomorrow after the race," yelled Dave across Jimmy to the guard with the now aimed pistol.

Mr. Pistol-packer moved away from the window as Dave hit the button, and turned the headlights back on.

"Now what?" Dave asked. "That didn't work."

"There has to be a servants entrance. Always is and I'm a servant. So are you, Steve. Fancy a spot of wall climbing? Be like when you were kids scrumping apples. You game?" asked Kane.

"I am, Kane. But a man ..." Steve wasn't allowed to finish his sentence.

"Too old? That what you were going to say? Of my age? I may be older, but I have a wife in her twenties. Mr. Rogers here can tell you exactly how old she is. Probably right down to the last second." Kane's words reflected his darkening mood. "Drive."

Jimmy flinched. Dave backed the car out of the long drive with a certain caution. He turned the car into the lane behind the house, turned off the headlights, and parked. Kane opened the doors and stepped out. His eyes looked towards the house. Kelly was in there and he knew it. His Kelly. He took off his top shirt and threw it in the back of the car. Underneath he wore a black T-shirt and he still had on black jeans. From his pocket he produced a band procuring his hair tightly behind him at the back of his head. How he wished he hadn't forgotten Kelly's gun, and knowing his own gun was somewhere in that house. Kane turned back to Steve.

"You ready?" Kane's tone was severe.

"Sir, you think this is a good idea. What are we going to do when we get in there?" asked Steve a little concerned that as an officer they were gong to break into a house.

"Don't remember saying we were going in the house. What time do you English have dinner?" Kane was getting impatient. His old partner would have known his moves.

"About now…you think they'll be in the dinning room?" Steve looked at his watch.

"Good bet. We're gonna just take a peek through the window. See who has Kel and who we are gonna take out tomorrow."

"We're going to do what tomorrow? Commander, this is England, not New York or the outback. You just can't go round taking people out!"

"You think these people would hesitate? Do you?" Kane was angry.

"No, but…"

"No buts, Steve. It's my way or the highway. Your boss took the file on Alexander. That puts him in the line of fire. He knew where we all were at any given time. Right now he's our main suspect." Kane looked back at the three men. "You two make sure that Mr. Rogers doesn't do anything but breathe," and Kane was gone.

How Kane could see in the dark lane amazed Steve. He followed the blonde hair like a beacon in the night as Kane moved stealthily over the road and across the grass. A huge roman-stoned wall lined the perimeter of the property, a wall which was built to keep people in, not out. It didn't stop Kane, nor did his cracked ribs. He hoisted himself up the stone, a hand then a foot, and the same again, and peered over the top of the wall. His chest hurt like hell. He ignored it. Kane had to find Kelly. Yin was no good without Yang.

"What can you see?" whispered Steve from the bottom of the wall.

"Not a fucking thing. A goddamn bunch of trees in the way. Gonna climb over and drop into the grounds. Give me fifteen minutes. If I'm not back by then, take off and get Michael to the hotel. He has to race tomorrow." and Kane dropped down into the onslaught of ivy.

Steve heard him moan.

"Kane, you okay?" Steve murmured.

"Yeah, now get going back to the car." His voice was subdued.

Steve turned away and scurried back to the others, glancing back over his shoulder.

Kane pulled pieces of ivy from his clothes while looking towards the location of the house, and could see the chimney tops rising out like spires to the darkened sky. What he couldn't see was the dinning room. The trees blocked the bottom part of the house out completely. He needed to get closer, and moved across the grass through the rose gardens, snagging his shirt on the bushes.

"Fucking hell!" Kane muttered.

Kane kept on going as the majestic house loomed in front of him. Kane figured there must be several men walking around and this was one time he didn't want to get caught. If he'd been the guy in the house, he would have taken every measure of security to keep people like him out. A noise near to him disturbed his thoughts, a noise that sounded very much like a growl, which got louder by the second. Kane turned very slowly and behind him stood a Rottweiler with ivory teeth gleaming in the night. Kane didn't move. Neither did the dog. He stared into its eyes and the dog stared back. It also bared its teeth some more, and still it didn't move, but Kane did. He moved one step closer. Still he looked into the dog's eyes and whistled in a low tone as the dog moved towards him, slowly. Kane put his hand out to the big black and tan creature.

"Hi, pup. It's okay," he whispered. "Knew a dog like you once. Yeah, man. Just like you. Come on, pup," and he reached out to the animal.

He touched it lightly on its nose, and then it's head. The dog sat down as Kane's hand slid down its back and he stroked the fur. He slid his hand back and took hold of the collar and hooked it to a sturdy rosebush.

"Good boy. You just stay like that for a few minutes."

Kane crept forward. Soon he wouldn't be in the shadows, but right there in the floodlit yard. One quick look in the windows was all he needed, but fate intervened as the gates opened, and a car entered by the front drive. The goons in the grounds were distracted just long enough for Kane to make a move. There was a path right through to the windows. Kane seized the opportunity and sprinted across the paved walkway that led to the side of the house. He figured that the dinning room had to be somewhere around that area. Jimmy had given him a rough idea, but now he was on his own. Kane skirted along the bottom of the old English house, inching his way from shadow to shadow. He came upon the study first, thus determined by rows of bookshelves. Kane was surprised that Jimmy Rogers could even read. Kane laughed to himself, but he kept on going. Voices filled the night air then, bingo, he'd hit the right room. Cautiously, he stepped around the corner, and glanced into the driveway where the approaching car was nearing the front of the house. As it did the porch lights brightened. Kane looked back into the room to see someone departing through the dinning room door, but he wasn't quick enough to see who. He could, however, see Maria very clearly, her flaming red hair hard to miss. She sat on a chair at the dinning room table, black dress, high heels and smoking a cigarette. Her hand moved down to the ashtray on the table.

But that's not what caught Kane's attention. Something else did. Lying next to it was a gun, not just any old gun, but his gun with the weather-beaten handle. He'd know it anywhere, and especially at only eight feet away. Maria's hand touched the barrel. She stroked it lovingly, and then gently she turned it in the direction of the other wall. Kane had to move to see at whom it was pointing. The back of a person came into his line of vision. Long tan legs, a short red dress split up the sides, and short spiky hair. He'd know those hips anywhere. He'd held them too many times not to know. Feelings welled inside him, and Kane wanted to burst through the glass and pull her out of there. But he needed to find out who else was involved? He peered harder. By the door a figure leaned in the shadows, but Kane couldn't quite make them out. The room was long and the door was at the far end of the room. Kane watched as Maria pulled a lighter from her purse and flicked it open. The man walked across the room and leaned down with his fat stomach and balding head. Kane only knew two men that smoked cigars like that and one was back in the car.

Peter Graham was arrogant when he looked across at Kelly. Not so much, at but up and down, and it was obvious to any fool he wanted a Kelly model one way or another.

The cigar caught light and Peter puffed hard on it. Sitting down next to Maria, his hand rested on the back of her chair and he motioned for Kelly to sit down. Kelly stood.

Kane couldn't quite make out what was being said. He could see Maria and Peter's mouths, but only Kelly's back. Kane looked through the glass and around the room and realized he needed her to come to the window. He noted only one entrance to the room and could not decide who had left through that door? Sergio maybe? He thought not. Sergio was menial and probably was not included in the dinner party. Kane edged an inch around, knowing his fifteen minutes were probably nearly up. There was time enough to make it back across the lawns and to the waiting car.

Without warning the dinning room door opened. A man dressed from head to toe in black stepped through the archway and into the light. The Italian sauntered into the room and walked over to where Kelly stood backing her up a little. Kane could see the aquiline feature perfectly though the paneled window. Bruno van Camp was the mastermind. Kelly took a step back. Was he threatening her? She backed into the window ledge, almost blocking Kane's view. Without even realizing, he put his hand on the windowpane and even with glass in between could feel her back. His hand slid down the glass and whether she sensed his presence or what, Kane never found out, but Kelly turned towards the garden. She saw his face behind the glass and her eyes widened in disbelief. Big pools of blue with oceans of love swimming through them, with her mouth forming a word.

"Vincentia," she whispered.

Kane saw Bruno move towards her and Kane shot back into the shadows. As he did, his boot made a loud scrapping noise of the pavement, and as he moved he disturbed a flower pot sitting right behind him. He heard the men yell from in the room, and Kane took off, darting back the same way he came. Suddenly there seemed to be men everywhere. The noise was enough to wake the dead, and Kane could not be caught. Sprinting across the lawns, back through the rose garden, Kane came face to face with his old friend the Rottweiler. This time the dog was not so subdued and influenced by Kane's ways. The noise coming from the house heightened the dog's curiosity for the man in front of him. The Rottweiler growled and Kane didn't have the time to pacify him. The dog lunged and Kane sprang aside. Speed was not his ally right now, but he made for the trees, dog at his heels.

Outside the wall, Steve waited. Dave sat patiently in the car with the engine now idling. It was way past fifteen minutes, Steve noted, as he glanced at the luminous dial on his watch. Kane had been gone too long. He felt a strange loyalty to Kane, perhaps because he admired what he stood for, and maybe because someday he would like to be the same. For whatever reason, Steve wore a hole in the ground with his pacing. Then he heard the noise of dogs and men from as far away as the car was parked. Michael wanted to help and moved to the wall, when suddenly there was gunfire. Steve knew Kane wasn't carrying.

At the base of the wall, Kane scrambled, knowing the goons were right behind him, and possibly the high-powered rifle was sighted right on his back. As he leaped for the stonework, the bullet caught his leg instead and he growled in pain.

"Steve," yelled Kane, "you there? Oh God, be there," Kane breathed hard.

"I'm here," Steve shouted. "Give me your hand."

Steve sat onto the top of the wall, his legs straddling over the sides, and now he leaned down with his arm out stretched to Kane. Kane had one foot on the ground and one on the wall. His hand reached up to Steve until their fingers touched, and Steve pushed the extra mile to grab Kane's arm. Kane reached it and hung there while Steve felt someone take hold of his own leg.

"I have you, Steve. Pull him up," urged Michael.

"Kane, hold on to my arm and climb," yelled Steve.

For once in his life Kane did as he was told and inched his way up the wall. Didn't seem so far on the way down. Steve pulled him up and Kane reached the top, as they both sat on top the bricks.

"You okay?" Steve asked, looking onto Kane's face. He could see the man in front of him sweating profusely.

"Not thirty any more," Kane breathed hard through his speech and clutched his chest.

Steve pulled Kane's legs over the right side of the wall and he felt something sticky touch his fingers. Kane dropped in silence next to Michael. With pain shooting through his leg, Kane was trying to decide which hurt the most, when Steve landed beside him.

"Let's get the fuck out of here. Those bastards are right behind me." Kane urged.

The three men took off across the grass to the waiting car. Climbing in, Kane caught sight of Jimmy. There was still a desire to kill him on the spot and Kane stared at Jimmy's face.

"Go! Go, Dave. They must not see the car." Steve slammed the door shut after him.

Dave flipped on the headlights and they took off more at 'Branson' speed than at a Dave speed.

Kane leaned back on the upholstery and let things sink into his brain. He'd seen Kelly. He'd seen Maria and Peter. Bruno was in charge. That would explain a lot. Or would it? If Bruno was police gone bad, like Sergio, why would they all be holed up there? Why not have skipped the country after Alexander's death? Maria had the money. What had Peter to gain from this? Except ...a Kelly model? Or was there more? Something none of them had seen. Time to call Gina. He reached down in his boot for the cell-phone, but his hand touched the wound first and Kane moaned.

"Something wrong, *Mister Branson*?" asked Jimmy.

Kane's eyes flashed. "Yeah, I'm sad they won't let me kill you right now. But I will after I win."

"You still going to race to win?" asked Jimmy, almost dumbfounded.

"You said I had to, cop or no cop. Remember?" responded Kane.

"I remember," and Jimmy laughed. "But when you cross that line they're going to kill you. Win or lose. You do know that, don't you? Just like they did Alexander because he wouldn't play ball. I tried to warn him the other day. That's what you saw me telling him, Michael. I really didn't want him to race. That is the truth. I didn't think they would kill him. But you, Mr. Branson... I hope they do kill you." Jimmy was playing with his life.

Kane reached straight over the seat and grabbed Jimmy by the throat, before anyone had time to stop him. Jimmy gurgled and tried desperately to shake the hold that Kane had on him. Kane wrapped his arms tighter around Jimmy's throat.

"You're killing him!" screamed Michael.

"That's right. Very observant. You want to try and stop me?" Kane yelled back and his eyes pierced Michael's.

"No, sir." Michael wasn't even going to go there.

Kane turned his attentions back to Jimmy. "You had better hope that they don't, Jimmy Rogers, cause by God, you'll be hunted for the rest of your days, Kelly's father or not. Something only a blood test can determine. You knew all the fucking time who rented the house, didn't you? The whole fuckin' time. You want to enlighten everyone else in the car who it is? You want to do that, *Mister Rogers,* and then I can strangle you to death with my bare hands. No fuckin' wonder they didn't want you up here, 'specially not at the hospital. You're not that good an actor. You were told to stay away all right. The day Michael saw you arguing with Alexander was down at your place, before Alexander came up here to practice. Then Michael was set up very nicely to hear Alexander and Maria arguing. How much were you paid to keep quiet? Did you all really think you could get away with this? Peter should have known better. Did he really think he could fool me?" Kane paused. "Actually, he did. All I have to do is confirm it with Gina. There was discontent between them at dinner. And when I called Peter on the phone, coming over on the plane, he didn't really sound that surprised to hear I was coming. How long did it take to set it all up? Or did it all just snap into place? Dave, stop the car."

"What? You can't just kill him?" Dave was having a hard time with this.

"Stop this fuckin' car now or I will snap this bastard's neck." The veins stood out in Kane's neck as he spoke.

Dave screeched to a halt and made sure no one was following them. Dave was clever enough with his new driving prowess to make sure of that. He steered the car into a side road.

"Turn the inside light on," Kane demanded.

It flickered into light.

"Roll up your sleeve, Jimmy." Kane slackened his grip on Jimmy's throat just enough for him to be able to maneuver. "Dave, roll the sleeve up for him. Now pull his hand out so we can all see his inside arm."

Dave pulled, and the arm stretched out before them. A band-aid covered the skin.

"Pull it off, Dave," stated Kane.

The Mickey Mouse band-aid came off easily, and in front of all their eyes was a fresh pinhole.

"Now that wouldn't be from a paternity test would it? When did they get Kelly's blood? While she was unconscious? It was her they wanted to take all the time from the bedroom. Am I right, *Mister Rogers*? Am I?" Kane screamed in Jimmy's ear.

Kane pulled tightly again on Jimmy' neck. Jimmy spluttered.

"Yes," he coughed.

Kane released him. Jimmy struggled for breath.

"Peter wanted the paternity test done, and being head of MI5, he got it rushed it through in a few hours. It was one more thing to hold over me. I am Kelly's father. They took her from your room to find out exactly that, and then to keep her so you would race. Also, because Maria was jealous and hated Kelly on sight." Jimmy paused and sighed. "I had a daughter for twenty-seven years that I didn't even know about. You had her. You're old enough to be her father…and yet you had her! You even have children by her. She is so much like Jenny…"

"That's positively, incestuous fucking thinking," interjected Kane.

"Maybe...but I didn't know she was an agent, and I certainly didn't know you were a commander in the AFP. They didn't tell me that. I only just remembered where I saw you." Jimmy's speech was still slurred.

In the car there fell a silence. Michael Ryder sat like a wooden plank and couldn't take this in, yet it all seemed to fit. Steve wiped his sticky hand on his jeans and that alone reminded him that Kane was bleeding. How did this man keep going? Dave sat with his hands on the steering wheel, keeping one eye on the rear view mirror just in case.

Steve broke the silence. "I don't believe you answered Commander Branson's question yet. Do you know who is the head of this operation?"

"An Italian," came the Mercedes man's subdued reply.

"We fucking know that, you bastard. Keep going," prompted Kane.

"Vincentia," Jimmy was hardly audible.

"Maria Vincentia?" asked a totally astonished Michael. "I don't believe that!"

"That's cause it isn't true. She's only part of it. I do know she has my gun. Saw it on the table in the house back there," remarked Kane. "What did she plan to do with it? Kill Kelly and blame me, or kill someone else with it, and still blame me? Right now there are too many witnesses. They have a glass with my fingerprints on. They could take out a couple of people with a loaded .38. All so convenient." Kane paused for effect. "You can do better than that. Man, tell them all who it is. They are *dying* to find out, mate. Tell them who is the big boss, the head honcho. Whatever you want to call him. Kelly knows. She saw him. She told me through the window. Now you can tell us and enlighten the rest of our team here."

"He'll kill me! He's not who you think he is. You never really knew the adult man. You were right when you kept mentioning the tires. That was the link. He made it so, stuck them all on the Mercedes cars. Even the one you borrowed from your pal, Peter. The man got involved with a company that was making defective ones, bought them out and planned to operate the whole thing from back in Italy. It all made sense. We all would make money from it. Nice and neatly tied up. All Michael here had to do was…"

"To die?" interjected Kane.

"Yes. But you, Kane, had to play the hero. So they switched plans and you had to race. You can bet all the money you want to win, Commander Branson, but he can top you, him and his syndicate." Jimmy Rogers was shaking. Sweat poured down his face.

"I won't have to bet will I? Cause if I win you and he will lose everything. You're all betting I lose. Then they'll kill me. They want me to cross the line so it doesn't look fixed. And who didn't want it fixed the most… Michael?" Kane turned and looked the man straight in the face.

"What are you all looking at me for? It's not me? Good god, you don't think that, Kane? I nearly got killed." Michael shook. Kane had to believe him.

"Yeah, you did. So did someone else. But they didn't did they, Mr. Rogers? Cause it wasn't them racing. You put some poor sucker in that car that you fixed to crash. Some poor rookie who didn't know what he was doing. Thought he was getting a break. " Kane's tone changed. "Tell them, you fucking bastard! Tell them who is in that house or I will! Tell them! Or you die right now!"

"It's Vincentia. Alexander Vincentia!" Jimmy screamed at the top of his lungs

CHAPTER 13

A pin dropped and bounced across the floor of the car.

"This some sort of sick joke? Alexander is dead," Michael said, but with a feeling that Kane wouldn't lie. Australian he might be, liar he wasn't. "Are you sure he's telling the truth, Kane?"

"Unfortunately, yeah he is. On all counts. Alexander is alive and well and living in Jimmy Rogers' house where I saw a man leaving the dinning room. I thought I recognized the figure. Then I saw Peter and Maria, and, of course, I saw Kelly. Bruno came into the room while I was watching and I thought at first it was his operation, but he's not bright enough for that. For some reason Kelly turned at the window and saw me, and whispered 'Vincentia'. It was then it hit me which person she meant."

"But you went to the hospital. You saw him," argued Michael.

"I saw the shell of a man so badly burned that I couldn't say for sure who it was. And then Maria distracted me long enough for my emotions to set in, me, the original tough Australian cop. They must have really fallen for that one. Laughed all the way home. Somehow, this doesn't shock me. Don't know why, but it doesn't. Maria and Alexander were always ambitious. Peter, well that's a little more of a shock. He has everything…"

"Except a young and sexy wife," commented Steve without thinking before he spoke.

"And now he has yours and a chance to make a lot of money…"added Dave.

"Yeah. He does. And that would explain why they didn't cut and run. They couldn't till I was in place. We should see what private airstrips are round here…" Kane hesitated. He blinked and the lines creased on his face. Pain had set in, and for once, Kane faltered. He tried desperately to hide it from everyone.

"I think, Dave that we should get the hell out of here and back to the

Devere. Our driver here needs rest. Right, Commander?" Steve was taking charge again.

"Yeah, right. Man, I'm tired," replied Kane in a lower tone.

"And you are still going to race for us tomorrow, Mr. Branson?" asked Jimmy. He'd rolled his sleeve down and was trying to get some sense of composure and dignity back.

"Of course he is. Why don't you just be quiet and let him rest a little. Or would you prefer it if we tied and gagged you till tomorrow?" Steve was almost overpowering. "And Dave will stay with you tonight, just to keep you company. Make sure that you stay put and arrive in one piece at the track. We wouldn't want to spoil the Commander's fun now, would we?"

Jimmy shuddered. He realized just how close he had come to being terminated. The only thing that had saved him was the Commander still needed him to get on to the track. What Jimmy didn't know was that Kane and Michael had planned to switch roles. Jimmy would never suspect the switch twice.

Dave turned the engine over and drove them at a reasonable rate back towards the hotel. When the car pulled into the lot at the Devere, Steve climbed out and held the door for Kane. Dave waited for them all to climb out and then turned to face Rogers.

"You, *Mister Rogers,* stay right here, and if I were you, I'd tighten my seat belt. Been taking driving lessons from the Commander!" and Dave hit the pedal.

Even in the dark Kane's snakeskin boot looked stained. Michael noticed this as they walked across the lobby entrance.

"You have d..." Michael hesitated. "Not dirt is it?" he whispered.

"No," and Kane kept walking through the lobby.

Size 36 was on her usual watch.

"Good evening, Mr. Branson."

"Evening. Great night, huh?" replied Kane without a care in the world.

"Yes, sir," and as Judy watched him go by she gave him the usual once over which, tonight, extended from the bottom of his pants to the waistband.

She waited till they were round the corner of the lobby then picked up the phone and dialed a local number.

"Sir...yes, it's me. Mr. Branson is limping." There was a pause. "What's he wearing? Black top and black jeans. Why? In the garden. I don't know. He had a shirt on. Color? Black. I said he was limping." Long pause. "You shot him? I don't want any part of this. You said just report his movements. He's a decent guy. No. I won't do this anymore! Count me out," and she hung up the line. Size 36 shook.

Kane made it to the suite. Steve took the key from him and opened the door.

"Think we should all stay together. There's room in the suite. I..." Kane got through the door and fell against the doorpost, almost passing out.

"Grab him, he's blacking out," and Steve closed the door behind them.

Michael slung his arm under Kane's shoulders and ushered him to the couch, where Kane fell back and, for a second, everything went black.

Steve bent down on the floor and carefully removed Kane's boot. Kane winced, but he made no sound. Steve looked around for scissors.

"Michael. In the bathroom there's a first aid kit. Get it," Steve yelled.

Michael disappeared and reappeared with the kit. Steve opened it and pulled out a pair of scissors, and slit Kane's new jeans up the side.

"How bad is it, Steve?" asked Michael. He sat on the table opposite Kane.

"Bullet went straight through the flesh." Steve took a good look. "Need to clean it up and bandage it tightly. Shit! We used all the bandages earlier. Kane. Kane, can you hear me okay? Commander, we need you."

Kane stirred slightly. "Yeah, I hear you. Front desk will have more bandages. Tell her I cut myself shaving," and he tried to make a joke of it. "She thinks I'm wonderful. See if you can get some things, and while you're there, bring back some whiskey or beer or something," Kane replied sarcastically.

"You're driving tomorrow. I don't think you can drink," proposed Steve.

"Not driving, Mikey here is." Kane was slipping in and out of reality.

"Kane. Come on. Snap out of this. Michael, see if you can get those things from the desk." Steve smacked the side of Kane's face. Not a smart thing to do on any given day.

"On my way," and Michael was gone out of the door.

"Kane. Try and sit up. Here let me help you..." Steve was worried.

Suddenly an eye winked at him and Kane managed a smile.

"You son-of-a-bitch, Commander. You're not half as bad as you're making out," Steve laughed, and sat back from Kane.

"Mate, four cracked ribs and a scratch from a bullet is not going to keep this man down. But Mikey has to think the worst. He has to drive that car. I haven't got a fuckin' chance, but he does. You stick with him at all times tomorrow. I can manage on my own. Michael's a good bloke and just needs a little help now and then. And don't smack me so hard next time." Kane heard the door open and he fell back on the couch.

"No one down stairs in reception. I thought we passed that receptionist on the way up?" asked Michael. He looked confused.

"We did…" added Steve. "She was looking at our man here. Maybe a little too hard."

In his mind Kane was agreeing. He assumed consciousness.

"What's going on?" Kane's eyes dared Steve to say anything.

"Receptionist has gone…" Michael didn't finish.

"To the other side or maybe she always was. Steve go take a look, and also call Dave and let him know to be on his guard with Jimmy. This is beginning to have a smell to it. How many people are in on this little conspiracy?" Kane's eyes turned to Michael and saw his empty hands. Steely blue and penetrating. "No bandages huh? Then improvise. The Devere has good sheets…use them. Then go in that bedroom and get some sleep, and I mean sleep. There is no way now I can drive. My leg hurts now so how can I put pressure on that pedal? But you, you can win. It's what you have always dreamed of, and it can be yours. You race for us and for Kelly. You do this and you'll be set for life. Everyone will want you on their team. You think you have money now? Just wait. Your life will be a dream."

Michael stared back at Kane. He did want it, but not at this price. He also wanted to know the truth. Was Alexander still alive?

"Okay, so I'll race. But you have to go out there first, wave to the crowds and do the sportsmanship thing. I'll be waiting in the wings to take over. How the hell you going to get back to me?" and Michael's younger age gave way to Kane's experience.

"I'll think of something," smiled Kane.

"He's Kane Branson, remember? Australia's answer to 007," added Steve laughing.

"How can we forget?" said Michael, rolling his eyes.

Kane looked at the two men then focused on Steven Asher.

"When the race is underway tomorrow, we have to get Kelly out. With no insurance policy, won't matter if Michael wins or not, but she has to be out before the end of that race. You know what to do. Storm the house if you have to. Take MI5 in. Use the local police, but get her out. If they plan to kill me, that means Peter intends to take Kelly with him. Switzerland would be a good place to hide for a while." Kane saw both the men's reactions. "You're wondering why I didn't do that tonight? 'Cause we didn't have proof. We had the lying tongue of Jimmy Rogers. We now have some people holed up in a house waiting for a race. My gun is there. Wouldn't have been if they had known we were coming. And they have some pieces of my clothes on a rose bush, and they probably are aware they shot me. Check mate." Kane glanced at Kelly's gun still lying in the same place. No one had been in there since they had left earlier today.

Michael cleaned the wound, and then started bandaging Kane's leg with the Devere's expensive sheets. Blood seeped straight through and onto Michael's hands.

"Shit! We need gauze and real bandages. You probably need a hospital, but I'm not even going to suggest that. Would be a waste of time suggesting it to you. The hole is too big and the blood won't stem." Steve was doing his best.

"Will if it's stitched," interjected Kane.

"That why I said…" and Steve saw the grin on Kane's face. "Oh no. Noooooo!"

"Then I'll do it myself. In the bathroom. There's always sewing kits in these places. Michael, get it," Kane ordered.

"You're joking?"

"Do I look like it, Michael? You want me to bleed to death?"

"No, sir." Michael felt sick.

"Then for Christ's sake get it," replied an arrogant Kane.

Reluctantly Michael fetched the kit.

"Slit the jeans up some more. I have one more pair here. Don't just stare at me, do it!" Kane was the proverbial Hitler.

Steve made the incision on the jeans another six inches higher to clear any material that might fall down on him. The wound was just below Kane's knee, right where the flesh was soft. The two men watched as Kane pulled the longest needle from the kit and then he pulled the lighter from his back pocket and flipped it open. Holding the needle over the flame, until it was red hot and sterilized, he threaded the strong cotton through the eye. Without fear or hesitation he plunged the needle into his skin, giving off a sickening burning smell.

For all his years as a police officer, Steve could not have done what Kane did. He watched as slowly he sewed the hole up. Kane never made a sound as sweat dripped down his face and onto his T-shirt. Blood oozed down Kane's leg and dripped onto the expensive carpet. Michael counted six stitches and turning away, he wanted to throw up. When Kane finished he held the cotton taut so that Steve could cut it. Some more of the Devere's sheets came in useful as bandages, and this time the bleeding did not seep through.

"I need to go wash my hands and use the bathroom before you go to bed, Mr. Ryder," insisted Kane.

Michael nodded to Kane, watched him go into the bedroom and turned to Steve.

"Did you see what he did? How did he do that? No anesthetic…nothing. It had to be unbelievably painful. They must raise them awfully tough in Australia," Michael stated. He stood up and rounded the table, totally astounded by what he had just seen.

"Yes, they must." Steve stared in admiration at the man and cleaned up the mess left behind.

In the bathroom it was a different story. Kane leaned over the luxurious washbasin and turned on the gold-plated taps. His hands were sticky with his own blood and the crystal-white basin swam red with foamy soap and blood. He washed the basin clean and looked up into the mirror above the basin. An unhappy man reflected back. He looked tired. Very tired. His hair was matted with his own sweat and his T-shirt dirty with his blood. His chest ached and his heart even more. Only one day gone and he missed Kelly, but more that that, he was afraid for her. The lines on his maturing face looked wiser than of late, and stubble from the last few days was growing though gray. His thoughts were disturbed by a knock on the door.

"Commander? You okay?" Steve whispered.

"Yeah, fine. I'll be right out." Kane was anything but fine. He used the toilet, zipped up what was left of his jeans, and opened the bathroom door.

"You're like a mother hen, Steven Asher. You know that?" Kane smacked him on the back as he walked out of the bathroom.

"And you are Superman, Kane Branson. You don't have to pretend around us. Your face says what your mouth doesn't. I don't know how you keep going," said the younger man. "First Kelly, then finding out about your friends. A bullet wound and four cracked ribs. Most men would snap."

"I'm not most men," replied Kane.

"No, sir, you are not. I'd be proud to cross the line with you any day."

"You already did, Steve. You already did," and Kane extended his hand in friendship.

The two men shook hands and returned through the room.

"You…bed!" Kane yelled at Michael.

"Sir, yes, sir!" replied Michael.

Kane stopped in his tracks and stared at him.

"That was a joke, Kane. Just a joke. I didn't mean anything by it," Michael wilted under the ice king's stare.

"I'm sorry, Mikey. That's Kelly's favorite line. You didn't know. How could you? Man, maybe this is getting to me. I'm getting too old for this kind of thing. All I wanted was a nice vacation in peaceful old England." Kane sat down on the couch. "Think I'll just take a nap. Just close my eyes a little…" He swung his leg up onto the couch and hoisted the injured right leg up beside it. Kane pushed cushions under his head and within seconds was asleep.

"Maybe not Superman after all…just a damn fine commander who is missing his wife."

With that statement Steve stretched out on the facing couch. It was much smaller than Kane's. But then Steve figured that Kane was a bigger human being.

"You heard the man, Mr. Ryder. Go get some sleep. You two are going to make history tomorrow. Switching lanes. Go!" Steve whispered.

Michael closed the door behind him and quiet descended on the Branson penthouse suite at the Devere.

At the Rogers house it was still anything but quiet.

"So, Kane was outside zee window? No? For an agent he is daring. I give my friend all zee credit he deserves, especially for picking a beautiful wife like you."

Alexander Vincentia stood in front of Kelly. He was extremely attractive. Deep brown eyes complemented short black hair and dark Italian skin. He was dressed from head to toe in expensive clothes, cream sweater and pants and Gucci cream shoes. Kelly thought that was going just a little too far, but at least he had shoes. If they thought shoes would stop her from leaving the house they were wrong. Kelly was used to running round the outskirts of Sydney without shoes, making this lush English countryside was a cinch. All she had to do was get out. A trifle more difficult. One thing was sure; they would all go to the racetrack tomorrow. Kelly had to persuade them to take her with them. Once there, she could find some way to get away from them. Maybe she should play along with Alexander's flirtatious ways and unsettle his wife just a little. And, also, Peter Graham. Kelly purposely left the pearls upstairs in the bedroom. She glanced at Peter. He looked a little perturbed at the situation. Kelly could also see Kane's gun on the table. They planned to use it for some reason and then frame Kane. That much she did know. But on whom?

"So, Mr. Vincentia, how did you manage not to be killed? Your wife was devastated at the hospital. She clung to Kane like a leech, or was that all part of the plan?" Kelly sat down on a red velvet chair and crossed her legs letting the dress rise to half way up her thighs. It always worked on Kane.

By the look in Alexander's eyes, it worked on him, too. He started at her bare feet and his eyes worked their way up.

"My wife did zat? You did zat, Maria?" Alexander called over his shoulder.

"You said to do zat," Maria replied irritated.

"Let me ask you, Kelly. You think zat my wife was coming on to your husband? Would you say zat?" Alexander's accent still came through very heavily.

"I would say that." Kelly chanced it. "Has she always been in love with Kane or was it just after he slept with her?"

"How astute you are, my dear. It is no wonder Kane married you, for zat and several other reasons." Alexander laughed and rested his eyes firmly on Kelly's legs. "You are also looking at the gun. That is to kill Jimmy Rogers with and set up Kane, just in case he should by some remote chance win zee race tomorrow, which he won't now that we have you. Jimmy knows too much and has by now told your loving husband a few things. Jimmy and Kane will die and Peter will take care of his own boys. We have a plane standing by waiting to take us all to Switzerland."

"How cozy. And which one of you gets me, mate?"

"An interesting thought. Maybe Peter and I should toss for zat honor." And Alexander laughed.

Maria stubbed her cigarette in the ashtray and pushed her chair back with a resounding thud. She didn't like the way this was going. She was losing her own husband, but more importantly, she would lose Kane.

"The child makes a ridiculous statement, does she not?" asked Maria.

"Is it so ridiculous? And from here she does not look like zee child," remarked Alexander. "Are you hungry, Kelly? We would have eaten long ago if not for zee heroics of your husband."

"You don't know it was him?" stated the young woman.

"No? We found pieces of black T-shirt in the bushes. Was zat not what he was wearing on the news conference tonight?" asked Alexander.

"Lots of people wear black T-shirts. That doesn't prove a thing." Kelly was doing well.

"I agree, except the hotel receptionist confirmed it and also zat he was limping. You see we shot the man in zee grounds. And who else would come after you? Well, maybe I would." Alexander still sat opposite Kelly.

Kelly stood up. "You shot Kane? How? Where?" She looked flustered.

"You really do love zee man. He is very lucky...well, maybe not so lucky." Alexander stood up and moved around the table picking up the gun.

Kelly noted he didn't touch the handle, only the barrel.

"Cannot be too lucky if he is going to die. You wonder why I would kill my friend?" asked Alexander.

"That thought had popped into my head," replied a sarcastic Kelly.

"He became useful to us. We were having some problems, ones that we couldn't find a way around. You and Kane just happened to be in zee right place at zee right time."

"You bet we were, and you really think he is just gonna let you set him up? He's just a little bit too smart for that." Kelly replied sarcastically.

In the back of her mind Kelly was wondering just how badly Kane was hurt. She knew him well enough to know how much pain he could take. And that was a lot.

"By the way, Mrs. Branson, we have zee news for you. We will wait until everyone concerned is present and tell them the glowing news. And..." Alexander didn't finish his sentence.

The dinning room door reopened and Sergio and Bruno stepped in. Hanging on their arms was size 36 from the hotel.

"I said get her, not kill her. She did after all do zee good things for us. She gave us reports on Kane." Alexander lifted the girls face with his long dark fingers.

"Is there anyone not in your little plot?" asked a sarcastic Kelly.

Peter Graham intervened. "My boys are not involved nor is Michael Ryder. They all think Alexander died in the crash."

Kelly let out a chilling laugh. "Do they?" and she stopped. She nearly told them what they wanted to know. Better they didn't know that she told Kane through the window.

"They couldn't know anything else unless the girl here told them," butted in Peter.

Alexander hit size 36 across the face, and then wrapped his fingers once more round her chin.

"Did you say anything, missy?" Alexander squeezed her skin between his fingers.

"Noooo. I didn't say a word," she cried, and her head flopped down as Alexander let her go.

"Once in, missy, never out. You knew zat was zee way. Take her downstairs and dispose of her. Use Kane's gun, but still wear gloves. No one can hear her cry down there! One bullet down." Alexander dismissed a life with a mere comment.

Kelly had no choice but to use the girl and now she would die for it. Kelly turned away as they dragged the girl kicking and screaming from the room. She begged Kelly for help.

"Mrs. Branson," she screamed hysterically. "Don't let them kill me, please," she begged. "I didn't know they were going to shoot your husband…please, please help me…" and her voice trailed away down the hall.

They all heard one chamber of Kane's gun empty. There was no noise in the room, a pretentious air hung around. Minutes ticked by in total silence.

"Ah, Sergio and Bruno you are back, and with a present for Kelly. Now we can tell Mrs. Branson the great news. She will be so happy. Peter here did some checking into zee background. Seems Kane killed your father while you watched. And you maybe will get zat chance again. Well, your father will die by Kane's gun anyway. And, before I forget. We had someone shoot at your car. It was only to scare you all. But back to your father…"

Kelly froze. She turned slowly and looked Alexander in the face. In his hands he held the pearls. The Jimmy Rogers look alike pearls from her room.

"My pa is already dead." Kelly trembled. Fear rushed through her brain. She clutched the back of a chair to support herself with what she knew was coming.

"I think by now you have zee guessed. Your face tells me that the pearls mean something to you so give the girl the prize. The man that Kane killed zat you knew as Walker…"

"Alexander, stop it! Just tell her." Peter couldn't stand this. Alexander was deliberately hurting her.

"But it was zee fun. Okay. Kelly, Kane killed zee wrong man. Your father is the Mercedes owner…Jimmy Rogers." And Alexander Vincentia laughed an evil laugh.

Kelly screamed. "I don't believe you! It's all lies. All of it. My pa was Walker and Kane killed him. It's lies. Lies!" she argued.

"Kelly, calm down," and Peter put his arms around her. "Come on, Kelly." He half turned to Alexander. "You wanted to hurt Kane not Kelly. Stop it right there. I won't let you do that."

Kelly smelled the strong odor of cologne.

"You have no zee choice, Peter. You have served us long enough." Alexander pulled on a glove.

Sergio handed Alexander the gun. Kane's gun, and Alexander raised it high. He shot Peter Graham once through the head and blood splattered straight out on to Kelly. She let go with a long piercing scream.

Peter slid down her body and onto the Persian rug. Peter Graham had lost everything, including his life.

And it was then that Kelly fainted.

"One down…zee two to go." And Alexander laughed.

CHAPTER 14

Grand Prix day was always total chaos at Silverstone and this year was no exception. It started for Kane around six a.m. when he woke to a throbbing leg and a chest that hurt like hell. Sleeping on the couch without his wife was the pits. He sat up on the makeshift bed and lit a cigarette, which made him cough. A stupid move even for him, and he put the thing out.

Kane moved to the window and pulled back the curtains, letting sunlight bubblier than champagne greet him. He opened the paned window and the noise of a busy courtyard filled his eardrums. The place was alive with confusion, even at this hour. This was the day, the day to win or lose. The noise of Silverstone race track could be heard even at this distance. Striking odors of oil filled the air, obscuring out the sweet smelling honeysuckles that shrouded the building. As quietly as he could Kane pulled the window shut.

"Morning," came a voice from behind Kane.

Steve was awake, just barely. Kane turned to see a bleary cop sitting there.

"Morning, mate. You sleep well?"

"Yes, actually. You?" Steve realized that was probably a stupid question.

"I guess. Need to use the bathroom, get a shower and get to that track. Mikey has to be awake by now..." Kane was doing his best to sound calm. Inside he was a wreck.

"Good morning," a bleary-eyed Michael came out of the bedroom. "Feel like I haven't slept and I am starving. Can we get some breakfast?"

"Go ahead and order. I need the bathroom. Gonna take a shower and then one of you guys is gonna play mommy hen again and bandage this humpty dumpty together again," and Kane disappeared into the bedroom.

"How's he doing?" asked Michael.

"As good as anyone would do. He was moaning in his sleep and called Kelly's name a couple of times. If only we could get her out now before the race." Steve's mind considered the possibilities. "Call room service and order for the three of us. I need to touch base with Dave after you use the phone and make sure everything is okay there. Jimmy Rogers has to be in our sight at all times today. One message to his compadres and it's all over. They only suspect it was Kane in the ground. They won't know for sure. So you all fit to race, Michael?"

"Yes, I guess so. He could do it you know. Kane could race and win. He has nothing to lose and that's what makes a winner. Kane has what it takes. All he needs is the right breaks. I'm just a little afraid that Camery is going to be too good. He knows this track well and how to play it. Camery will have studied the races on video for hours and will know every turn and curve. I've studied them and I know them, but he knows them better. John Camery is one smart guy and plays to win at any cost. He has the same determination as Kane." He paused. "Alexander had that fire. Why in god's name did he change lanes? What made him do it?" Michael was puzzled at all the events.

"Money and power, by the sound of it. It has to hurt Kane like hell. Both his friends that he grew up with turned on him. One for lust and one for money." Steve paused.

"What are you thinking?" Michael asked as picked up the receiver.

"Was wondering how Kelly was doing. Same probably as Kane. You wait till you meet Kelly. She's…" Steve turned at the sound of the door opening.

"Tough as any guy. Feminine as all women put together, and mother of my kids and someone we have to get out. They knew it was me last night. I left too many clues and they'll be more guarded now. They will also bring Kelly with them, a 24/7 watch on her. So now which one of you smart blokes is gonna help me with the bandages." Kane stood in the doorway just in a towel. Long wet hair hung down his back. His ribcage was visibly badly bruised and the bullet wound looked red and almost infected.

"Sit down here, Kane. Michael is going to order some food. We can eat as we go."

Kane did as Steve asked and propped his leg up on the table.

"Oh, yeah. We have to feed Mikey. He's gonna be Britain's new champion. And we won't let anything happen to you. No one is gonna blow your head off at the end of the race," added Kane.

"I hadn't thought of that. If they think you are in that car they will do just that," stammered Michael.

"They won't cause I'll have them by the balls by then, mate. You just race and leave the rest to us. Superman and his aid will have your safety at priority level," laughed Kane and coughed.

Michael ordered the food. Kane could hear him asking for coffee, fruit and bagels to go. As Steve bandaged Kane's leg he whispered in his ear.

"He can't win, can he? The truth. Mikey told you he can't do it, right?"

Steve looked into Kane's concerned face. "He's scared he'll lose. Michael doesn't want it on his conscience."

"Hm-m-m, thought so."

Now, there was a problem.

Bandaged tightly in two places and dressed in black gear, Kane was ready to go. He was also getting impatient.

"How long does it take you two to find clean T-shirts? I told you where they were. For God's sake, man, come on."

Michael and Steve emerged from the bedroom. Kane was munching a bagel and swigging down some steaming hot coffee.

"Nice choice, Mikey. Steve, that's Kelly's sweatshirt. No time to change. Let's go," and this time Kane picked up Kelly's gun and stuck it down the back of his jeans.

Outside the hotel, the three waited for the car. Amid all the traffic Kane saw the gray Mercedes pull into the driveway. Kane noted as they walked through reception that there was a new clerk on the desk. Poor size 36 was no more. The courtyard was bustling, drivers, wives, girlfriends, crew, TV cameras. The whole place was alive and this before they even got to the track. The Mercedes blasted its horn and made a path through the crowds. Jimmy Rogers sat in the passenger seat making himself very visible.

The TV crew saw him and besieged the car with a microphone shooting through the open window.

"Mr. Rogers, what do you think Branson's chance are of going the distance?"

Jimmy Rogers stuck his head out of the open window and shouted down the microphone. "Same as anyone else's."

Kane pushed his way through the crowd. "'Scuse me."

"Mr. Branson, Mr. Branson, how do you feel this morning? Any comments?" asked the over zealous reporter. "I mean it's a chance of a lifetime."

"No comments," and Kane opened the car door and climbed in.

They pounced on their next victim… Michael. "Sorry you're not racing, Mr. Ryder. You hold any grudges against your teammate here?"

"You want a punch on the nose?" and he followed Kane into the car.

Steve tucked his precious cargo of drivers into the Mercedes.

"Fucking hell. They always like this?" asked Kane staring back out of the window.

"'Fraid so. So, Dave," asked Steve, "how was your night with Mr. Rogers here?"

"Uneventful really. Yours with Superman there?" chimed in Dave glancing at Kane.

"Bout the same." Steve smiled.

Jimmy was dressed in Mercedes colors and looked more than a little nervous now, Kane was in the back seat behind him.

"Morning, Kane. How are you? Just fine, Mr. Rogers. Am I ready to race? Sure I am. Thank you for asking, Jimmy. Glad you are so interested." Kane had the whole conversation with himself.

Michael was trying to suppress laughter. Steve didn't succeed.

"Oh, by the way, for your information, Jimmy, I will win today. So your little friends better let my wife go or you die right there on the track, and they'll just die later." Kane leaned back in the car. He was psyching himself up… for the kill.

There was a very pregnant pause and electricity vented through the air. Traffic this morning was slow moving, and no one spoke again in the car till they reached the racetrack, where the gray Mercedes entered the grounds. There were fans everywhere and Kane was overwhelmed with the presence of people. Getting through them with the car was something of an adventure, until a police car, with sirens blazing, appeared and escorted the lagging Mercedes into a spot near the garage.

Jimmy Rogers was allowed out first closely followed by Kane. Michael was right behind and they were escorted with the bundles from Britain into the locker rooms.

Women clamored behind the group of men, trying desperately to get a glimpse of the drivers, especially the new one from Australia. Kane used it to his advantage and swaggered behind Jimmy. Over his shoulder he whispered to Michael.

"Hey, Mikey. Hope you can swagger like this," and Kane continued walking with an air of confidence making every pain staking step count.

In the locker room the suits hung on the pegs. As Kane unhooked his, he noted it was a slightly different one from practice. This one carried every racing manufacture going that he had heard of and some he hadn't. On the back of the suit Kane saw a name in big bold red letters he didn't want to see...Tyroler. He stared at it. Jimmy saw him.

"Your best friend's company. You're racing on his tires. Ironic, huh?" laughed Jimmy and chewed on the now familiar kind of cigar. "He'll get you one way or another."

Now Kane was nervous, nervous for Mikey. They were gonna kill someone...one way or another.

Kane pulled his clothes off carefully. He couldn't let anyone see one set of bandages, let alone two. Michael stood alongside him and pulled the spare suit on. Jimmy Rogers disappeared, with Steve and Dave at his side, out to the pit area. Every driver in the locker-room was in their own world, and were not aware of two men equally dressed.

"Why did you put the fireproof wear on? You'll be safe enough just driving round in the exhibit cars." Mikey stayed in a confused state of mind around Kane.

"Yeah, I know that, Mikey. I just want to look good. You know, get the feel of things. Has to be convincing," lied Kane. He flipped his locker shut and carefully felt the weapon was secure inside his suit where no-one would see it.

"Oh, right. When are you going to go after Kelly?" Michael asked as he was finishing his own zipping.

"Sooner than you think. Steve is gonna send the troops in as soon as you start racing. But I think probably they will come to us, so let's concentrate on this event. Man, I need the bathroom. You know where it is?" asked a well-suited Kane.

"I'll come with you. Better use it myself. Sixty laps around this place and that will make you...well, you know." Michael closed his locker.

"Yeah," and the two strode off together. Both clad in Formula One racing-day red and silver-gray suits, sporting Tyroler and the kiss of death on their backs.

The night had been hard for Kelly. When she fainted, they carried her to the bedroom where they cleaned her face and arms, leaving no trace of blood. Assured that she was coming round, Kelly was left to her own devices. When she finally awoke, Kelly wasn't sure if she had dreamed the whole thing. She still had on the red dress, but her arms looked like they had been scrubbed. On the bedside table sat a tray of food. Slowly Kelly climbed off the bed and pulled the cloth back to reveal food. English muffins, fresh strawberries and freshly squeezed orange juice. She actually felt hungry and then it occurred to her why… No dinner. Why no dinner? Someone dying had interrupted dinner.

"Oh, my god!" Now she remembered. Peter had died while holding her.

She looked down her dress where she could see dried blood staining the material, making Kelly want to rip the dress right off her body. That was Kane's job and she laughed hysterically. Then she cried. When she finished crying, she forced some food down her from the breakfast tray. The next thing to do was shower, and find the shorts and shirt she arrived in. She moved to the bathroom door, opened it, and disappeared inside.

Showering didn't help any, except to clean the body, but not the soul. She couldn't wash away the thought of Peter dying on her and she couldn't get Alexander out of her mind. He was a cold bloodied killer. When had he crossed the line? And when exactly did he plan to kill Kane? Presumably after Kane's gun was used on Jimmy Rogers. Jimmy Rogers. That name flooded her brain. That could not be true. He could not be her father. Yet deep down she knew it was, knowing right from the start when he pulled the locket out of his shirt. She turned off the shower. As she did, she heard a noise in the bedroom. She looked for something to hit someone with from the bathroom, some kind of weapon. There was nothing. Kelly wrapped a towel round her carefully, opening the bathroom door.

"What do you want? You're as sick and guilty as your husband!" yelled Kelly.

The red and gray suits moved out onto the track as the grand parade was about to start. All the drivers filed out as they were announced, climbing on top of the awaiting cars and clung on to whatever they could find to support them. The British crowd went wild clapping and shouting for their favorite driver. John Camery, the home-grown hero, went first acknowledging the cheers. One after one they went until it was Kane's turn to be announced.

"And racing for Mercedes is the Australian rookie, Kene Branson in car number 21."

The rookie Mercedes driver positively swaggered onto the track with no sign of a limp. Nothing. He'd pulled the mesh down already on his head and all the crowd could see was a great body in a red and gray suit. He climbed onto the wing of the waiting car and waved ferociously at the applauding fans. This was just for show... for the admiring public. The display cars set off round the track at a slow speed, with a police escort heralding the show under red, white and blue flags of the British nation which were flying overhead. Alongside of those were the colored drapes of all nationalities of the world. Red, yellows, greens and orange lit the Silverstone day.

"You okay up there, Kene?" his driver yelled.

"Yup," the reply came and the Mercedes driver never looked down from his perch.

One lap round the track, with the pace car way out in front of the leaders of the pack, and fans continued to go wild and huge cases of confetti floated in the air. The cars stopped amid loud music, countless flimsily dressed girls clutching pompoms, the smell of burning oil and revving engines. It looked like July 4th in New York.

The drivers jumped down from their prestigious seating accommodation and walked to their cars. Climbing in one driver crossed himself; another kissed a picture of his child and pushed it inside his suit. Jimmy Rogers hovered round the car complete with his two protective escorts. There was no outwards sign from car number 21.

"Remember, Kane, listen to what we tell you. Just cross over. No more and you'll get Kelly back. Win and you'll never see her again. All Alexander wants is the money. It's Peter that wants your wife," Jimmy lied.

There was no reaction from the car. Steve stepped forward.

"You hear him, Kane?"

Still no reaction. Then something occurred to Steve. When did the two guys make the switch? Kane was supposed to go back after the parade to the changing room and switch with Michael. He hadn't. Who was in the car? Suddenly, Steve thought he saw something gleam round the driver's neck. He blinked, looked again and the image was gone.

"Kane? Michael?" his words were lost as car Number 21 revved its engines. The mechanics moved away in haste to escape the fumes of the engine.

Steve turned to bang on the helmet trying to reach the driver; he failed and car 21 took off out of the pits.

The first lap was to warm the tires. The cars skidded from one side to another on the steamy track, and then they headed into their pole positions. Car number 21 was near the back, very near the back. Only a miracle could make car 21 win. His foot touched the pedal and he felt the power. He couldn't hear a damn thing except for car engines and screeching tires. The drivers watched with anticipation for the green flag, feet firmly attached to the metal, and then the flag dropped and the 2001 British Grand Prix was under way.

The black Jaguar with the tinted windows pulled into the car park. Maria and Alexander rode in the back with Kelly sandwiched between them. Sergio drove the car with Bruno riding an intrepid shotgun. Kelly wriggled in between her captors, making life generally uncomfortable for all concerned. Today she wore the shorts she arrived in at the household and a bright pink T-shirt that Maria had given her. That wasn't all Maria had given her. She'd given her a way out. Maria didn't want Kane to die, and she couldn't warn him either, but Kelly could. Framing him for Peter and Jimmy's death was one thing, shooting Kane after the fact was another. Alexander said no witnesses and more importantly Maria wondered if that also meant her. Back in the bedroom, Maria had made an arrangement with Kelly. If Maria let her go then the English police had to protect her. Kelly agreed. As yet Maria had killed no one. When they went to the bathroom Kelly had to go her own way, any way but preferably out of a window.

The Jaguar stopped, but the engine still ticked over, purring majestically. They waited somewhat impatiently. Bruno picked the high-powered rifle parts off the seats, collected the sights, and hid the whole thing neatly into a long canvas bag.

"And don't bother coming back if zee job is not completed. I'll take care of zee Jimmy Rogers," and Alexander produced Kane's gun.

Kelly gasped. Now she knew what they intended to do. They sat in the car for what seemed like an eternity. Sixty laps would take a while, and Bruno needed to get in a good position for a nice clean shot. When Kane crossed over he would take his helmet off. Bruno was not hired as an expert marksman for nothing.

"I need the bathroom," whined Kelly.

"Hold it!" snapped Alexander.

Tension in the car ran high.

"Can't," she replied and shuffled about in her seat.

"You will," and he forcibly turned her face to him with his hands.

"Said I can't," argued Kelly.

"Then you pee in zee seat," Alexander scowled. He didn't look so handsome now.

"Not that kind of bathroom use," moaned Kelly writhing in pain.

Alexander stared at Kelly. "If you were not so valuable I would kill you right now."

His hand slid from her face down her neck. He hadn't noticed the butterfly on her breast till this morning, and now he was having a job not to look. His hand carried on down till it touched the butterfly.

That was enough for Maria. Staring at Kelly was one thing, touching the butterfly on her breast was another.

"I will go weth her. Sergio can come weth us." She intervened.

"Okay. Be quick. Go with them, Sergio, and don't let them out of zee sight…except for zee bathroom." Alexander was irritated.

Alexander lay back in the seat with his hands behind his head, while his wife and Kelly climbed out. He watched the women and Sergio walk across to the main arena where there would be bathrooms.

"Over there," and Sergio pointed to the ladies room.

"You will wait here for us. I can manage zee slip of a girl like her," and Maria ushered Kelly through the ladies room door. She turned to Kelly. "Zee rest is now up to you. Just remember I helped you."

"Sure you did and we have to make it look real. So," Kelly brought her right fist up and hit Maria square on the jaw.

Maria dropped like a brick to the floor and Kelly grabbed her by the arms. Pulling Maria into one of the cubicles, Kelly closed the door, and moved back into the bathroom.

"Kane, you would be proud of me," she quoted as she shook her aching hand.

It was now or never. At the end of the Ladies room was a window, not a big one, but big enough for Kelly to climb through, and low enough for her to almost reach. In the corner stood a rubbish bin. Kelly pulled it over and propped the bin under the window, hoisting herself up onto it. The window gave easily and Kelly pulled herself onto the ledge and out through the window. She dropped down onto the grass much to the amazement of folk outside.

"Door's jammed," she said to the astonished passers-by on the other side and took off running.

Kelly had a fair idea of where to go, but getting in the pits dressed like a woman would be something else. She needed a suit, and what Kelly needed she got.

"And car number 3, Camery, takes the lead. In second place is Villeneuve for Honda, followed closely by Schumacher in the Ferrari car. And here they come now on the tenth lap. In third to last place is the Australian Branson for Mercedes. There seems to be some problem at the front!" As the commentator got louder, the crowd rose in their seats.

"Camery is in trouble! There is smoke coming from the engine and he's pulling into the pits. John Camery's car is on fire! He's pulling into the pits. My god, Camery is out of the race. The red hot favorite is out!" screamed the commentator. "Now the race is wide open." He pulled his handkerchief form his pocket and mopped his brow. This was too much even for him and his years at Silverstone.

The audience in the stands stood as one, watching and waiting with the prospect of fate all part of the day.

Word came down the wire to car number 21.

"Kane, pull into the pits. Now!" Jimmy screamed down the line.

"For once listen to him, Kane. Pull in now and change tires. Its gonna rain. Pit now, damn it, Commander!" Steve wasn't so sure it was the commander in the car. In fact he wasn't sure who was driving car number 21. "Pull in, Kane! I sent the troops to Rogers' house. It's clean. No traces. They have to be here. Come in, please."

Jimmy Rogers laughed. "Told you you wouldn't find anything. They're long gone."

As he spoke neither men's eyes left car 21. It left the track and headed for the pits where the mechanics leaped into action. Then the yellow flag went down and all the cars descended to the pits. Steve wasn't suited and this time the marshals held him back.

"I need to speak to Kene!" Steve tried to shout over the engines roar.

Two eyes watched him. Two steely blue eyes, with a fixed stare, shone through the visor. Steve could hear car 21 revving with the foot hot on the metal. Steve had to tell him that the last statement about the house wasn't true. The police had found two bodies, one man and one woman.

One was his friend, and Steve's boss. Steve stared at the visor. He still could not tell. Both Mercedes' drivers had blue eyes!

Then the flag was up and they were gone back in the arena to do battle. Number 21 pulled out at a fast and dangerous speed, narrowly missing the leading Ferrari. He drove with everything he had learned over the years. This was his one and only chance to win this race.

"Funnel down in the turn, Kane. Find a hole, make a hole! Go after the leaders. Go, Kane, go!" Was this the same Jimmy Rogers yelling down the microphone on his headset?

"Since when did you want him to win?" asked Steve with a startled look.

"Since I realized I didn't want to die. There gonna kill me too, aren't they? If he wins, maybe he can help me clear my name. I never agreed to kill anyone," Jimmy protested.

"But you didn't stop them either, Jimmy. You could have. You could have stopped it long ago," Steve reminded him.

"I wanted to be out from under the debts and the blackmail of the Vincentias and I didn't know I had a daughter till just a few days ago; seems the only way to Kelly is through her husband. If I help will it go lighter on me? Alexander is the head of the ring. It was all his idea. Maria can tell you that." Jimmy was pleading for his life and was fidgeting nervously with the headset.

"You'll help him? Though by the way he's driving he doesn't need much help. Talk to him and we'll see."

Steve gave Jimmy free range on the mike. Now it was up to the two of them to help Kane across the line.

"Kane, this is Jimmy. Kane? Answer me," his voice droned on. "Kane, you hear me?"

Then with a sudden crackle on the line there came a reply. "Yup."

"Do as I tell you. You can do this. You can get a place," Jimmy murmured.

The line crackled and the voice was deep and gruff. "Win!"

"Okay, win. You get one more scheduled pit stop. We're going to put different tires on the car. Not Tyroler. The tires you have on now won't hold you. You understand?"

"Yup," came the reply and the roar of the engines deafened him.

He could feel the rush in his chest and his eardrums were filled with the noise of his own heart beating fast and furious. Adrenalin pumped through his veins as his foot went farther down on the pedal, and he eased it back up just a little. He felt the harness tight on his chest. His vision blurred with the speed of one-seventy then one-ninety. He blinked his eyes just for a second to try to see better and almost clipped the car next to him. Someone was passing him.

"Let him go, Kane. Let him go! Stay behind him. Get in his draft. Stay behind him. You still have twenty laps to go. Let Ferrari take the line. Stay with him. Keep your speed even." Jimmy urged him on.

The loud speaker once more sprang into life.

"The Australian is racing the race of his life. He's only one lap behind the leaders. Ferrari and Schumacher are in first place. Still its an open race." The commentator paused. "And here comes the rain ladies and gentleman."

Umbrellas shot up all over the ground with the British used to downpours and always carrying the required essentials with them. Big drops of rain hit the visors of the driver's cars. Now it really was a race. But the rain had stopped one thing. Bruno van Camp couldn't see clearly enough through the rifle lens to get a clear shot at Kane. He could fire the gun, but from the position he had found, but he couldn't take the chance of not killing Kane first shot. Unless the rain stopped he had failed and the people he worked for did not tolerate failure. Bruno had his own gun ready by his side just in case.

"And now it's really turning into a Grand Prix ladies and gentlemen The Australian is catching up nicely, but he's taking the corner too fast. He'll never make it at that speed. He's doing what Vincentia did right at the same corner. Oh, my god, not again!" and the commentator's voice reached fever pitch.

The crowd stood up and the noise dropped.

"Kane, drop back!" Jimmy screamed down the mike. "Drop back. You can't take him there. That's what the rookie did. Drop back now. You hear me?" yelled Jimmy. His hands shook on the headset, which he held tightly to his head. "Please, Kane, not there!"

The car dropped back.

"Thank god," yelled Steve and he breathed a sigh of relief. "Kane, listen to Jimmy. He doesn't want you to die. Kane? Kane is that you in that car?"

"Yup," came the reply.

Suddenly, from behind number 21 the following car span round and round on the wet surface till it hit the balustrade with a fierce thud. Two cars after him ploughed straight into the battered car. The explosion rocked the overcrowded stands, and disturbed the afternoon air.

"Eyes ahead, Kane! Don't look in your mirror. Don't let it distract you. When you see the yellow flag pull up. The pace car will stop you. You understand me?" Jimmy pleaded.

This time there was just a grunt.

"It isn't Kane in the car, Jimmy… it's Michael Ryder!" Steve shouted.

"What?" and a wide-eyed Jimmy didn't believe it. "Can't be, we all saw Kane get in."

"Did we? We all saw what we thought was Kane. Did you see his face? Well, did you?" Steve was yelling at Jimmy.

"No, but it has to be." Jimmy was red and flustered.

"Why, Jimmy? Why does it have to be? You just said you wanted to help. Help whom? Is someone sitting out there with a high-powered rifle just waiting for him to glide over that winning line? Is that it?" yelled Steve.

"Yes," replied Jimmy in a low and condescending tone.

"What? Where? I thought you changed sides a little too hastily." Steve took hold of Jimmy's shoulders.

"On the hill over there," and Jimmy pointed to the embankment. "Soon as he crosses he's dead," and Jimmy hung his head. He was killing Michael Ryder, not Kane Branson.

"Dave," Steve yelled to his partner at the back of the box. "Go and get the security and backup to check out that hill. Arrest anyone that seems suspicious. Most likely Italian, and send a couple of cops in here to guard Jimmy."

"On my way," and Dave ran out into the afternoon rains.

"Michael, listen to me. They think it's Kane racing in the car. There's a sniper on the embankment by the finish line just waiting to kill him. Do not cross that line. I repeat pull in now. Do you understand?" Steve's eyes were wide and he was frantic at the prospect of it not being Kane in that car.

"Nope." Car 21 replied.

"Michael, just do it! Or you'll die for Kane." Steve pleaded.

"Do what?" came a familiar voice behind him.

Steve turned around and his eyes widened. Steven Asher got the shock of his life.

CHAPTER 15

"You? You're in that car," stammered Steve, not quite believing his eyes.

"Apparently not. That Australian can pack one hell of a punch. He left me out cold in the bathroom and he's been out there the whole time." Michael rubbed his black and blue jaw and peered onto the track.

"And I just told you what you wanted to know," moaned Jimmy. He'd spilled the beans just minutes before for no reason.

Two local police officers appeared with Dave to take Jimmy Rogers into custody. He went without a struggle, handcuffed between the officers. He looked at Michael, then back at the track for the last time in his life. He walked away from the Mercedes group despondent at losing, but more because he'd never got to know his daughter...now he never would. The police ushered him through the gawping crowd towards the waiting police car. There were no sirens and no bells. As Jimmy bent his head to step into the car, he caught sight of a small Mercedes red-and-gray suited person running through the crowd. They turned their head slightly and Jimmy Rogers saw her face.

"Jenny," he whispered and the policeman closed the door.

As they drove away, Jimmy Rogers' face pressed against the windowpane. She was safe and that's all that mattered. The daughter he never knew he had, till now, a remembrance of his beloved Jenny.

"Michael? If you're not in the car, who is? Kane can't drive like that, can he?" Steve was staggered.

"I guess we're about to find out. Think Commander Branson has been holding out on us." Michael paused and picked up the spare headset. "Kane?"

"Kane? Answer us, damn it," yelled Steve. "Michael is here. Talk to me, Commander."

No response and Michael tried again.

"Kane, it's me, Michael. Answer me. How are you feeling?"

The driver's headset burst into life. "Tired," whispered the Australian accent.

The two men stared at each other.

"Kane, listen to me. You can win this. I'll talk you through the final laps. You can make all our dreams come true." Michael said the last part with a tinge of regret.

"Except mine. No Kelly," once more the accent came through.

"We have Jimmy Rogers in custody, Kane. There's a sniper on the hill by the winning line but Dave and local Bobbies will take care of him." Steve hesitated telling him the rest." I lied, Kane. The house wasn't empty. The local police found Peter's body with a hole clean through his head along with the receptionist from the Devere."

"Kel?" asked car number 21.

"No sign of her," answered Steve and he curled his lip.

"Find her first. And you better find Alexander before I do," uttered the Australian.

The air was fraught with electricity.

"Would that be zee threat?" a voice cut in the line.

"No, Alexander. That would be a fuckin' promise. Where is Kelly, you son-of-a-bitch?" Kane's voice boomed over the helmet's microphone.

His speed dropped automatically and he lost the momentum he had attained. The yellow flag dropped.

"Kane? Kane, can you still hear us? Vincentia get off the line! You want him to crash?" Michael yelled down the mike in the pits.

"Stupid question, *Mikey.* Of course I want him to crash. If he doesn't, my guy is zee waiting to take him out," replied Alexander.

Steve grabbed the mike. "Don't think so, Mr. Vincentia. We already have your hit man and Jimmy Rogers is in custody. All we have to do is find you and Kelly."

"And that you won't do. Maria has her," and a shrill and piercing laugh echoed down both their lines. "And I will be leaving England as soon as zee race is over."

"Kane, you have to come in, now. Do you hear? The yellow flag is down. Bring the car in. Rogers said the tires were faulty. We'll block out Vincentia somehow." Steve was taking over again.

"Do it in eight seconds," Kane demanded. "And don't block that bastard! I want to hear what he has to say before I kill him."

Kane pulled into the pits, and the Tyroler tires were discarded, with new ones replacing them. This time no one stopped either Steve or Michael from going to the car. Michael tapped on Kane's helmet as Kane revved the engine.

"You have to wait, Kane. Flag is still down. Keep revving. Stay in the Ferrari's line, Kane. Keep pace with him. Get in his draft and stay. I will tell you when to go. You understand?"

Kane raised his thumb up. The accident took a lot longer than any eight seconds to clear.

Kane flipped the visor. "Water!"

Michael grabbed a water bottle and pushed it to Kane who sucked hard on the straw. He downed half a bottle of liquid and tossed the bottle high into the air. He patted his chest with his fist.

"Too tight."

"Release his harness a little," demanded Michael.

"We can't do that, Mr. Ryder. It has…"

And the mechanic realized he was staring down the barrel of a .38.

"Yes, sir." The mechanic immediately did as he was asked, and released it just a couple of notches, which eased the pain somewhat in Kane's chest.

"Where are you keeping that? Kane, give it to…" Michael's voice was lost in the dust.

The flag went up and Kane was gone, complete with .38 at his side.

Michael turned back to Steve and just stared at him, the pair taking giant strides to get back to the stand and their headsets.

"He has Kelly's gun with him, Steve."

Steven Asher smiled. Why did that not surprise him?

"Really? So you're going to go catch him and take it from him?" Steve laughed.

"Funny," grimaced Michael.

The line crackled through the earpieces.

"Mikey, you still there?" asked Kane.

Michael grabbed the microphone to the front of his face. "I'm here, Kane. How's it in the car? Your speed out of the pits was good."

"Car is fine. I'm tired, Mikey. My ribs hurt. I hurt. I can't do this, Mikey. I can't do it." Kane moaned. "Can't see straight."

Michael stared at Steve and whispered. "You think he means that or is it just for the other party's benefit?"

"The latter. Play along till we know for sure," whispered Steve.

"Kane, it's Michael. How's your leg? Can you control the pedals okay? How is the rain affecting you? Some of the drivers didn't go back out."

"Some problems, Mikey. Funny we all call you Mikey." Kane hoped he was lulling Alexander into a false sense of security.

Big blobs of rain dropped on his visor. That part was true, he was having difficulty in seeing and the track was slick. Seven more laps to go. He was tired. Very tired. He wondered how much Alexander had heard. Had he heard the part about the bodies? Kane thought not. He would have chimed in the conversation a lot sooner. All they had to do now was find Kelly or he still couldn't risk it. Most of the big names were out of the race and he, Kane Branson, really did have a chance here. Funny, really. He had a shot at a boyhood dream and his boyhood friend stood in his way.

Back in the car, Alexander was becoming a little worried. Neither Maria nor Sergio had returned and he sat alone. When he called Sergio from his car phone, Sergio answered on his cell. He could barely hear his boss for the noise from the track.

"So where are zee ladies?"

"They went in to use the bathroom, but have not come out, Mr. Vincentia," replied the not so bright Sergio.

"Then go look. Women don't just disappear…unfortunately."

"I cannot hear you, sir," replied Sergio putting a finger in his ear.

"I said go in zere…" Alexander was agitated. "Kane only has zee few laps left. Go get Kelly and we'll put her on zee line here."

"Go in there, sir..?" he couldn't hear properly.

"Just do it, Sergio and stop with zee whining."

"Yes, sir," and Sergio knocked on the ladies bathroom door and stepped inside and saw no-one. One of the stalls was closed, and he knocked. Hearing no sound he pushed the door open. Immediately he saw Maria.

"Oh, my god!"

"What is going on, Sergio?" demanded Alexander, still hanging on to the call.

"Mrs. Vincentia is out cold on the floor," he blurted down his cell

"Shit. Where is Kelly? Where is Kane's wife?" Alexander asked, dreading the answer he was about to get.

"Gone, sir. The bathroom window is open." The frame was swinging freely.

"Get Maria. Bring her round, zen get back here, now! We need to get zee hell away from here." Alexander disconnected the call.

He climbed over the seating and into the driver's seat. If they weren't there in ten minutes he planned on leaving.

But they weren't coming back period.

Five laps left. No more contact with Alexander. Kane tried yelling things at him in Italian. No response. Strange. Had something gone wrong? Kane kept his foot on the pedal. His leg hurt like hell but still he kept driving. If only he knew about Kelly. If she was safe he could go, but he had to know where she was first. He did what Michael said and kept behind the Ferrari.

"I can pass him, Mikey," the Australian accent boomed.

"No, Kane. You have to wait. Wait, Kane! I'll tell you when. Save the speed. Save your energy. Don't overdrive the car. Keep a steady drive. How do you feel? We are monitoring you from here. Your heartbeat is a little fast. Try and calm down. When you were talking to Alexander the beats went right up. If he comes on line again ignore him. Concentrate on the race. We'll get Kelly out…"

Steve interjected. "Police just picked up Maria and Sergio. A woman reported a strange looking man going into the ladies room. They found an unconscious Maria and a very conscious Sergio who was more than happy to talk. Kelly wasn't with them. Apparently she knocked Maria out and went through the bathroom window. Kelly's in the grounds somewhere. She'll get to us. Vincentia doesn't have her. You copy, Kane? Vincentia does not have Kelly."

"I hear you," came Kane's muffled voice. "But where the fuck is she?"

Kelly scrambled through the crowds. Then she saw the Mercedes camp. She pulled the stolen Mercedes suit tightly around her and the mesh down over her head. They had to let her through. There wasn't time to give the police any details right now. She had to reach the guys and tell them she was safe. It was then she heard the commentator.

"Ferrari still leads. But the Australian racing for Mercedes is in second place. How in God's name… it's a mystery? But he's there. Something is holding him back and he seems reluctant to try for the lead. Maybe the rain, who knows. He could actually win this race if he went the extra mile," yelled the over zealous commentator. He pulled at his stiff and starchy collar wanting to be down there racing with them. He could almost feel the power from the commentator's box. "Something is holding him back."

"Yeah and that something is me!" and Kelly ploughed on.

Then she saw them all grey and red in the stand. She could see Steve's blonde hair and the Mercedes team, but the barrier was across the entrance at the pit. And she couldn't get through. She grabbed at a policeman's arm.

"Please, I have to get in. I am an Australian Federal Police Agent," she told the young and soaking wet police officer.

"Of course you are? And if you are why are you dressed in Mercedes clothes?" he asked pushing stray wet hair from his eyes.

"I can't wait for you! My husband is in car 21. Kene Branson. Please let me through," Kelly screamed.

"You're a woman?" the officer asked.

Kelly didn't hesitate. She unzipped the front of the suit.

"*Oh, you're a woman…*"

"What is going on out there?" Steve turned to look at the distraction. He caught sight of Kelly pleading with the officer.

He didn't even stop to tell Michael, just ran outside into the rain.

"Let her through, officer. She's fine. Let her in," Steve yelled through the pouring July rains and the noise of engines.

The young officer cleared a path for her and people fell out of her way to let her through.

"Steven," Kelly cried and fell into the young man's arms.

He hugged her to him and with wet fingers pulled the mesh from her hair. Her short choppy hair spewed out and she pulled the zip up the front of her suit. With no thought for herself, Kelly's first words were for Kane.

"Is he okay? Is Kane okay? I saw him on TV. He was holding his chest and you do know, don't you, he had a heart attack some years back. Is he okay?" She peered up into her friend's face, rain dripping down her cheeks.

"Kelly, Kelly! Kane is fine. No, he never mentioned anything about a heart attack to me. I do know he is racing the race of his life. How about you? How do you feel? We should get a doctor to you…"

"No, doctor. I have to talk to him. He can hear me on the headset, right?" she pleaded.

Steve didn't know if those were tears or raindrops on her face. He did know she needed her husband right now, and he himself was not a good substitute.

"He can hear you. Let's go inside and you can talk to him. He has cracked ribs," he hesitated, "and a bullet wound in his leg…"

"A bullet wound? You let him race like that?" she condemned him.

"He knocked Michael Ryder out cold… Kelly, you know about Peter and the girl right?"

"Peter died with me in his arms. He was protecting me." and she turned her face away. "Later, Steve. Ask the questions later. I can't talk about that right now. I just want to talk to my husband."

Steve ushered her to where it was dry and the rest of them stood. Michael stared at the young woman with the short spiky hair and the big blue eyes that cried out for her husband. She was indeed extraordinary beautiful. No wonder Kane would not risk losing her. Introductions were fast.

"Michael, Kelly. Kelly, Michael. Kelly the microphone. Michael watch his heart beat now," commented Steve as he whispered to him out of Kelly's earshot.

Kelly clutched the spare headset to her and put it on her head. Steve adjusted the mike for her so she could speak to Kane. Michael was still attached intently to his. This he could not miss.

The line crackled as Kelly began to speak.

"Kane," she whispered down the line and tough little Kelly cried. "It's me. Kane, it's me… Kelly." Tears of joy exploded down her face.

"*Baby*," Kane whispered and they could hear both pain and relief in his voice.

Kane's heartbeat increased a thousand times on the monitor. Michael raised his eyebrows and looked towards Steve. They exchanged glances with each other. Now Michael knew what Steve already knew. The Branson's were a team.

"Don't cry baby. Kelly? You with Steve?"

"Yes," she murmured and stemmed the tears. Crying would only distract him and that she didn't need to do.

"Did they hurt you, baby?" Kane's line crackled.

"No," she lied.

"Kelly, I love you." The tension down the line was electrifying, with Kane's voice sensual in its tone.

"I love you too, Kane. Come back to me," she begged, her voice low and seductive. "Always." He coughed, remembering who might be listening. "Steve, you there"

"Here, Commander."

"Keep her with you. Remember what I told you?" reminded Kane.

"Yes, I remember. If anything happens to Kelly, you'll kill me." Steve stated the obvious.

"You remember. Now, I have a job to do. Put Mikey on." Now Kane could go for it. The .38 lay beside him. "Let's do this!" and Kane's speed increased dramatically.

And as suddenly as it started the rain stopped. Steve hoped that Dave and the local Bobbies had the sniper by now. If he knew Dave he would have.

Time for Michael to get serious. Kelly sat down next to Steve, who put his arm around her shoulders, feeling that she was soaking wet.

"Kelly, climb out of the suit," and Steve helped her pull it off.

Underneath the suit Kelly had on the shortest of shorts and a low-cut pink T-shirt. She was stunning, and Michael couldn't keep his eyes off her. Now he definitely knew why she was with Kane. They were a pair to draw to.

"Mikey, you there? Stop staring at my wife!"

"How did you know that?" asked Michael surprised at the statement, and jumped back a couple of inches.

"Cause I know Kelly and what she can do to a man," replied Kane huskily.

Kelly blushed and her eyes sparkled at the compliment.

"I'm here, Kane. So watch your speed. Stay in his line. Stay there, Kane. Increase your speed. Put your foot down hard." Now Michael took charge.

They all heard him moan as he accelerated. Kelly flinched. Her man was hurting and she longed to comfort him. But none-the-less his speed increased. Almost two hundred miles an hour.

"Hold it there, Kane. Hold it!" Michael urged.

"Need a hole, Mikey. Need a hole," the voice from the track boomed.

"Make a hole, Kane. Make one! Go, Kane, go. Do it!" screamed Michael into the mouthpiece. "Go raise Kane!"

They could hear Kane breathing hard. Two laps left. He could do it. His hands shook on the steering wheel, but he knew he could do it. One more burst. Find the space. Open the space. His mind raced as well as the car. The .38 shuddered by his side. And then the space was there. The Ferrari moved a fraction too far over to the right and Kane saw the hole. So did Michael.

"On the left, Kane. Go for the left of the Ferrari! The hole is there. It's now or never, Kane! Do it! Do it! Take him on the bend!" Michael's voice echoed round the booth.

"I can't do it, Mikey… I can't…" Kane pleaded.

"You can, Kane…you have to! It's all up to you my friend! This is your chance…go for it!"

Kane couldn't see anything except the blur of speed, and felt nothing except the power of the silver-dream machine beneath him. He was one with the motor around him and suddenly he could taste the sweet smell of success. It flowed like fine wine through his veins.

They watched the monitor from the booth. Kane was keeping speed, in fact it increased. So was his heart, which raced along with him.

"Take him now, Kane. Take him!" Michael yelled uncontrollably, perspiration dripping from him.

Kelly grabbed hold of Steve's arm and squeezed it. Steve smiled. He didn't care she was cutting off his blood supply, only that she was safe.

And Kane pulled to the left, making the car vibrate violently. He took the inside path and pulled ahead with inches to spare. He was ahead for the first time in this race, in fact in any race ever. The Ferrari fought instinctively and the two cars were neck and neck again. Dead level and flat out on the home stretch.

The crowd stood in sheer amazement, cheering like crazy for the underdog. The commentator was uncontrollable, positively leaping up and down in his box

"Neck and neck! Dead even. One has to go. One car. Can he do it? Can the Australian do this?" Red and ruffled, the man yelled. "He can do it! He can… he's pulling ahead! Look at this guy go…he's flying! Branson takes the lead! All depends now what he has left in him. He has my vote…"

The crown at Silverstone went wild standing on their feet, clapping and cheering. Half a lap left to find out who would be champion.

Kelly leaned into the microphone, her voice low and very seductive.

"Go, baby, go. I'll be waiting for you, Kane. Do it, baby. NOW!"

The two men stared at her and then at each other. It was totally obvious what she was implying to her man.

Kane put one last pressure on the pedal, and he felt the stitches pull in his leg while the harness tugged on his chest. But Kelly had put the fire in him that he needed the most, making the pain seem like nothing now. Crossing the line had never been so rewarding. Kelly was waiting for him. He saw the checkered flag drop as his sleek silver dream machine slid over the line at two hundred and twenty miles an hour. He had done it. He, Kane Branson, had done it. Kane slowed the car and raised his arm in salute to the cheering crowd with his red and gray gloves in mock salute. The British Grand Prix was his! Confetti fell from the seemingly cloudless skies and the sun once more shone on Kane's adventurous life.

In the booth Kelly jumped up and down. Steve clutched the excited young woman to him. Michael leapt around like some maniac let loose, and the Mercedes crew were totally out of their minds with joy.

Alexander knew he was on his own. Sergio would squeal like the stuffed pig that he was. Maria never wanted Kane to die, and she and Bruno were probably in police custody by now. He could leave England a broken and bankrupt man, but at least he could leave, but for where? His partners in Italy wouldn't take too kindly to failure.

Alexander had started up the car's engine before the end of the last lap. He'd kept it revving ever since. Now was the time to pull out of the car park, and he cruised through the traffic heading towards the entrance. The black Jaguar with the license plates V2 drove out onto the main road. V2 was Maria's car and no one gave it a second glance. Alexander had to get to the airstrip where the pilot was waiting with the plane. Pilot, butler, one and the same. He stepped on the gas and drove out of this life. No eyes were on him. That honor belonged to the Australian.

Kane flew round the track, his one arm still raised. Spectators began to descend towards the pits as Mercedes men rushed down to the track. But car number 21 didn't stop.

"What's he driving?" came the voice from the helmet.

"Black Jaguar, tinted windows, V2," replied his partner. Kelly smiled. She knew his moves well.

"I'll be back. Be ready," Kane replied in a low sexy voice.

"For you, Kane, always!" Kelly replied quietly and handing Steve the headset, moved back out of the way.

Now Steve knew what Kane meant about partners. Kelly knew instinctively what Kane wanted. On duty… and off.

At that point Kane saw an opening in the balustrade. He crossed the track and took off ignoring flag waving officials. The crowds parted to let the speeding car go past them. The popping of champagne corks could wait.

Alexander got as far as the entrance to the motorway before he glanced in his rear view mirror, and he did a double take. A silver speed machine was turning out behind him and catching up to his car with great speed.

"Kane Branson… I hate you!" The man with the Italian accent declared.

Alexander stepped on the gas, knowing now he had no chance. The silver formula one car got closer. Now he was behind him and then beside him. Alexander was doing one hundred mph. Kane was passing him without any difficulty and began to cut him off. He thought about that and then realized he would cause a severe crash if he did so. He backed off just a little. Cars on the motorway cleared out of the paths, pulling into the side, with screeching tires trying desperately to get out of the way of thunder. Kane could hear the police sirens and could see flashing lights in his mirror. He didn't want Alexander taken by some damn police. He wanted him for himself and he wanted answers.

Kane flipped the visor on the helmet and pulled his glove off with his teeth, at the same time reached in the base of the car for his gun. He had it. He dropped his car back alongside Alexander and aimed the gun at the car tires, gesturing to Alexander what his intentions were if he didn't pull over. Alexander knew, laughed, and kept going, driving like some maniac with a dry maniacal smile on his face. He could outpace a rookie driver any day. Alexander pulled ahead. Kane pulled along with him.

"You don't have zee balls, Kane! You would not shoot me!" yelled Alexander over noises that even he couldn't define.

Overhead the choppers flew in noisy procession. They yelled down the line at Kane who chose not to hear. Kane aimed, firing the gun just once so that it hit its mark. The front right tire burst on the Jaguar that was riding on Tyroler tires. Alexander desperately tried to control the car and pulled it towards the pavement. Kane had only meant to stop him, but

Alexander tried to continue. The Jaguar mounted the curb doing the speed that Kane had forced the cars to race. The Jaguar flipped up in the air and turned once, landing upside down, with a resounding thud of breaking metal. The force shattered glass, shooting it from the windows, and gas spewed from the full tank. Kane saw it in slow motion, and stopped his car with a resounding screeching of tires. He unhinged his slackened harness and jumped from the car. But he wasn't quick enough to save a life.

Alexander's car exploded in front of Kane's eyes, a big orange ball of metal and fuel. The blast sent Kane reeling back against his mobile, with flames shooting into the sky, and Alexander Vincentia died the way he wanted to go out.

Kane pulled the helmet from his head and tossed it in the car. Removing the mesh from his hair, he held his head in his hands and tried to compose himself.

Kelly stood in the pits waiting with the guys. She shivered in the damp air and Dave offered her his jacket. She snuggled into the coat, and stood listening to the chopper's report. One driver dead, with the other driver now on his way back by helicopter.

Outside in the stands the crowd was unusually quiet. They waited for the conquering hero, till then, no champagne flowed. No celebrations.

The chopper camera crew relayed pictures back to the track's monitors. Pictures flashed on there of balls of orange smoke and steaming metal. Kelly watched Kane fall back against his car, his head buried deep in his hands. Without hesitation, she flipped her monitor off. This was his time to grieve.

The rescue chopper landed on the parking lot amid the scurrying of racing folk and cars. Police escorted Kane through the crowds to the pits, and the Mercedes team. When she saw Kane walking towards her, tired and blood seeping through the suit, Kelly shed the coat and ran to him. He engulfed her in his arms, and she clung desperately to him. Nothing could keep them apart. He kissed her nose and then her mouth, whispering in her ear, and she nodded her head, while he ruffled her spiky hair with his other hand. Then he let her go just for a few seconds. He looked up towards his comrades, two great cops and one Mercedes driver. They had been a team, and he was used to teamwork. Had been all his life.

When he had seen the balls of orange smoke and tangled metal from Vincentia's car, it reminded him too much of his hundredth mission and the Forts of Lantau. But instead of finding a son in Lantau, this time he had lost his friends in the same fort. Kane wondered what he had done to deserve such justice. Maybe they had never been a team, he, Alexander and Peter. Where had it all gone wrong with them? An answer he would possibly never know.

Right now he didn't want to talk to anyone. He turned and walked away across the shimmering tarmac, silhouetted in the late afternoon sun. He stopped, and turned slightly, stretching his hand out to Kelly. She looked at him in the slowly fading light of the summer afternoon. If not for the love of Kane, Kelly knew she would be nothing.

"When they raised you, Kane, they broke the mold," and Kelly moved on to the tarmac to join the conquering hero.

Breinigsville, PA USA
04 December 2009

228664BV00003B/28/P

9 781593 933500